The Medium Is Murder

THE MEDIUM IS MURDER

MOLLY McKITTERICK

St. Martin's Press
New York

Library of Congress Cataloging-in-Publication Data

McKitterick, Molly
    The medium is murder / Molly McKitterick.
       p.   cm.
    ISBN 0-312-07032-2
    I. Title.
    PS3563.C38224M4   1992
    813'.54—dc20   91-403615
                                                      CIP

First published in Great Britain by Scribners, a division of Macdonald & Co.

First U.S. Edition: March 1992
10 9 8 7 6 5 4 3 2 1

Special thanks to Linda Cashdan,
who held my hand and,
often, slapped my wrist.

CHAPTER ONE

AT FOUR P.M. IN THE KYYY newsroom the contestants were running the game show. 'Give me the man with the fast fingers in editing room Num-bah Five!' a reporter yelled across the newsroom. 'I'm in a hurry.' Tucking a video tape under his arm he charged towards the opposite end of the rectangular room, where a chubby tape-editor bounced and beckoned. 'Come on down,' the editor squealed, 'Come on down.'

The Channel Three newsteam was making its daily hectic scramble for the five p.m. jackpot. From the news director's glass-enclosed office, which officiated at one end, to the other where doorways led to editing booths and photographers' quarters, the newsroom was full of noisy turmoil. Writers slammed out sloppy scripts on battered typewriters. Reporters scurried to and from editing rooms. Assignment-editors monitored screeching police radios and conveyed story information to photographers in urgent shouts. Cameramen skedaddled, grabbing coats and equipment as they went. Producers hastened around the room checking and rechecking on everything.

For all the chaos, newsroom staffers were playing out a regular ritual: a practised liturgy in deference to the Great God, News. Those who served, knew the news had to be dished up in one final glorious burst of panic. Thus, whatever items were picked for public consumption were the very latest, the freshest, if not always the most considered.

The running reporter tripped over a piece of torn carpeting and bumped into a desk, rattling one of his colleagues, who rolled with the jolt and continued banging on her typewriter. The reporter resumed his trot, determined to let no obstacle keep him from the news, a formidable resolve since the newsroom was full of impedimenta. Mismatched and battered desks had been manipulated into every conceivable space. They formed odd clusters. Among them teetered untidy stacks of video tapes and papers. Old schedules and torn cartoons adorned the breeze-block walls, where they hung in various stages of falling off. Broken pieces of styrofoam ceiling-panel jutted down; stalactites, breaking the pall of stagnant cigarette smoke.

Yet the privilege of working in the newsroom overcame its discomforts. That they were privileged, newsroomites had no doubt. To serve an important god was to assume consequence and surely they, who administered the news to an information-hungry public, were elevated by it.

'Here's a chance to do something creative.' Waving his video tape, the reporter passed the waiting tape-editor without so much as slowing down. 'The amaryllis show at the botanical gardens,' he tossed over his shoulder. 'I want to edit it to some music, *The Waltz of the Flowers* maybe.' Humming, the editor fell into a dance behind him.

Consumer reporter Laurel Michaels took off her quilted coat and hung it on its peg in the corner of the gloomy cubicle she wishfully referred to as an 'office'. She pulled a notebook and some papers out of one of the coat pockets and tossed them on her desk.

Then she walked to the doorway of her cubicle and regarded the newsroom with distaste. 'I need quiet!' she screamed. 'I'm try-ing to workkk.' For two seconds there was complete silence in the newsroom. Then as if someone had flipped a switch, the din was on again and noticeably louder than before.

Disgusted, Laurel flopped into her typing chair, slapped a pair of earphones on her head and punched the 'play' button on her tape recorder. Immediately, her head was filled with the sounds of the sea. If her ears were the gauge, there was no more newsroom. Its noisy confusion had ceased to exist.

Laurel took a deep cleansing breath and let the taped tide carry away her tensions. One by one they left her as her breathing slowed into time with the rolling surf. The cry of a seagull echoed through her slackening body. Soon, she knew, she would be at one with the noises of nature and from them she would draw strength. She had only to come back to her inner self, away from the inconsequence that surrounded her: breathing out and breathing in.

Now. Now it was time to strike! Ritualistically Laurel raised her index fingers to the space in front of her eyes and blessed each of the digits in turn with a look before driving them on to her typewriter keys. There they waited as she took one last, toe-deep breath and collected her thoughts in the now receptive pocket of her mind.

One of the fingers hit a letter, then the other, popping like the first kernels in a batch of popcorn. Slowly the pops gathered speed and, as they did, established a furious rhythm of their own. When an errant strand of frosted hair brushed the top of the Olympia, Laurel did not stop to remove it nor did she shake it away. Except for the movement of her hands she remained immobile, balanced cross-legged on the typing chair. In that posture, wearing a pink jump-suit, she appeared girlish. Laurel was, however, forty-three. In proximity she looked every day of it.

The ocean tape ran out and clicked off but Laurel typed on until she had filled a little more than half a page with everything she remembered from the conversation. She checked it with her notes to be sure she hadn't forgotten anything. Satisfied, she pulled the paper out of the type-writer and put it on top of those she had taken from her coat pocket. She had it all: the story and the documentation. Laurel peeled back the typewritten page to look at the papers underneath.

All she needed now was one more on-camera interview.

Laurel flipped through her notebook until she found the telephone number. She dialled it. After a few rings she identified herself to the person who'd answered. 'I need to do an interview,' she announced.

The person on the other end asked a question.

'Well, I have some . . . information. I'd rather wait and

tell you in person.' Then in a sudden burst of uncontrolled maliciousness, Laurel added. 'You probably know what I'm referring to. I've got everything I need to air the story and I'm going to do it whether you go on-camera or not. But you'd better do the interview; at least that way you'll have a chance to defend yourself.'

Laurel listened.

'All right, I'll call you tomorrow and we'll set something up.' She dropped the receiver back on the phone and hugged herself in anticipation. To stick a microphone in someone's face and ask discomfiting questions was Laurel's greatest pleasure. She loved to see the victim squirm, caught and held by the camera's eye.

Laurel suddenly gathered up her notebook and papers and put them back in the pocket of her coat, stuffing them way down so they wouldn't fall out. She gave the coat a compulsive little hug and rubbed her cheek against its purple quilting.

On the other side of the concrete wall, anchorman William Hecklepeck tossed his sheepskin coat into the air. He left it on the floor where it fell.

His cubicle and Laurel's were in a string of doorless niches lining the far side of the KYYY newsroom. These spaces had been granted to the people considered important in the newsroom hierarchy, although they had nothing to recommend them but semi-privacy.

Hecklepeck tugged down his vest where it had ridden up and tried to assess the feeling of uneasiness that had come over him some time between the time he'd left for work, walking, and his arrival in the newsroom. He checked his fly and put a hand on his hair. But the fly was zipped and the hair was lying flat.

Hecklepeck's six-foot-three frame was topped with a likeable face. In repose his deep-brown eyes and regular features contributed to a general sort of attractiveness. But Hecklepeck's face was almost never in repose. His features worked in unison to produce a running commentary on the world around him. As he gazed out at his skittering colleagues in the newsroom his expression was benevolent.

10

While he was just arriving for work, they had been busy most of the day. What was truly gratifying was that their activity was aimed at making him look good on the air; in his honour, so to speak.

If there was a time to look good, this was it. The February ratings period was beginning. Hecklepeck enjoyed ratings. While the Neilson and Arbitron rating services carefully took the pulses of St Louis television viewers, it was he who made their hearts beat. He knew it. Four times a year he mentally challenged the other anchormen in town to beat him in the ratings. It was a competition he didn't expect to lose and he never had.

Thirty-eight years old, Hecklepeck had been the number one anchorman in St Louis for more than six years. It was surprising because he was not a St Louisan. When he first arrived he had been a stranger in a city that didn't like strangers. By now his Virginia origins had been completely forgotten. Most viewers simply assumed Hecklepeck had grown up among them. One University City resident went so far as to claim that his house in the St Louis suburb had been Hecklepeck's childhood home. The house had previously been inhabited by a Dutch family named Hoeklpoehl.

Richard Markowitz, producer of the ten o'clock newscast poked his head into Hecklepeck's cubicle. 'Little Richard,' proclaimed Hecklepeck. 'What's doing?'

'Aw, heck, Heck. And yourself?'

'Don't know. I have this feeling, this premonition or something . . . I don't know.'

A self-conscious little smile played under Richard's black moustache and beard. 'Well, I would say you have ESP.'

'Say what?'

'The place is going berserko.' At twenty-nine, Richard still suffered the agony of adolescence: feeling not only the smart of his own shortcomings but a preternatural pain derived from those of others. Richard's affliction had not served him well on the outside but in the Channel Three newsroom he thrived. It was his medium, his Petri dish in life. He grew and prospered there.

'The new music debuts tonight. It makes the beginning of

11

the show sound like a game of Pac Man.'

Hecklepeck shrugged. News management was continually fiddling with the sound of the show on the erroneous assumption that the viewer cared which electronic beeps prefaced the day's news.

'Bill Kinslow threw up in the middle of shooting open-heart surgery today. All over the patient.'

Hecklepeck chuckled. 'Every medical reporter we've ever had has done a piece on open-heart surgery during ratings. They work on the premise that the gorier it is the more people are likely to watch.'

'Yep,' added Richard, 'And they always put a disclaimer at the beginning: "The following story is fairly graphic. You may want to restrict your viewing." So, of course people watch.'

'Well, you can't argue with success,' Hecklepeck commented wryly. 'The consultants never do.'

'The gore passes the goosebump test,' said Richard, referring to a time when a KYYY consultant had attached electrodes to a group of viewers to measure their skin responses to various newscasts. 'Here's your script.'

'The big ratings punch,' said Hecklepeck, flourishing the stack of papers. 'Anything in here pass the "Who gives a shit?" test?'

'Probably not.' There was an evil twinkle in Richard's green eyes. 'It definitely fails the "Is this really news?" test.' Leaving Hecklepeck with the script, he slipped back into the newsroom and walked back to his desk. Richard's stride had a self-conscious lilt to it, a discomfort he tried to hide with his sardonic manner. The sarcasm was as much a part of his costume as his ubiquitous cords and running shoes. It was greatly appreciated in the newsroom where it materialised in the form of somewhat unpleasant jokes.

'Watch. There's a man who's about to have the chair pulled out from under him,' Richard said to the five o'clock producer, whose desk was next to his. 'When his overpaid ass hits the floor, he's going to rebound right through the roof.' With an eager eye on Hecklepeck's office, Richard carefully arranged himself in his chair. Humming under his breath and tapping in time, he waited. It wasn't long.

12

A howl emerged from Hecklepeck's office and soared out of the darkened doorway: 'Drivel!' The cry of rage muffled the bustling newsroom. In the sudden silence, heads at most desks bent further over their typewriters. Those in transit leapt forward as though licked with a riding crop.

Richard's black beard twitched with delight. 'Right through the roof and into the ozone layer,' he chuckled.

Beside Richard, the five o'clock producer raised her pale, protuberant eyes but not her head. 'What's he screaming about?' she whispered.

Richard hooted. 'Oh, K . . . why . . . why . . . why?' he intoned.

Hecklepeck stormed out of his cubbyhole and strode into the glass-enclosed office where Ken Marshal, the news director, sat, his face hidden in his hands. The door slammed.

Richard rose. 'Te — ll me why . . . K . . . why . . . why . . . why?' he sang, wringing his hands in an operatic gesture. A series of twitters swept the newsroom. Richard took an elaborate bow and sat.

All eyes tilted up to the scene in the news director's office. Hecklepeck's roars filtered through the glass walls. His words were indistinguishable, but their meaning was made perfectly clear by the way he pounded on Ken's desk. The reverberations rattled the news director, who sank deeper and deeper into his big chair.

'What is it?' the five o'clock producer whispered. She watched Hecklepeck drive home another point.

'It's the *Caustic Consumer*. He's finally seen her series for the rating sweeps.' Richard assumed a falsetto: 'Michaels on Mistresses – Get down and dirty as Laurel Michaels reveals the shocking truth about Mistresses behind the scenes of St Louis' politics and society. Let her tell you who's doing what to whom.' Richard leered.

'Well, this time he's right.' The five o'clock producer let out her breath, relief spreading over her babyish face. 'We have no business going on the air with crud like that. It's not exactly going to do anything for the consumer. I just wish it wasn't going to be on my show.' Although her tenure at KYYY had been short, she was well-acquainted with station series. They invariably aired during quarterly rating periods in the hope of hooking the viewer with a captivating subject on Monday and bringing him back for more during the rest of the week. But with repetition the gambit had lost much of its effectiveness. To compensate, series subjects had been getting flashier and flashier.

'TRASH!' boomed Hecklepeck in Ken's office, where he was still pounding the desk. 'Give me one (bang) goddamn (bang) good reason (bang) why I should go on the air and be associated with that shit (bang, bang, bang). It belongs in the *National Enquirer* and not in a self-respecting news show! Of course self-respect is not something we strive for around here.'

The news director had slipped to eye-level with the surface of his desk. Affable but forgettable, Ken was generally described as a nice guy in the way women describe dates who have nothing at all to recommend them. He had been lucky in the minor leagues, successful as news director in Paducah, Kentucky and Zanesville, Ohio. As a result, he had been hired by KYYY. But his competence simply did not extend to big city news. He had fallen victim to television management's most over-used maxim: What works in one place will work in another because all television markets (big cities, small cities, east or west) are the same.

'The ABC affiliate in Washington DC, did a series on mistresses,' Ken said as he pulled himself up from the underside of his desk. 'It got a good response. It's also been done in other major markets.' He merely offered the argument; Ken never took a stand, if he could help it. He especially avoided postures that put him in opposition to Hecklepeck. Hecklepeck had outlasted the last eight news directors and was indisputably the most powerful and best-paid man in television news in St Louis.

'This is *not* Washington,' Hecklepeck bellowed. 'We don't have any damn frou-frou senators and do-nothing bureaucrats here. This city's got better things to do than to reflect on the bedroom habits of its prominent citizens.'

It was at this point that Laurel Michaels burst into the

14

office. 'I understand there is a problem with my series?' she demanded.

'Yes, there's a problem,' Hecklepeck drawled. He raised the right corner of his mouth in a delicate sneer. 'It's garbage.'

'I wasn't aware that you had seen it.'

Hecklepeck shrugged. 'Don't need to. The subject doesn't qualify as news.'

'Well, I think you need to see it. It's news all right. At the very least it's an in-depth look at a fascinating subject but. . .'

Hecklepeck snorted.

By now the newsroom was watching this scene behind the glass walls. 'Godzilla meets King Kong,' whispered Richard, sounding for once more awed than sarcastic.

'But,' Laurel spat the word out, 'I've uncovered something big, a major story. It's . . . well, it's going to be part of the series.'

'Ooookay,' said Hecklepeck generously, magnanimously he thought. 'Show it to me.'

'I can't. It's not edited. And anyway, since when did stories have to be cleared by you? That's his job.' Laurel swept a hand in the direction of Ken who was looking as pleasantly neutral as he possibly could.

He cleared his throat. 'That, uh, is my job.'

'Yes? What did you think?'

'Well, I, uh, haven't, uh, actually . . . Laurel is a good and trusted reporter. . .'

'I don't care how good she is and how much you trust her, there are other considerations like little things called lawsuits. But *that*, as you say, is your business. Mine is this: lacking evidence to the contrary, the subject of people's sex lives *does not qualify as news.*'

As Hecklepeck left the news director's office swathed in angry dignity, newsroom personnel immediately dropped their heads over their desks. But it was hard to resume work. The voice of Laurel's fury had risen to a grating scream. It filtered through the glass walls, hitting unpleasant peaks.

Ken sat and took it with folded hands and head bowed.

15

CHAPTER TWO

AT FOUR FIFTY-FIVE HECKLEPECK entered the gloom of the KYYY studio. He walked across the filthy concrete floor towards the bright lights at the far end. Several steps above floor level under the station logo, a large silver three, was the anchor desk. It was a pulsating, vibrant blue. Three empty chairs awaited the KYYY triumvirate: Anchor, Weather, Sports.

Blinking, Hecklepeck tripped over the torn carpet on the steps. He took his seat carefully. Through the camera's eye, the set would look like a space-age structure built of some technologically advanced laminate. It was in fact made of painted plywood and apt to splinter.

Hecklepeck reached under the anchor desk and fished up a big pink mirror. He scowled at his image and went after a wisp of hair that was refusing to lie down with the rest. He batted at it furiously.

Hecklepeck was sensitive about his hair, even though there wasn't a viewer in St Louis who saw any variation in the neat brown waves from one night to the next. If they wanted hair, they watched Channel Six where the anchorman's features melted away beneath his gloriously sculpted coiffure. Hecklepeck knew the competition was a head of hair. He competed accordingly.

The floor crew anxiously watched the tonsorial tussle. It was an excellent gauge of Hecklepeck's disposition and the state of his disposition mattered. In a passionate mood he could render scripts and cues meaningless. He was capable of reworking an entire show in progress.

In addition Hecklepeck shared his feelings with the viewing audience. He couldn't help it. As he read the

17

news, his views were written all over his face. One had only to listen to his salutatory pronouncement: 'In the news tonight . . . ' to know whether Hecklepeck regarded his lead story as good news or silly news or not news at all. He had a way of raising one of his dark eyebrows that conveyed utter contempt. He could scowl just a little or, in severe cases, deeply and damningly.

Unable to prevent his face from talking, Hecklepeck had made a virtue of it. He dismissed the thin line between news and editorial. He crossed it. He trampled; he danced all over outlawed editorial territory. He let the audience know he didn't fit into the soft shoes of most anchormen.

St Louis viewers took it as a mark of respect. Hecklepeck didn't talk down to them. He let them have it, all of it. He seemed to assume they were intelligent, rational human beings. St Louis, a city with a poor opinion of itself, was flattered. News managers, who took the stupidity of the viewing public for granted, were less enamoured of the Hecklepeck style; so were crew members, who had to work with it.

One of the camera operators squinted through a studio camera, the size and shape of a Gatling Gun. He squared his shot and locked the camera down. As he did, the floor director sidled up, underhandedly offering a vial of valium. The camera operator started to wave it away. Then he accepted the vial and took out two tablets. He had been persuaded by the sight of Laurel Michaels taking her place in the sports chair next to Hecklepeck. Laurel presented her *Cautious Consumer* reports live from the set during the five o'clock news. Because KYYY's leading players, its anchor, meteorologist and sportscaster were all male (and the weatherman, Irwin Samuels, was black), it was considered important to feature a female in a prominent way.

Tonight Laurel's humourless face was cast in a dangerous mould. All her tricks with make-up only seemed to mock her, overruled by the force of her unreleased anger. The pent-up emotion drew her features closer together, creating an effect that was rodent-like and mean.

18

Pointedly ignoring Hecklepeck, Laurel clipped her microphone to the lapel of her suit jacket. Underneath the jacket she still wore the hot-pink jump-suit. Laurel always dressed in a one-piece pants outfit. She owned them in all colours and styles; some, whimsical adaptations of safari outfits or mechanics' uniforms. They fitted her campy idea of style and her desire for practicality.

Laurel took a sip of water, shuffled her script, adjusted her mike, made a note on her copy, wet her lips, leaned into the camera as though about to deliver her story, changed her sitting position, sipped her water. . . This was Laurel's ritual. After years of reporting she was still nervous about appearing on the air. She believed the right combination of adjustments, notations and sips would guarantee her a smooth show.

'. . . when you want to know why. Turn to KYYY, the news with answers.' The disc-jockey voice of the station's announcer filled the studio with the opening of the news show.

'With our Channel Three news family: Anchorman William Hecklepeck, Meteorologist Irwin Samuels, Sportscaster Bucky Ballwin . . . and featuring special consumer reports with Channel Three's Cautious Consumer Laurel Michaels.'

The floor director cued Hecklepeck, who fixed the camera lens with an awful stare and pronounced fatalistically, 'In the news tonight. . .'

Halfway across town in the quiet post-deadline newsroom of the *St Louis Post Dispatch*, newspaper media critic John Alden stared intently at the Channel Three monitor. He sensed something unusual. Alden was watching all three major news shows simultaneously on a row of monitors sitting on a high shelf. He intended to review their ratings efforts in his column.

Alden watched closely as Hecklepeck read a dull story about development in downtown St Louis. It was followed by a house fire and the announcement of a new county programme to provide summer jobs for young people. There was also some national news. It was all perfectly straightforward. Alden shifted his focus to Channel Six.

In the darkened KYYY studio behind the cameras, however, the vial of valium was circulating among members of the floor crew. It reached the last one just in time, just as Hecklepeck arrived at the tease line before the first commercial break. The words unrolled on the teleprompter in front of him.

> LAUREL MICHAELS REVEALS THE MYSTERY BEHIND ST LOUIS' MISTRESSES AS SHE BEGINS A SPECIAL SERIES OF REPORTS. WE'LL BE RIGHT BACK AFTER THIS MESSAGE.

Hecklepeck glared at the tease but did not open his mouth to read it. For ten awful seconds he sat and stared. It was an eternity in television time, enough to attract the attention of the most phlegmatic viewer and make more sensitive watchers squirm with discomfort. But Hecklepeck did nothing to save the situation. Instead he deliberately leaned back in his seat and folded his arms across his chest.

In master-control four horrified technicians gazed at a wall of television monitors. The recalcitrant Hecklepeck stared back from each of them, a repeated insult, a series of slaps in the face. To the technicians his silent figure embodied the worst that could happen in television: dead air.

Simultaneously three pairs of eyes swung towards the five o'clock producer. It was her show and she was responsible for salvaging it. But she sat stunned, with her mouth open, a little pool of saliva collecting in the space between her bottom teeth and lip. Her eyes were similarly flooded.

When no directions emerged, the man responsible for the show's mechanics groaned. 'For Christ's sake go to commercial,' he shouted. It was too late. One of the engineers had killed Hecklepeck's camera. But in his panic he had failed to roll the commercial. KYYY went to black.

Across the hall in his glass-enclosed office news director Ken Marshal covered his face with his hands and sighed deeply. Outside in the newsroom his employees stared open-mouthed at their lifeless television monitors.

'Jesus H. Christ,' murmured Richard Markowitz, as the screen finally flickered to life, mid-commercial. 'What we have just witnessed is anchorman-suicide.'

At the *Post Dispatch* John Alden was furiously taking notes. Ratings forgotten, he was going to take Hecklepeck to the cleaners instead. Alden did not believe that journalistic rules were made to be broken and he had thoroughly berated local journalists for infractions far more minor than Hecklepeck's. It was his little revenge on a business that wouldn't have him.

At the centre of the storm Laurel Michaels was still playing out her ritual in the studio but she had become rigidly tense. She took a precise sip of water, lined up her script so that the corners matched, delivered a killer smile to her camera, squared her shoulders. . . The tranquillised floor crew watched her with benevolent torpor.

'All right, Heck, what are you going to do when we come back?' the show director spoke through the plastic piece in Hecklepeck's ear. He had bypassed the five o'clock producer completely.

Hecklepeck drew a telephone receiver out from under his desk and spoke into it. 'I'm not doing a damn thing. I told Marshal I'm not going to be associated with this crap and I meant it. Let her intro her own story.'

At those words Laurel stopped short. Incredulous she lifted her eyes from her desk to the camera. Her face showed a new radiance, all but erasing the lines of ill humour and age. Laurel had heard the call, the call to more on-air exposure. During all her years of reporting she had never stopped seeing herself as a great, undiscovered talent in the television news business. Discovery hadn't happened, in her view, because she never got adequate air-time; nobody ever saw enough of her in one sitting.

Laurel picked up her phone and told the show director,

'Sam, I'll just rewrite the intro to my series. After the break you can come directly to me.'

The show director accepted the only solution offered to him. He ordered the repositioning of camera two to take Laurel rather than Hecklepeck.

Laurel faced the camera lens and assumed a look of utter portentousness. When the floor director flicked his wrist, she began: 'It is well known that mistresses have played pivotal rôles in politics and business throughout history. But it may surprise you to know . . .' (here Laurel favoured the camera with a look of intense severity,) '. . . that many of St Louis' most well-known government and business leaders keep mistresses today. What the Cautious Consumer wants to know is how the practice of keeping a mistress affects their ability to perform their jobs. We also wonder how the rôle of mistress affects the women themselves. In our five-part series, *Mistresses: Mystique or Misery?*, we name names and reveal the sometimes shocking lives of mistresses in St Louis.'

In the newsroom Richard Markowitz commented to the group of colleagues surrounding him: 'There's no question in my mind. It's misery. You'd think the Caustic Consumer had just uncovered a crime or something. All she's really doing is prying into some poor bastard's private life.'

On the newsroom monitor the live Laurel was replaced with tape. It showed a series of artists' drawings of couples edited in time to an instrumental rendition of 'Blue Velvet'. Hugging an invisible lover, Richard sang along with unpleasant nasality.

The music soon gave way to Laurel's recorded voice. She rattled off some figures demonstrating that the divorce rate, even in a conservative town like St Louis, was rising. Here a shot of the Gateway Arch was intended to represent the city. She went on to surmise that men and women need to be involved with each other in some sort of relationship. If marriage wasn't the answer, there must be something else. This was confirmed in an interview with

Dr Tim Siliciano, a psychologist called upon by reporters at KYYY whenever they needed a psychologist to comment on anything. Dr Siliciano's chief recommendations were that he was always available to talk about anything and always did it in easily edited twenty-second paragraphs.

In the studio Hecklepeck had ceased to pay any attention to Laurel and was baiting weatherman Irwin Samuels: 'You were two degrees off the low last night.'

'Yes, but the weather service was off by four,' Irwin replied. His handsome brown face, however, revealed that he took his own error more to heart than the weather service's greater inaccuracy. Every degree mattered to Irwin.

Over their heads, in the television set suspended from the studio ceiling, Laurel was seen walking through one of the local shopping centres. The live Laurel watched from below with self-righteous satisfaction while the recorded Laurel stopped to address the camera. She pulled her dubious tenets together into an even more dubious thesis. In summary: People need people but divorce rates reveal that marriage today isn't a satisfactory answer. Therefore, men and women are looking for alternative relationships. One of those alternatives, for men, is to take a mistress.

Richard shook his head as if he were trying to shake all of Laurel's thoughts into an order that made some sense and quipped. 'If A equals B then B must be greater than C which is less than A and the whole mess adds up, but god knows how, to Z.'

The television screen in front of Richard displayed pictures of famous mistresses, Nell Gwynne and Madame de Pompadour. What a glamorous life they lived, gushed Laurel. Did today's mistresses also live that kind of life?

The tape cut to the silhouette of a woman. She had been photographed against a white background and flooded with white light from behind to protect her identity. In an electronically altered voice the shadowy figure said, *yes it was fun, man.* It meant sharing lots of good times: 'going to clubs but never having to take orders from no man.'

'That's easy. It's Tareesa,' said Richard. Tareesa Wells

was the well-known companion of St Louis' Eighteenth Ward Alderman, Walter 'Tiny' Payne. 'What's so revealing about that? She goes everywhere with Tiny. He's not even married.'

As Richard spoke, a second backlit apparition appeared. This one was taking the opposite view. There were lonely times, the shadow averred, hanging her head, as well as times when she felt used.

In his office, Ken Marshal sank his face even more deeply into his sweating palms. He knew that one. It was Rita Cullen in the art department. She was having an affair with the station manager.

From behind his fingers Ken heard Laurel's voice press on. 'Why do women continue to act as mistresses?' she asked. A third silhouette chuckled. It was, she said, a question of love and the sacrifices one was willing to make for it. She laughed again, creating an electronically modulated warble.

'Maggie,' murmured John Alden. Maggie Johnson had consorted with St Louis' fertilizer magnate for years. While his eastern wife had spent most of her time in New York, the late Warren Billings had spent most of his with Maggie. St Louis knew it and loved Maggie for it. What the city couldn't forgive was the wife's preference for New York.

As her outline dissolved to that of another woman, Maggie's chuckle gave way to teariness. She wanted out, the next silhouette sniffled, but didn't know where to go. Besides, *he* wouldn't let her go. Alden strained to hear the rest but it was too soft to be heard through the electronic manipulation.

In the studio Hecklepeck became abruptly aware that the shadows on the monitor screen were human beings with real troubles. He stopped trying to assure Irwin that the difference between eight and ten degrees is insignificant to the average viewer who just feels cold, and asked, 'Who was that?'

24

Laurel merely looked smug. As the last interview resolved slowly into a freeze frame, she prepared to go back on the air.

'During the rest of the week,' she pronounced, 'you will learn the identities of these women and hear their stories. Their situations, you will find, are not enviable. They are characterised by neglect, abuse and, even . . . ' Laurel paused significantly, ' . . . crime. Join us tomorrow for part two of *Mistresses: Mystique or Misery?*' She bowed her head in triumph, while the station went to commercial.

CHAPTER THREE

IN THE WAKE OF HECKLEPECK'S sit-down strike the newsroom was a relatively subdued place. Normal loud banter was not heard the next day, just the sibilance of whispering under the clack of the wire machines and ringing of the phones.

'How could Hecklepeck. . .'

'Who does Laurel think. . .'

'What about the rating*ssss*?'

News staffers were in agreement about the enormity of what had happened. It was the very hugeness that reduced them to a hush. But their interpretations varied and, as the day wore on, they began to separate into two groups: champions of Laurel and supporters of Hecklepeck.

Viewers, or at least those who called into the station, were less divided. What they had seen was an anchorman in the throes of temperament. The subtleties that delineated news from non-news had not been presented to them and would have been lost if they had.

'What's the matter with that Hecklypeck?' boomed one viewer.

'Nothing,' breathed a news writer into his receiver.

'Well, he sure looked like he had a mad on about something last night. Is he having problems with management over there?'

'No. He just . . . just . . . felt like he couldn't go on.'

'Just felt like not working you say?'

'Uh, yes.'

'Well, hey, I work over here at the Chrysler Truck Plant. What would happen if I decided I didn't feel like working? No bumpers, that's what. We would lose even more to furreign imports.'

'Yes, well. . ."

'You tell that Hecklypeck not to be doing like that no more. He's got a job to do too. It's tough, I don't deny that but we all got to pull our own weight. You tell him I said so.'

The news writer hung up with a small sigh. His name was Joe Osifchin, which worried him because he didn't think it would sound well on the air when he got his big break. Joe Osifchin sighed again and raised his eyes from the dirty melamine of his desk top, only to come eye to eye with Laurel.

Laurel, usually out of sight in her office or in the field, had been apparent in the newsroom all morning. In a creamy-white jump-suit she hung around the newsroom, looking like an eager ice-cream vendor waiting for a horde of children.

But the children hadn't been buying. They scuttled around her in silence or they tripped over her and hurried on with an indistinguishable whispered something.

'A lot of people seem to be calling in about my series,' Laurel said pointedly to Joe after he had the misfortune to make eye contact.

'Yes,' he said, not bothering to set the record straight. Joe Osifchin was a little egg-shaped fellow in a grey woollen vest. News writing at KYYY was his first job after journalism school and he was hopeful it would lead to bigger things. 'Yes,' he said again, edging his chair closer to his desk and letting his glasses slip down on his nose.

'Wait until later in the week, Thursday,' said Laurel softly. 'This is going to be the most important story I've ever done.' She hugged herself and rocked back and forth on her feet in what looked to the writer like some kind of sexual excitement.

Joe reached his hands out to the outer extremities of his desk and pulled his body closer to its shelter. 'Why?'

Laurel dropped her arms and looked at him with contempt. *'You'll* just have to wait and see.' She leaned forward tauntingly. 'I'll give you a little hint.' She whispered something. Then she straightened up. 'A real reporter would be able to figure it out from that.'

Osifchin watched her snake back to her office before he let go of his desk and pushed his glasses back up on his nose. 'Tootle?',' he repeated to himself. *'Tootle? Tootles?'*

The five o'clock producer put the styrofoam box with her salad in it on her desk and sat down. 'Have you noticed that blue car over at the car wash?'

Richard Markowitz and a photographer shook their heads.

'This morning it was parked at the abandoned gas station next door. I noticed it when I came into work and it was still there when I went to the dentist. But now it's across the street at the car wash.'

'Yeah, so someone's getting a wash?' Richard wasn't impressed.

'The car wash is closed. But that's not it. The car looks empty but when I went into Holden's to get my salad I could have sworn I saw somebody in there move. It was like somebody was watching me or something.'

'Maybe it was the gas station ghost,' suggested Richard.

'What kind of car was it?' asked the photographer.

'It's blue. A what-do-you-call-it . . . Sedan. Not a station wagon.'

'Yeah, but what kind, what make?'

The producer opened her pale, bulgy eyes very wide. 'I don't know; I can't tell one car from the other. It wasn't a Mercedes.'

'Well, that pins it down to a few hundred foreign and domestic models,' commented Richard.

'What if . . . what if there's some kind of rapist in there or something?'

'There probably isn't. Somebody just needed a place to park.'

'Yeah,' added the photographer, 'most parked cars don't have sexual deviants in them. Most of them contain ordinary people doing ordinary things.'

Richard grinned suddenly. 'Remember the guy who hid in the bushes out front waiting for that woman who anchored the morning news? What was her name? Michelle, what?'

'Michelle Gray,' supplied the photographer.

'Yeah. He was a paroled murderer and he jumped out at her in the dark. It was five-thirty in the morning. But he didn't want to murder Michelle. Or rape her. All he did was point a pen at her and ask for her autograph. And she started screaming.'

'Yeah,' said the photographer. 'What was it he wanted her to write?'

'Best wishes for your future endeavours.'

'He was talking about his new job as an auto mechanic. So you see.' Richard and the photographer chuckled and the five o'clock producer smiled uncertainly.

In her cubicle Laurel dialled the number again. No answer; still no answer.

She put her coat on and went into the newsroom. 'I'll be out for a while,' she announced to the chief assignment-editor. 'I'm going to lunch. But after that, sometime this afternoon, I'm going to need a crew. I have to do an interview as soon as I can get hold of the person I want to interview.'

'Oh?' The chief assignment-editor put on his interested face. 'Something I should know about?' It was not unreasonable. The chief assignment-editor was the newsroom traffic cop. It was his job to know where his reporters and photographers were.

But Laurel appeared to be deeply offended. 'No. This is for my series,' she snapped. 'Why doesn't anyone around here understand reporter confidentiality? If I went around handing my stories out to everyone, what would I have left to put on the air? And this is a major investigative piece; it's going to be the biggest story of the year. But I suppose *you* think it's not important?'

The assignment-editor pulled back and waved his hands in front of his face. 'No, no,' he said. 'It sounds great. It'll really help our ratings. You do what you have to do.'

Laurel smiled with something that might have been sweetness. 'Then I guess you can reassign that piece you wanted me to do on the Good Consumer Fair.' The assignment-editor nodded. Nettled, he watched Laurel flounce into her office. Then he let out a huge sigh and bent over his schedule. If Laurel didn't cover the Fair, who the hell was he going to send?

After some study, he picked up the two-way radio. 'This is KY333 base to Unit One. Unit One?'

'Go,' said a wary voice on the other end.

'I need you guys to spray the Consumer Fair at the convention centre. Have you eaten and are you finished getting your car washed?'

'We've eaten but that's a big negative on the car wash. There's an empty car sitting there but the place appears to be closed. We're on our way back, about to turn into the parking lot.'

'Well, head on down to the convention centre and get me enough for a thirty-second voice-over.'

When the outer door slammed loudly at three p.m., everybody in the newsroom started and glanced up. Hecklepeck looked back at them sternly and continued looking for a while after he had stared them all down.

Then he ambled to his office, removed his sheepskin jacket and tossed it on the floor in the corner of his office. He sat down in the squeaky chair and contemplated the four-foot heap of trash on his desk. The pile of old show scripts, news releases and soft-drinks cans was a living sculpture, an ever-eloquent commentary on the news business.

Richard stuck his head in the door but he did it tentatively like a turtle ready to retract into his shell at any time. 'Hey . . . hi . . . how're you?'

Hecklepeck raised an eyebrow. 'I am fine.'

'Oh, good. I guess you haven't, perhaps, seen this?' Richard held out a section of the afternoon paper, the *Post Dispatch*.

'Nope.' Hecklepeck was speaking in a normal voice but it sounded loud in contrast to everybody else's hushed tones.

He settled back to read, lifting his legs, one after the other, on to the typewriter. They were so long that Hecklepeck's black alligator cowboy boots extended past his door and hung out into the newsroom.

31

'Laurels for Laurel, Boos to Hecklepeck,' the headline read. 'Yesterday evening, Channel Three watchers were treated to the most reprehensible display of anchorman temperament this reporter has ever seen.' With that sweeping statement John Alden got right down to dogma. 'The television anchorman is the spoonful of sugar that helps the news medicine go down. He is the evening news host, responsible for welcoming the viewer and making him feel comfortable. He should never be less than polite and congenial.'

'A sort of ringmaster,' murmured Hecklepeck. 'Silly me, I've been thinking of myself as a general assignment-reporter, only I have to be a little better and know a little more than most generalists because in any given newscast I have to know and write a little bit about everything.'

Richard looked at Hecklepeck with mock pity. 'You shouldn't even be thinking, according to Alden,' he said. 'Read on.'

'Last night William Hecklepeck was guilty of gross impoliteness. He exercised what he calls his "news judgement" by refusing to introduce a colleague's work. In the opinion of this reporter, he was indulging in news jealousy. Hecklepeck was afraid he would be upstaged by the accomplished work of consumer reporter Laurel Michaels, so he tried to dismiss it. His unprofessional conduct should clue the viewer that the Michaels series is well worth seeing.'

Hecklepeck tossed the newspaper to the top of his trash pile. 'Alden is the one who should be paid not to think,' he commented. 'It must hurt him a lot. I'll give him one small point only. My behaviour was unprofessional as all get out.' Hecklepeck didn't sound contrite. 'I look at it this way: this business isn't old enough or honest enough to have a true professional tradition. Hell, we don't even have any moral standards.' Hecklepeck was now poised to soar on one of his favourite themes. 'If we did we wouldn't be so goddamn eager to find new ways to shock and titillate. We should be worrying about content rather than manners. The please and thank-yous can come later.

'Let's face it: all the etiquette in the world doesn't excuse this Michaels-on-Mistresses business. She can politely swear it's news from here to Friday, but her series isn't going to change anything. It won't feed the hungry or expose the corrupt. It will merely be Laurel-as-usual. She will make people, who don't deserve it, look bad so that she can look good. She's got a talent for splashing dirt on the spotless. One day (and by rights, it should have happened before now) she's going to run into some real contamination and the shit's going to splatter on her.'

Richard pictured a besmirched Laurel with pleasurable disgust. He knew that what Hecklepeck had said was at least partially true. Laurel had a way of condemning her subjects without benefit of trial. She used her camera to draw and quarter them publicly.

Richard remembered with a twinge the small brides'-wear shop in South St Louis that had custom-ordered an expensive gown for a young bride. The day before it arrived, she walked into the shop, cancelled her order and demanded a refund. Her fiancé, she claimed, had been killed in an automobile accident. Fiancés are always getting bumped off in the bridal-wear business and, stuck with a 'size 18' mountain of ecru lace, the store owner refused the refund. It was, in any case, against stated store policy. The erstwhile bride phoned Laurel and Laurel marched into the shop with her camera rolling. In front of all St Louis she accused the store owner of callous behaviour and worse. A week later the fiancé surfaced. He had been drinking all week on his sailing boat at Lake Carlyle. He had gone there to console himself after his erstwhile bride had given him the boot. Laurel never reported that part of it.

But she had also done worthwhile stories. Whether by accident or happenstance, some of her stories had helped people and exposed wrongdoers. Richard had not forgotten them, even if Hecklepeck had. 'What if Laurel really does have some news in this series? Some big story she's going to break?'

'Then I say let her show it to me,' said Hecklepeck expansively. 'She won't do that so I say she's bluffing.' It occurred to Hecklepeck as he said it that Laurel took herself too seriously to bluff. 'Even if she's not, her definition of a major story varies widely from mine.'

'But what if . . . ' Richard's voice got very small even by the standards of the hushed day. 'What if she *reeeally* does have something? Something like she said last night, a crime she's going to expose.'

'Then she'd better show it to someone. One thing I learned in my years as an investigative reporter was to cover my behind. I tried to get witnesses to everything. That meant making meticulous records of my investigations and leaving them with various people. It was simple self-protection. That way I ensured that nothing would happen to me because the story was going to get out regardless.

'And that's why I think Laurel may be full of shit. If she really had something, she'd want someone to know. She's taking a hell of a risk otherwise.'

'I take it then that you are going to continue boycotting her stories?' Richard asked.

'Show me a reason not to,' said Hecklepeck with a wry smile.

'No! The story's about macaroni but the name's Muldoni. That's Mul-doni! Ask for Mrs Muldoni.' The dam had broken. At four p.m. the chief assignment-editor was screaming into the two-way radio handle he held in front of his mouth. Everything else forgotten, he was directing one of his two-man taping crews to the location of a live shot scheduled for the end of the five o'clock show. Time was running short.

So was his temper. He would have needed an army of photographers to comfortably cover all the stories that day. As it was, he had spent the afternoon hurrying unwilling crews all around town. The last minute decision to do a live shot from the house of a woman with her own home pasta business was the final straw. But, the chief assignment-editor reminded himself bitterly, the five o'clock producer had needed a kicker, a happy story to end her show with. She didn't want her audience to go away depressed. *Tooo* bad! Too goddamn bad for them.

34

'Does this Mrs Macaroni know we're coming?' The voice responding over the two-way was deliberately provocative. It had been a hard day for the crew too.

The chief assignment-editor pulled the receiver back from his mouth and glared at it. Puffing forcefully he prepared to deliver the last, crushing word.

'Have you seen Laurel?' The five o'clock producer was there, looking at him with her big, babyish eyes.

The chief assignment-editor slammed down the two-way. 'No!' he yelled. 'No, no, no, no. . .' Loudly chanting 'No', he stalked out of the newsroom.

The five o'clock producer jerked nervously with each 'No' until the chorus faded and she was left looking around her in bewilderment. But it wasn't the assignment-editor's behaviour that perplexed her. It was Laurel. She wasn't in her office and she wasn't in the ladies' room putting on make-up. Nobody seemed to have seen her. The five o'clock producer looked at the clock and began to worry.

At seven minutes to five Ken put his pen down on his desk. 'Let's review a few scenarios,' he said ponderously to the five o'clock producer and Richard, who were sitting in his office.

'Laurel could get here in time to go on the air at the beginning of the second block and I'm sure she will.' Ken nodded to himself. He liked the sound of that.

'If she doesn't,' he held up two fingers indicating the second alternative, 'we could move her series down further in the newscast to give her more time.' Ken paused. By now the five o'clock producer was frantic and even Richard was beginning to fidget.

'If all else fails, Hecklepeck can read the intro to the story and we'll air the tape without Laurel.' Ken wound up his list with a flourish of three fingers.

'No way,' Richard burst out scathingly. 'Heck won't do it.' He glanced at the clock. 'You'd better get to the studio and sit with the show. It's beginning,' he said to the producer. Richard came into his own in a newsroom crisis. 'Move Laurel's piece down after the weather. I'll see if I can locate her. If I can't, we'll just have to stretch the pasta thing to fill in or take something from the network. Go!' The five o'clock producer went, with Richard right behind her. As the door closed behind them, Ken began to nod with at least partial understanding.

In the newsroom Richard issued orders to phone Laurel's home and he shouted to editing to find a feature story among those sent down everyday by ABC. Then he picked up the two-way radio. 'This is KY333 base to Unit Two. Unit Two?'

'This is Unit Two. Go ahead.' The voice on the other end came through the static.

'What's your status. Is that live shot set up?'

'Naw, we just got here. We're trying to figure out how we're going to light this place and still show all these different noodles.'

'Well hurry up! We may need to have you go on early.' The reply was an angry squelch.

'KY333, out,' said Richard reprovingly. Federal Communications Commission guidelines require that two-way talkers open and close by identifying themselves.

Hecklepeck favoured the studio camera with a look of scepticism. He was reading a story about the city prosecutor, who was dropping a tax-evasion case against the comptroller for lack of evidence.

A member of the floor crew lit up a cigarette and blew the smoke away from the camera lens. It curled upward, blue in the magenta cast of the studio light. On the news set all was serene.

'Do you suppose she just forgot?' asked a photographer. He was perched on a desk in the newsroom.

'Only if she had amnesia or was in a deep coma,' replied Richard with less cynicism than usual. His mind was still on the content of the five o'clock show. 'Laurel doesn't miss air-time. Of course,' he added with a flash of his normal style, 'I suppose she could have had a date or something.'

The photographer chuckled. 'Yeah,' he said, 'maybe her prince came and took her to Never Never Land.'

'Laurel lives in Never Never Land.' Richard stopped abruptly as the two-way radio squawked. It crackled and screeched. Somebody was trying to get out an urgent message. 'She's dead . . . ' were the only two words that emerged intact.

'Does that mean they can't get a signal out?' Richard was getting angry. He grabbed for the two-way handle.

'This is KY333. For heaven's sake just move the truck and see if you do better at another location.' A television live-shot is created by bouncing a microwave signal off a hill or tall building. Large obstacles can get in the way and have to be manoeuvred around.

Richard was pleading. 'We have to have that story. Laurel hasn't shown up and everything else has gone down on us. *Please*, make it work guys.'

But the two-way squawked back something about Laurel and impossible and dead. Richard was suddenly furious. 'What the hell are they talking about?'

'It sounds like they don't think they should be responsible for filling in for Laurel and the shot is definitely dead,' ventured the evening assignment-editor.

Richard considered that briefly and pressed the two-way talk button. 'You guys had better have a damn good excuse for not doing that live shot,' he said murderously. 'Why don't you call me by landline and explain it? Your transmissions are breaking up.'

Richard sent the evening assignment-editor to see if editing had indeed found a stand-by feature to replace Laurel and the live shot. He also phoned the five o'clock producer in the studio to suggest she stretch out the sports and weather segments. When the newsroom phone rang he pounced on it.

'You guys are going to pay for incompetence like this,' he shouted. 'The catty consumer's taken a hike and without your live shot we're in deep shit. What the hell happened?'

Richard's anger faded as he listened. It was replaced gradually by a look of incredulity. At one point he moved his mouth as if trying to ask a question but was unable actually to frame it. He gave up the effort. After several minutes he muttered something and dropped the phone back on the hook.

It took some prodding from his colleagues before he announced confusedly: 'The shot's dead and so is Laurel. I mean Laurel's dead. They found her lying in the van . . . dead in the live van.'

'When he lifted that stick and started to bring it down, I had to close my eyes. I was sure that guy was committing murder.' Sportscaster Bucky Ballwin spoke with relish until he glanced at Hecklepeck's face and recollected himself. 'Of course, fighting is not good sportsmanship,' he said. 'The game of hockey would be better off without it.'

Hecklepeck looked off-camera at the floor director with an expression that said 'get me out of this'. Normally the pre-sports chitchat was curtailed but tonight it seemed to drag on forever. 'On the other hand,' Bucky was saying, 'if a fight happens you simply can't ignore it and last night. . .' The producer let him continue. She wasn't sure where the rest of the show was.

When the show ended KYYY viewers also wondered where it was. They never saw the second part of Laurel's series. Nor did they see the pasta live-shot which had been touted at the beginning of the newscast. Instead they were unexpectedly treated to a long story on mud-wrestling championships in Sun Valley, California.

CHAPTER FOUR

ART MACKE AND PHIL CLADSTRIP were eating pasta. Seated on the concrete steps of the Maria Muldoni bungalow they were working on steaming plates of fusilli, rigatoni and vermicelli.

The afternoon breeze was dying. A cold February damp drifted in heavily behind it. The photographers didn't seem to be affected either by the cold or by their recent encounter with a corpse. They were used to both.

Art viewed a piece of fusilli with one eye as though he were looking at it through a camera. It loomed large and fleshy. Art wanted to be taking pictures but his camera was in the van with Laurel's body and the van was surrounded by the police. They had moved in quickly and completely after Art had called them from the Muldoni residence. Their presence, more than the body inside, gave Art the feeling that the familiar van had been violated. It was always that way, it seemed to him, when non-news people got involved.

He considered what the promotion department had done to the van in its fall advertising campaign: nothing short of mutilation. Except for the microwave dish lying on top, the entire vehicle had been painted with great day-glo green and yellow question marks all purportedly asking the question, 'Why?' In glowing rejoinder, 'KYYY has the answers!' had been scripted on the van's flanks. The promotion department was not inclined towards moderation. All the station vehicles had been painted in this ghastly eye-catching fashion.

'Hey, a little of my special marinara sauce for you boys.' The president and owner of Muldoni's Home-made

Macaroni approached with an aluminium pot and ladled some of its contents on to their plates. Mrs Muldoni had cooked up great vats of pasta and sauce for her television appearance. She wasn't going to let them go to waste.

Without a break in the rhythm of his consumption, Phil shovelled up another mound of pasta. It filled his cheeks but didn't rumple his placidity. Nothing did that, especially not the demands of his job. Most KYYY photographers worked alone, but Phil had been assigned to work with Art because at critical junctures he couldn't always be trusted to lift his camera finger and shoot.

Art stared at the mess of pastas and sauces on his plate. It was actually his fault. If he had remembered to lock the van's sliding door last night, it wouldn't have happened, at least not in the van. Art had noticed it was unlocked when he went to get his equipment out for the live shot and saw her lying there dead. He extracted a strand of vermicelli from his plate. From what he had observed, Laurel had been strangled. The murderer, Art noted glumly, had used Art's longest and newest mike cord. 'I shouldn't have left my equipment in the van last night,' he grumbled, sipping up the vermicelli. Each KYYY photographer was assigned his own set of gear. The two photographers had been using Phil's car and equipment that day until they switched to the van for the live shot.

'If we hadn't been in such a hurry to get to that alleged fire this morning, I'd have gotten my stuff then.' Art devoured a piece of fusilli. As he chewed he considered his own words dolorously. 'Oh, my God, it will have my fingerprints all over it. What if they think I did it?'

The born-again Phil smiled. 'I'll vouch for you,' he said serenely, scooping up a large forkful of pasta.

'That's great. That's just great. All I need is a deadbeat like you for a character witness.' Art regarded his plate with disgust. He put it down, reached for a cigarette and lit it, staring at the book of matches he had picked up off the floor of the van. It was baby-blue and satiny. The word 'Tess's' was scripted across the cover in gold letters.

Staring at it, Art brightened. 'Wait a minute. You are my alibi,' he said. 'We saw Laurel this morning, remember?

After we came back from that fire, before we went to the Checkerdome to shoot that hockey story for Sports. We were together the whole time after that. We couldn't have done it.'

Phil smiled again and tranquilly chewed a large mouthful.

'Mud-wrestling . . . in California?' Hecklepeck's objections could be heard down the hall and into the newsroom. He appeared in the doorway. Outrage was written all over his face. '*Mistresses* wasn't bad enough. We had to do *mud-wrestling*. Why don't we just choose a centrefold each month and. . .'

'Can it, Heck,' Richard was still seated by the phone. 'Laurel's dead. They found her in the live truck. Macke says it looks like a strangling.'

Hecklepeck hardly seemed to shift gear. To the assignment-editor he said, 'Get another crew and a reporter out there *now*!' The assignment-editor was about to object. Hecklepeck shook his head. 'We can't rely on the live crew. The police will have to interview them,' he said, 'and we can't afford to be beaten out of our own story by the competition.'

He strode to Ken Marshal's office where he informed the news director that a short announcement was in order. He wrote it himself and delivered it at the top of the six o'clock news. It said merely that Laurel was dead and details would be aired as they became available.

Hecklepeck returned to the newsroom after the show. 'Come on,' he said to Richard. 'We're going over there.'

Without a word Richard reached for his jacket and pulled out his car keys. Hecklepeck often left his car at home and walked to work, making Richard his reluctant chauffeur. This time, however, Richard was eager to drive. He had often encountered murder on newstape but never in person.

Maria Muldoni's block looked more like the scene of a nightmarish carnival than a murder investigation. Other news vehicles, some as brightly painted as the KYYY van, had been allowed to park inside the barricades. They flanked the van like freaky circus wagons. Some were equipped with television lights, which threw a brilliant white blanket over the scene, turning news photographers and their police subjects into peculiar faceless paper dolls.

Mrs Muldoni was the only three-dimensional figure there. But, over made-up for her TV appearance, she was hardly a comforting sight. Her lips cut through the light in a garish red swath. The pink circles of her sagging cheeks hung like melancholy full moons. A harlequinesque figure, she circulated with huge trays of pasta dishes. These she was now offering to her neighbours since the police had turned them down.

The lawmen stood about idly in sad little groups, men trained to help with nothing to do. The captain in charge of the City Homicide Division had called out all his troops in a camera-oriented show of conscientiousness. Most of them were superfluous and there was nothing they could have done for Laurel Michaels anyway.

Richard and Hecklepeck took it all in from the dark of the onlooking crowd. Unable to convince the uniformed policeman at the barricade that Richard's battered Toyota was a newscar, they had parked outside and walked.

Richard shivered. The nightmarish quality of the scene was not lost on him. He had seen Fellini's *Satyricon* eight times; five of them stoned. One of those times he had smoked several bowls of miracle hash outside the movie theatre and barely made it to his seat. This real-life phantasmagoria was giving him the same panicky, paranoid sensations he had got from that viewing. Richard glanced around wildly. With relief he recognised KYYY night-time reporter Barry Saire and his photographer. He ducked under the police tape and headed for the familiar comfort of news-gathering.

Hecklepeck remained on the sidelines. He, too, was affected by what he saw but, unlike Richard, he didn't let it distract him because to Hecklepeck it was a news story.

'The lab guys are wrapping up. The meat wagon's on its way.' One of the homicide detectives was reporting to Lieutenant Mike Berger.

Berger nodded. 'You and Tucker head on out to her apartment,' he said. 'Stake it out until we get clearance from the county. I want to know if anyone goes in there while we're waiting on the paperwork.'

'Lad-di-dah,' said the detective. 'Better get my passport in order if I'm going over to mingle with the county boys.'

'Don't worry,' Berger rejoined. 'The way yahr dressed you won't get lost in the crowd.' All of Berger's 'yours' emerged as 'yahrs'. It was a characteristic of almost any St Louisan raised south of Highway Fahrty.

He turned back to the van, his face taking on an expression of profound sadness. To Berger every murder investigation was a bereavement. He had been with the St Louis Police Department for more than twenty years and had attended scores of murder-scene vigils, but he still couldn't understand how anybody could take another's life. No motivation, no set of circumstances had ever been presented to Berger that justified the act of murder. He mourned every victim.

Berger was by nature a sad man so it was fortunate that his job provided him with the opportunity to grieve. There were victims aplenty and the work of crime investigation, which often succeeded in rendering justice, served as a palliative.

Berger's wife had long since recognised his maudlinism. She encouraged him to work out his troubles at the office and tried to prevent him from spending long periods of time at home. Holidays were sombre enough in the Berger household but longer vacation periods could stretch from being wretched to despairing.

Berger shoved his hands into the pockets of his cheap black raincoat to warm them. He regarded his men dolefully. Some were busy. Most were milling about in clusters. From behind one group emerged a tall, solid form, walking with the unconscious importance of the very self-assured.

Berger watched him approach. How many times, he wondered, had he seen Hecklepeck descend on a crime scene this way? Hecklepeck might be drawing an anchorman's paycheque but at heart he was still an investigative reporter, hungry for the big story.

Berger might well have resented Hecklepeck, given the anchorman's local celebrity status and notorious disrespect for police procedure. But he had nothing left for professional jealousy. It took all his energy to fight off melancholy. He plodded through each of his cases with deliberate care, hoping for an outcome that would relieve his feelings. If Hecklepeck could help him make an arrest, he would be a grateful man.

Hecklepeck had helped on several occasions. Berger had particularly welcomed his interference when a pipe bomb blew up in the office of a North St Louis veterinarian – killing the vet, a parrot and several dogs and cats. Berger had been more acutely affected than usual because of the hapless pets. The bloodied body of a pure-white Persian tormented him for weeks.

While the police were trying to establish unlikely connections with the Mafia, Hecklepeck had investigated a hunch of his own. It had led to the arrest of the vet's receptionist. She had discovered that the vet was selling animals for research and in the name of Animal Rights she blew him up.

'Bill Hecklepeck. Hey buddy, I know how you must feel,' Berger was sympathetic. 'One of yahr own, killed in the line of duty.'

Hecklepeck nodded and cut to the heart of things. 'Laurel Michaels was a pain in the ass,' he said. 'You're going to have a tough time finding her murderer. Half of St Louis wanted to kill her.'

'From what I read in the paper, you did too.'

Hecklepeck didn't bother to deny it. 'I'd like to see the body,' he said.

The area around the van was deserted. Having finished their photoing and probing, the police had made a tactful retreat. Laurel's body was being granted a few moments of quiet before the ambulance trip to the city morgue.

Hecklepeck looked through the open sliding doors on the passenger side of the van. In the television light Laurel's cream jump-suit seemed to leap out at him. There were dirty streaks on it and a few drops of blood on the right shoulder. She lay on her front with her head in the corner behind the driver's seat. Her legs were splayed, the right one bent backwards against the side of the van and the left straight out.

Berger's fleshy face seemed to sag in pity. He ran a hand over the top of his crewcut and began: 'The driver of the van says he didn't see her because he was in a hurry. The big fat guy riding in the passenger seat dumped his coat back here. It musta covered her up.' Berger sounded as if he didn't quite believe this.

Knowing Phil, Hecklepeck had less trouble with it. He noted that the body was as cold as the outside air and rigor mortis was becoming established. Laurel's arms were stiffening. Her right arm, looking thin and pathetic, stuck out between the front seats, while the left tightened at her side. Hecklepeck could just picture Art and Phil speeding to reach their live shot while Laurel's right hand waved between them.

'She must have met her assailant in the van,' Berger continued. 'Until those clowns took it, it hadn't been moved all day.' Hecklepeck nodded. The van had been parked at the far end of an area of the KYYY lot that was reserved for news vehicles. He had seen it on his way into work.

The rubbery cord around Laurel's neck had loosened when her assailant released it. Underneath, Hecklepeck saw a double ring of bluish bruises. They contrasted starkly with her cream suit. Yet, it wasn't the bruises but two little brown coils resting on Laurel's back that gave him a cold feeling in the pit of his stomach. After strangling Laurel with the microphone cable the murderer had carefully wound up both ends of the cord. The killer, Hecklepeck realised, would have wanted to keep the cable from getting caught in the van door where it might have been seen and the body prematurely discovered. But why not toss it out of the way? Why coil it up so neatly? Somebody, he thought distastefully, had taken precious time to be fastidious.

The rest of Art's equipment lay in an untidy heap behind the passenger seat. Lights, battery belts, cables, extension cords, microphones and the camera tape-recorder: it all seemed to be there except the microphone cable and the camera itself.

Laurel's left cheek was resting on the camera. Appropriate, Hecklepeck thought. She was going to her final rest, pillowed on a television camera. On the visible half of her face he recognised her bitterly self-righteous look. That, too, was telling. It was the look Laurel wore when she was on to one of her stories.

'See that cut on her fahrhead,' Berger pointed to a gash on Laurel's right temple. 'Somebody hit her head-on. They must have been sitting on the flahr, otherwise the assailant couldn't have gotten enough of a swing to bash her like that. Not enough headroom.'

Hecklepeck nodded. Laurel had been sitting face to face with her murderer. Death may have surprised her but it hadn't sneaked up on her. Whatever the chain of events that led to her murder, Laurel had obviously been a partner in the dance, not as guilty as her killer but not entirely innocent either. He felt relieved of any obligation to feel pity.

'What was she hit with?'

'Dunno, probably something in that pile.' Berger gestured towards Art's equipment. 'We're going to take it down to headquarters and sift through it.' The rest of the van's interior, Hecklepeck noted, was shipshape. There were latched drawers and cupboards for equipment storage. Panels of buttons were built into the rear and side of the vehicle. In the near back corner was a passenger seat.

'The victim would have slumped over,' Berger continued in a melancholy tone. 'Then her attacker pushed or pulled her on to her stomach and strangled her.'

'And took her coat,' said Hecklepeck. 'I don't think she'd be out without a coat.'

Berger took out a notebook. 'We wondered about that. What'd it look like?'

'Well, it was quilted . . . big and purple. Made her look like a huge grape.'

46

'We'll put out an APB for a grapeskin,' Berger smiled painfully.

'That coat had big pockets. She kept everything in them. Laurel never carried a handbag,' Hecklepeck explained, adding significantly, 'all her story notes were in those pockets.'

'Anything else?' Berger probed. 'You worked with her.'

Hecklepeck shrugged. 'I think you've got it right. She . . . met somebody she knew. Whether by prearrangement or not.' He finished, 'Listen, Mike. I've got to go. I have a show to put on.'

Berger turned back to his men. Hecklepeck hadn't told him much he didn't already know.

'Get a shot of that, that red stuff,' KYYY night-time reporter Barry Saire pointed to a sizeable pool on the pavement. The photographer obediently swung his camera lens in that direction.

'Why?' asked Richard with deadly sarcasm. 'Why are you shooting that puddle of spaghetti sauce?'

Barry opened his pretty blue eyes. 'I thought it was, might be, bl . . . blood.' Barry's *In the Dark* features were aptly named.

Richard was scathing. 'Can't you see the meatball in the middle?' he asked. The sight of Hecklepeck was a welcome interruption. Richard followed him to the car.

'Well, what? *What?*' Richard asked as he started the reluctant vehicle.

Hecklepeck told him what he had seen, concluding, 'There's no doubt she was murdered. Which of course begs the question why, and in turn brings up the distinct possibility that she may have been on to a big story after all.'

'Oh, *reeeeally*,' said Richard. 'Are you saying that if you had believed her and supported her instead of acting like a great big "I'm-a-star" baby that it might not have happened and Laurel would be alive today?'

'No, I'm not saying that,' Hecklepeck sounded irritable. 'My believing her would have changed nothing so long as she refused to cover her own ass and share what she had with somebody. She could have told me; I wasn't going to steal her precious story. But spreading the information around would have kept her from being killed.'

'You could have encouraged her a little more, been her news daddy.'

'Her what?' But Hecklepeck didn't wait to hear it again. 'No, Little Richard, you're not going to get me off on one of your guilt trips. Laurel was a big, grown-up reporter; she could have protected herself in a number of different ways. She didn't and now the evidence says she was killed because of it.'

'What evidence?' asked Richard.

'For one thing, whoever murdered her took her coat. All Laurel's notes for that series of hers were in those coat pockets.'

'Her wallet was also in one of those pockets. Maybe she was killed for money.' One of the manifestations of Richard's prolonged adolescence was his love of objections.

'No. If the killer had wanted her money, he would simply have taken it out of her coat pocket and made off with it as quickly as possible. This psychopath hung around to clean up.'

'Why didn't the murderer take the notebooks out of the coat pockets instead of stealing the whole coat? That coat wasn't exactly inconspicuous. It was huge and . . . purple. How did whoever took it get it across the parking lot without being seen?'

'I don't know,' said Hecklepeck.

'Ken is in with the station manager and they want to see you,' the voice of the evening assignment-editor stopped Hecklepeck as he charged across the newsroom. She was minding an empty store. Other newsroom-staffers had gone home or were taking dinner-breaks.

'I'm not officially back yet,' Hecklepeck growled. 'Richard, I need you.' He propelled Richard to the front of Laurel's cubbyhole office. 'You stand there and let me know if anyone comes.'

'What are you doing, Heck? Have the police deputized

48

you to work on this one?' But Richard stayed where he had been put.

Hecklepeck picked up Laurel's tape recorder from her desk. He detached the headphones and pushed the 'play' button. The little cubbyhole was filled with a giant exhalation. In spite of himself, Hecklepeck looked to see if the walls were caving in, and as he did, he heard the surf rolling in. 'What the hell is that?'

'Ocean sounds,' said Richard. 'Laurel's latest craze. She came in with that cassette a few weeks ago and made everyone listen to it while taking deep breaths. It's supposed to relax you.'

Hecklepeck let the tape continue to play as he turned to the rest of the items on Laurel's desk top.

It was covered with untidy file folders. There was a long correspondence with a local cleaners suggesting they soon would be figuring prominently in *Consumer Corner*. A lot of information on dietary fat and cancer coupled with sample menus from some of St Louis' best restaurants indicated Laurel intended to rate their meals for fat content. There were also a number of files on stories that had already aired which suggested to Hecklepeck that Laurel must have been preparing to follow up on them. What there wasn't was anything at all connected with her current project, the *Mistresses* series.

Hecklepeck glanced at the hook where Laurel's coat had hung before flipping through her Roladex. The telephone numbers were mostly consumer agencies or advocacy groups. There were a few individuals but they all had titles. There was nobody who appeared to be a personal friend.

Hecklepeck sifted through the books and video tapes on the shelf over Laurel's desk. None of them seemed pertinent to her death. Neither did her calendar which was taped on the concrete wall just under the shelves. The calendar entries were written in shorthand: 'Interview, 10.00' or 'Shoot cover tape, location A'. Laurel believed the entire world was out to steal her story ideas. She trusted no one with the details.

Was she also secretive about her private life?

Hecklepeck wondered. There was nothing on the calendar that appeared to be a personal engagement. But he remembered how many evenings Laurel had spent at the station, ostensibly reviewing tapes or editing. He wondered if she hadn't just wanted to avoid going home alone.

The cry of a seagull echoed through the cubbyhole. As the surf once again rolled out, Hecklepeck switched off the tape recorder and looked over the tiny room to see what he had missed. His eyes came to rest on Laurel's typewriter. Taped to the beat-up Olympia was a handwritten note. He pulled it off. It read '13.43:22'.

Hecklepeck considered. It could have been a combination, of course. Laurel might well have had a safe. But Hecklepeck didn't think so. He stepped outside. 'What do you make of this, Richard?'

Richard opened his eyes and dropped his wrist. He had been deep-breathing along with the ocean and checking its effect on his pulse.

'Thirteen,' Richard said rudely, 'comes after twelve. Forty three is a big number. It . . . ' Hecklepeck offered Richard a look of pure malevolence. 'It looks like time-code, Heck,' Richard spoke as though he were addressing a simpleton.

Hecklepeck nodded. That had been his assessment too. Time-code is digital numbering which is electronically applied to video tape. Since the tapes used by television photographers are twenty minutes long, it can be a time-consuming process for editors to locate certain shots. With time-code the photographers' field tapes can be logged in advance. The editor then has only to watch the digital clocking as he fast-forwards. When he gets to the time indicated on the log sheet, he has located his shot.

If the numbers on Laurel's desk were time-code, they referred to a shot that could be found thirteen minutes forty-three seconds and twenty-two frames from the beginning of a tape. Video tape has thirty frames or pictures per second.

'I wonder why she had it taped to her typewriter?' mused Hecklepeck.

'She probably just wanted to keep a certain shot in mind,' said Richard, still speaking in his tone for the very stupid. 'It's no big deal.'

Hecklepeck looked at the shelves of video tapes over Laurel's desk. Then he regarded a box of some fifteen tapes sitting on the floor under her typewriter table. The box was labelled '*Mistresses*' in black magic-marker. 'It *might* be a big deal.' He looked around and noted that the newsroom was empty, the assignment-editor had gone. 'We won't know till we look at the tapes.' He picked up the box and shoved it at Richard. 'Here.'

'What am I supposed to do with this?' Richard asked, alarmed.

'Keep it. I can't put it in my office. It's too obvious.' The trash pile on Hecklepeck's desk was entirely composed of paper. There were no video tapes in his office because he rarely covered any stories. Richard's desk on the other hand was piled with tapes. He kept copies of features for slow nights when he needed something extra to fill the ten o'clock show. He also wrote and produced original stories for KYYY's on-air reporters. For these he kept stacks of field tapes.

'Better yet. . .' Hecklepeck retrieved the box and dumped its contents on Richard's desk. He then filled it with part of Richard's tape collection and replaced it in Laurel's office.

Richard would have objected but Hecklepeck's abrupt removal of one tape stack had toppled several others, covering his desk in sliding tapes. He leapt to stop the cascade while some of the still-standing stacks wavered dangerously.

Hecklepeck regarded the mess on Richard's desk with satisfaction. 'That's perfect Richard. Nobody will find them there.' Richard muttered something obscene.

'I beg your pardon?' Station manager Wally Corette was standing behind Richard, who straightened up nervously as several piles of tapes collapsed.

Wally merely frowned at the mess. He turned to Hecklepeck with a big, phoney smile. 'Bill, my man, do you think you could come into my office? Ken and I would like

51

to chat with you.'

Hecklepeck seemed to welcome the opportunity. 'Right, Wally. I'm at your command,' he said purposefully.

As he followed Wally into the hall, Hecklepeck grinned evilly over his shoulder. Richard didn't respond. He was too busy clearing a small work-place on his desk. It wasn't until later that he remembered the appearance of the station manager's mistress on the first part of Laurel's series.

CHAPTER FIVE

WALLY CORETTE STRODE INTO HIS office and seated himself in the big fake-leather chair behind his large, empty desk. The station manager was a handsome, if hard-looking, man. From his Brylcreamed black hair to his lacquered black shoes he kept himself under careful control. Wally had been losing spontaneity for years. The more it drained away the more he had to drink to summon it.

Hecklepeck trailed him into the room, deliberately dawdling. He knew Wally's game. It was the only one Wally had: intimidation. Wally expected him to sit on one of two torturous straight chairs in front of his desk. From there he would be completely dominated by Wally's desk, Wally's recliner and Wally himself.

Ken was already in one of the chairs, his affable face tilted towards the man behind the desk; a blank slate, waiting for Wally to write on him.

Hecklepeck knew Wally was more likely to spit, and he turned to his left and ambled to the far end of the room where a sofa was grouped with some chairs and a coffee table. He settled himself on the sofa and looked expectantly at Wally. The room was large and there was a sizable expanse of shag rug between Hecklepeck's sofa and Wally's desk. Wally had shrunk.

Wally looked back at Hecklepeck. Hecklepeck knew he was supposed to be unnerved by the silence. He reached into the cigar box on Wally's coffee table, helped himself and lit up with a flourish. Hecklepeck looked at Wally.

Wally looked at Hecklepeck. Thuggery had always worked for him. He had no other strategy. Like other local television station managers he had come from a mid- to lower-management position in a larger parent company. Wally and the others were assigned to television in the early days when it was something of a joke and not expected to be profitable. As the years went by and the industry began to make large amounts of money, there was no need to change management. Through no effort of his own Wally had effectively become a king with the reputation of a Midas touch. He had a legacy of money-making stations behind him.

Hecklepeck puffed prodigiously on the cigar and looked at Wally. He knew that even the king had to answer to a higher authority: the family.

KYYY was owned and robbed by the Babson family media conglomerate. Babson Broadcasting regularly reaped the profits from its five television stations and used them to finance less profitable ventures, of which there were many. The Babsons rarely interfered in station management unless some decision was made that affected earnings. Then they descended like huns on the city of Rome and cleaned house so completely that even the station receptionist was fired and replaced.

Before Wally there had been a house-cleaning every two or three years. Wally had managed to survive for five, mostly by doing nothing. He never bought any new equipment. He refused to increase the budget for promotion. He added no new personnel and only replaced half of those who left, always at lower salaries. These policies kept Wally's expenditure low. They enabled the station to show ever larger profits. That they did so at the expense of future growth did not bother Wally or the short-sighted Babsons.

Wally looked down at his manicured nails. He would have gladly fired Hecklepeck and replaced him with an Anchor half as expensive. But he knew the Babsons wouldn't approve. Barry Babson loved Hecklepeck whom he credited with making KYYY number one in news, thus enabling the station to increase its earnings on newscast commercials. Wally looked back at Hecklepeck.

'We have been trying to formulate a strategy to

54

effectively meet this, uh, challenge of Laurel's tragic demise.' The forgotten Ken had finally been cowed into speech. 'We were wondering. . .'

'We're going to have to cancel this series of hers,' Wally interrupted. 'We can't possibly air it. We don't know what she had in mind.' Wally had to strain for Hecklepeck to hear. 'Ken and I think it would be better if we took a hands-off approach to this thing. We feel it's too close to home and might hurt our standing in the community.' Wally's eyes narrowed slightly. He took a deep breath so as to project clearly. 'I understand you went down there tonight, Bill. I hope that doesn't mean you're going to get involved in this one.'

Hecklepeck picked his feet up and placed them, one after the other, on Wally's coffee table. He crossed them. Wally wasn't so much worried about the station's reputation as he was about his own, Hecklepeck reflected grimly, and so far he was safe. Few people outside the station would have recognised Rita Cullen on the first part of Laurel's series. Only station employees were likely to connect her with Wally. If Wally could stop it there, he could keep it from the Babsons and from his wife.

Ken spoke up again anxiously. 'We've, uh, looked at several scenarios. We feel the best mode of operation is to lay low and just report the official statements handed out by the police.'

'I see,' Hecklepeck spoke softly. His tone had a dangerous edge. 'You want to put us in the news-suppression business rather than the news-dissemination business.'

'What?' snapped Wally, beginning to rock in his recliner in irritation.

'I said we're in the news business and not in the business of suppressing news,' Hecklepeck boomed.

Ken jumped nervously. 'Oh, we're not going to suppress anything,' he squealed. 'We want you to do a special half-hour news show one week from tonight about Laurel and her work, kind of a memorial.'

They want to keep me busy, thought Hecklepeck with amusement.

'We'll get a producer to review all of her stories and pick the highlights for a show you would write focusing on her work and her contribution to the community,' Ken continued loudly.

'I want Richard to produce it,' Hecklepeck all but whispered.

'What!' shouted Wally.

'I want Richard,' Hecklepeck returned in more penetrating tones. 'You'll have to free him up from the ten o'clock.'

Ken looked disturbed but Wally jumped in. 'Sounds good Bill, I'm sure it can be arranged. We'll schedule the show for one week from tonight in prime time. In the meantime you can leave the investigating to the police.' He stood, preparing to end the meeting.

But Hecklepeck was comfortable in his seat. He puffed on his cigar. He blew a series of smoke rings. 'Okay Wally. Now you tell me something. What was Rita Cullen doing in the first part of Laurel's *Mistresses* series?'

Wally looked at Hecklepeck. He walked to the opposite end of the room, to a vinyl-covered bar flanked with mirrors and poured himself a Jack Daniels. His measured return took him the entire length of the room.

'I don't know what you're talking about,' Wally said, looking directly down on Hecklepeck from the top of his six-foot frame.

Hecklepeck stood up. He paused while Wally adjusted his gaze upwards. 'Yes, you do,' he said. 'You and the lovely Ms Cullen have been seen stepping out together on several occasions. If I had to, I could produce witnesses.' Hecklepeck walked past Wally. 'You must have been livid when you discovered Rita was part of that videoed dirty-laundry list aired by Laurel Michaels yesterday and that was just the first part of the series. Didn't you wonder what Laurel was planning for the rest of the week?' He turned and leaned up against Wally's desk.

Wally stiffened. But he managed to swing around and deposit himself on the sofa. 'How do you know Miss Cullen was in that group? Those women were all disguised.'

'What?' bellowed Hecklepeck. Wally repeated himself.

Hecklepeck smiled knowingly. 'If I were the police,' he

boomed, 'I'd be checking the raw tapes for that series. I wouldn't be at all surprised if there weren't some recognisable shots of our Miss Rita. Who knows maybe she even mentioned you by name? It would ruin your future with the high-minded Babson family. I wonder just what you would have done to keep it off the air.'

'We'll let the police handle it,' Wally spat the words out. 'I suggest that you confine yourself to work on that half-hour show and stay away from matters that aren't any of your business. Your contract is not unbreakable.'

Hecklepeck grinned. 'Okay. Richard and I'll go to work on the show tonight,' he said. He headed for the door. Ken staggered out of the office behind him.

Wally remained seated on the edge of the sofa for several minutes after they left. Then he walked over to his phone and dialed two digits. 'Come to my office,' he growled. Wally hung up the phone and looked at his watch. It was about half an hour until the ten o'clock news.

In the newsroom Hecklepeck threw himself into the desk chair opposite Richard's. He draped himself across the top and helped himself to some of the French fries Richard was having for dinner. Richard ignored him. He was busy adding up tape and commercial times to see how they filled out his thirty-minute show.

'You know what's sad, my man,' Hecklepeck said with mock self-pity. Richard didn't look up. 'It's positively heartbreaking to see how little gratitude you have. Here I rescue you from the interminable drudgery of this tedious production line you're on and you aren't the least bit gracious about it.'

Richard stared at Hecklepeck, his black beard twitching suspiciously. 'What are you talking about?' he asked.

'I have gotten you sprung from the ten o'clock news to produce a half-hour special on Laurel's murder. It's going to air one week from tonight. We'll have to do some fast investigating to find her murderer before then.'

'What?'

'If we don't, we'll have to do a half hour on Laurel, herself, her life and times.'

'You've got to be kidding!' Richard wasn't at all pleased. 'Specials' were a lot of work and he had a feeling Hecklepeck wasn't going to dispense too much of *his* energy on the production of this one.

From the blur of her bleached curls to the rounded curves of her ankles, the young woman walking across the carpeted expanse towards Wally's desk had the sensual promise of a down pillow. She was encased in pastel polyester. With her pale-blue eyes directed myopically at Wally, the woman hooked her right toe behind her left heel and stumbled.

Rita Cullen had never acquired grace. But she didn't seem to feel the bumps and falls. Like a piece of white bread her flesh merely dimpled and rebounded. Those who failed to read the expression of greed in her eyes mistakenly believed she was soft to the core.

Rita seated herself on Wally's lap with a plop, wrapped her arms around his neck and kissed him in the corner of his mouth.

Wally pushed her abruptly on to the floor. 'There's something I want you to do,' he snarled.

The red puddle filled the television monitor. Barry stopped short of claiming it for blood but the implication was clear. His story was about murder not spaghetti sauce.

'Je-sus Kay-rist,' Richard wailed in the production booth. He slouched deep into his chair. As far as he was concerned the show was ruined. Somebody almost always ruined Richard's shows. Every night he walked into the booth with a newscast that went flawlessly on paper. Practically every night one of the many people whose job it was to translate Richard's script into television made a mistake and disfigured his perfect show. Night after night after night it was an embittering experience.

'. . . I'm Barry Saire reporting, *In the Dark*.' Barry's report ended and the camera took Hecklepeck. He too had found Barry's report lacking. He was shaking his head in utter disgust.

'Oh, fuck me,' Richard moaned. 'Why can't he pretend

for once?' He sank further into his chair.

When Richard returned to the newsroom after the show, the phones were ringing insistently and members of the police Forensic Unit were jockeying for a place in Laurel's cubbyhole. The rest of Berger's team milled idly about the newsroom.

Richard answered a phone. It was a furious Italian viewer who had recognised the puddle of red stuff for what it was. Perversely, Richard leapt to the defence. Viewers, no matter how justified, were not entitled to bother him with their protests. He sighed grandly and punched the button of another ringing line.

Feeling no compunction to help, Hecklepeck made for his own office. That was where Lieutenant Berger found him. 'Let me run something by you, Bill.' Hecklepeck assented with a gesture. 'Yahr colleagues tell us there should be some tapes in Ms Michael's office. Tapes fahr this thing she was working on. This *Mistresses* thing.'

'Oh, they're there,' said Hecklepeck with confidence.

'No they're not. There are no tapes in her office at all.'

'None? No tapes at all?'

Berger nodded.

Hecklepeck considered this. 'Maybe they were stolen,' he suggested.

'We've thought of that.' Berger slowly patted the bristles on the top of his head. 'We wondered if you knew anything about it. That girl. That whatchamacallit, assignment-editor, says you were messing around in there earlier.'

'True,' said Hecklepeck, 'I looked in briefly to see if Laurel's coat was there. However, I did happen to notice a cardboard box full of tapes under her typewriter table.' In his mind Hecklepeck excused himself. It was true he had lifted the real tapes but somebody else had taken the false ones. While *he* was out to see justice done, that somebody else was probably a murder suspect and well worth police attention. Hecklepeck decided the police owed him some credit for keeping the real tapes out of the hands of that unscrupulous person.

Berger nodded slowly. 'We'll find it. On another matter, she was apparently waiting for some phone call about an interview? You know anything about that? Does it make any connections for you?' Berger couldn't bring himself to say the name of the victim.

Hecklepeck shook his head. He didn't know anything about it. But he was glad to be told.

'No, we are not prejudiced against Italian-Americans here! I eat spaghetti, too, quite often. I love spaghetti. I sometimes have it three times a day, not including snacks. I wear it to parties!' Richard was screaming into the phone.

He pushed the button of another line and began again. 'This is the Anti-pasta Patriotic Association, dedicated to eradicating consumption of anything ending in "itti" or "oni" wherever it lurks.'

Hecklepeck stepped out of his cubbyhole and shook his head. He grabbed his jacket and Richard's from the coat rack and hurried over to Richard, saying: 'The poor guy. He's finally cracked under the strain. He and Laurel were very close, you know.' Hecklepeck winked at Berger as he took the receiver out of Richard's hand and hung up the phone. Before Richard could protest he yanked him out of his seat and steered him towards the door. 'I'll just take the poor guy home and settle him in for the night. Things'll be better in the morning.'

Berger looked sympathetic as Hecklepeck opened the door and shoved Richard out.

CHAPTER SIX

OUTSIDE IN THE PARKING LOT, Hecklepeck slapped Richard on the back. 'Good deal,' he said. 'Now let's get to work.'

Richard just stood, stunned. Hadn't he just heard Hecklepeck link his name romantically with that of Laurel Michaels? The expression of pain on his face deepened. In the yellowish cast of the KYYY anti-crime lights he appeared jaundiced.

The newsroom door from which Hecklepeck and Richard had emerged was on the long side of the concrete shoe-box that contained KYYY. It opened on to an expanse of pitted black asphalt. In the far right corner of the parking lot Laurel's BMW was marked off in orange police tape. Along with Richard's Toyota, the BMW was one of only a few employee-owned vehicles remaining.

The lot was, however, partially filled with police cars and to the left of the newsroom door, on the other side of a fifteen-foot-high chain-link fence, the station vehicles were parked. Some security-minded news director had put up the fence to create a safe parking area for station vehicles. It had succeeded too well. There was a morning when a warehouse fire had raged out of control in downtown St Louis. A special crew was called in to cover it. But crew members got no further than the fence's double gate. The news director had absent-mindedly taken the keys to the Radio/Television News Directors' Convention in Las Vegas. By the time a helicopter had been summoned to fly the crew the two miles to the fire, it was out. After that the gates were always open.

Even before the fire, the fence had had its critics. The

KYYY fault-finders were willing to concede it protected one side of the lot and the station building could be said to safeguard another. But the other two were defended only by a low concrete wall which a child could easily traverse.

Even these objections, the same station critics argued, were peripheral to the real issue. It was, they said, a question of philosophy: a television station should be accessible to its public, even if the public makes off with the occasional fifty-thousand-dollar camera.

Hecklepeck glanced at the police cars parked in front of the newsroom door. Then he grabbed Richard by the elbow and pulled him through the fence to the end of the row of newscars. 'The van was parked here,' he declared. 'You stand here and be it.'

Richard stood. He was still trying to rid his mind of that libellous coupling with Laurel.

Hecklepeck walked slowly around Richard. Laurel and her murderer could have met behind the van in virtual seclusion. The vehicle itself would have shielded them from the rest of the parking lot. On the other side beyond the concrete wall was a shallow wooded area. The two were unlikely to have been seen from there and they would not have been spotted from the station building since the KYYY shoe-box had no windows.

All the murderer had to do afterwards was get out of the van, jump the low concrete wall and walk among the trees behind the station building. Then the killer could have made his/her way to the Burger Chef on the other side of the station and got lost in the lunch crowd.

. . . If it weren't for the coat, the long, purple, quilted coat. That coat would have been spotted, even among the weirdos at the Burger Chef. And maybe when the police began questioning people that would be the case. But Hecklepeck wondered if the coat could possibly have been abandoned on the far side of the wall. He went to look but it wasn't there and from what he could see under the parking-lot lights there was nothing big and purple among the trash in the wooded area. Perhaps, he speculated, the coat had been dumped on the far side of the wall and the murderer had already returned for it. There had been plenty of time and, under the cover of nightfall, opportunity.

Laurel's murderer had been helped by the moving of the van. If her body had been discovered in the parking lot, the place would have been crawling with police a whole lot sooner. Instead, the van had been parked on the street in front of Maria Muldoni's bungalow when Laurel was found and the police had concentrated their efforts there.

But, as Hecklepeck walked back towards Richard, he was still unsatisfied about the coat. It was too purple. How could the murderer leave it and be sure that no one else would spot it and pick it up? And otherwise, how did the murderer make off with the coat without being seen?

'Here's what I think we ought to do.' Hecklepeck stopped in front of Richard. 'We've got to wait until the police are finished so we can go back and look at the tapes. Why don't we go to Tareesa Wells' nightclub and talk to her about Laurel's series. She was in it.'

'Not me. I'm going home.' Richard's disgust finally found words.

'Richard . . . Richard . . . Richard. Where's your spirit of adventure, your dedication to the truth, your. . .'

'Shut up, Heck. I've had it. I'm going home.' Feeling in his coat pockets for his keys, Richard marched off in the direction of his Toyota. Hecklepeck followed, watching him with amusement.

'Go ahead and leave if you like. But I'm borrowing your car.' Hecklepeck dangled Richard's car keys in front of his nose. 'I extracted them from your coat pocket for your own good, in the interest of protecting you from yourself.'

'Give them to me, Heck.'

Hecklepeck swung into the driver's seat of the battered Toyota. 'I'm sure the police would agree with me that you mustn't drive in this condition.'

Richard looked back at the newsroom door. As he did, an idling police car shifted into gear and merged away into the Kingshighway traffic. Richard got into the passenger seat and folded his arms across his chest.

'Well, I'm glad for the company. How do you start this

wreck?' The gear stick in Richard's aged Toyota stuck more than it shifted. They were off to a fitful start. The car tossed like a mechanical bull. 'Sha-boom, Sha-boom,' yelled Hecklepeck as the poor vehicle jerked its way out of the lot, on to Kingshighway.

Coming in from outside, Tareesa Wells removed her shaggy pink coat and hung it in her office closet. She looked at herself in the full-length mirror on the inside of the plywood door. She was a short, black-black woman with a mane of relaxed and gently waved hair. Tonight her thick features beamed with satisfaction.

She strolled out into her club. Wrapped in a blue satin sarong, Tareesa walked as though pulled by a string attached to her belly button. She had an attitude, a my-body-right-or-wrong bravado and it commanded attention.

Tareesa's club was just over the line separating poor and largely black St Louis on the North from the wealthy and fashionable Central West End on the South. However, she let her white patrons know that not only her club but also her heart was in the North. Called simply 'Tess's' the club was the centre of black society.

Central West End clubs were usually decorated in Art-Deco cool or country-antique cosy. Tareesa's place was a mixture of the bourgeois and the bordello. Customers sat in cushy synthetic red plush chairs that wheeled easily and comfortably on the red-and-gold-patterned carpet. They rested their elbows on parquet tables laminated in thick plastic and their eyes on wood-panelled walls covered with photographs of Tareesa: Tareesa with distinguished guests: Tareesa with Stevie Wonder and Jesse Jackson; Tareesa with government officials and city aldermen; most of all, Tareesa with Alderman Walter Payne, with Tiny – all three hundred pounds of him.

From behind the bar, the living Tareesa surveyed her patrons with satisfaction. The club was about half-full, good enough for a Tuesday night. Good enough, Tareesa decided, to have the Harmones back again. The Harmones was the current jazz group playing at Tess's.

64

Taressa had a knack for finding good, young jazz performers and her club was known for its music.

Tareesa herself was a product of Blues Alley. When she'd first performed there as a young singer, Blues Alley was one of the most thriving nightclub strips in the country. Barbra Streisand sang there. So did a host of other talented performers.

Blues Alley died suddenly and completely in the late Sixties from a fatal mixture of drugs and prostitution. (Tareesa, it was said, dealt in both.) The combination was so lethal it turned the nightclub strip into an urban desert, leaving only the music of the west wind rustling in the trash and hooting through empty buildings to the percussion of passing cars. Just a few blocks away, capitalized with cash, Tess's thrived.

On the outside Tareesa's club was in a low-slung, concrete building identified only by a small neon sign over the doorway. Standing by itself with empty lots on either side, it had a forbidding look, a demeanour that warned the uninitiated to stay away.

Richard would have been happy to stay away. However, he was even less keen to continue standing on trash-strewn Page Avenue where all kinds of menaces lurked.

Hecklepeck wasn't bothered in the least. He pushed open the heavy door, holding it for Richard behind him.

The Harmones were on a break. The stage was dark and the club filled with the roar of conversation. A bruiser who looked big enough, and mean enough, to take on the entire Cardinals football team was collecting five-dollar cover charges at the door.

Hecklepeck handed him a ten, smiling gamely. The bruiser only glared in response, letting Hecklepeck and Richard know that in his view the eighth mortal sin was being white in a club of black people. With a sinking feeling that left his stomach somewhere around his ankles Richard noted that he and Hecklepeck were the only white people in the place.

He followed Hecklepeck to the bar in a haze of fear, all too conscious of the sudden hush.

'We would like to talk to Tareesa Wells,' Hecklepeck said

65

to the bartender in a loud voice. Richard cringed.

The bartender merely stared. He had clearly gone to the same school of warm welcomes that the bruiser had attended.

'My, my, my . . . my, my, my, my,' from around the end of the bar came the curve of Tareesa's stomach, bringing the rest of her behind it. 'It's Mr Big-Time Tee-Vee, come to the ghet-to.' Patrons laughed.

Hecklepeck grinned. 'Yeah,' he said. 'I'm conducting a social experiment.' Another ripple of laughter went through the club.

Tareesa nodded slowly. 'Come, sit.' Her satiny rear twitched as she strutted over to a table set slightly apart from the others. It was her table, the place where she seated her special guests.

'What he got up his ass?' Tareesa cocked her head at Richard. Poor Richard's discomfort was making him appear stiffer than ever.

Hecklepeck slouched and stretched out his long legs as though Tess's was his natural habitat. 'He drove me,' he said offhandedly. Richard drew up in outrage.

Tareesa beckoned to a waitress. 'Would you like a drink?' she asked. Richard declined. He only drank alcohol when he didn't mind making a fool of himself. Now he longed for a shock-absorbing joint. Hecklepeck ordered a Carta Blanca beer.

'You here 'cause that Consumer bitch?' Hecklepeck nodded. Tareesa smiled contemptuously. She reached for a pack of Kools on the table and delicately extracted one, her long, red, plastic-hard nails gleaming in the half-light.

Hecklepeck picked up a satiny blue book of matches with 'Tess's' written across it and lit Tareesa's cigarette.

She smoked carefully, deliberately curling her creamy-red lips away from the cigarette. Teeth bared, she looked a little like an intelligent horse. 'Somebody took the bitch out,' Tareesa savoured the words, her eyelids dropping to half-mast. 'My, my, my.'

'Hey,' she said suddenly. 'That news report of hers, it ain't going to be TV now?'

Hecklepeck shook his head. 'She never put it together.

66

All she left behind was a box full of tapes.'

Tareesa smiled. 'Why you here, television man?'

'I'd like to know who killed her.'

"Fraid they be gunning for you?' Tareesa snorted. 'Shit. That bitch was on some kind of weird trip. I kinda got a kick out of her though. She come on like she some kinda high-minded so and so but she ain't nuthing but a garbage collector. She tole me she doing a story on, what she call,' Tareesa pulled back her lips and said the words precisely with her teeth, 'extra-mar-ee-tal relationships and their ro-ell in modern so-ci-et-ee. That ain't what she had in mind at all.'

'How so?' asked Hecklepeck.

'That white-assed Consumer bitch. . .' Tareesa leaned back as if she were enjoying herself. 'She scrooch'd around in that chair she was in and tied herself up in a grea' big knot and all this 'cause she's getting ready to put it to me that Alderman Tiny's been running around on me.' Tareesa laughed heartily. 'Me? You think I don't know that nigger got other women? Shoo-oot.' Tareesa paused as the waitress set a glass down in front of her and another beer before Hecklepeck.

The Harmones were coming back. Richard, whose case of discomfort was still acute, watched them pick up their instruments. Like glistening chocolate in gold wrappers the trio of band members all wore gold lamé. Richard wondered if they got their name from their musical synchronisation or their glandular secretions.

'That has the earmarks of her,' said Hecklepeck.

Tareesa took a sip of her drink. 'Dig it, television man. She come to me and want to do an interview 'bout all that marital jive. I say okay. She put the microphone in my face. I say Tiny and me got a good relationship. We do. We been together almost seven years.' Tareesa's blunt nose flattened and her nostrils flared. 'But that ain't what she after. she be more inclined to rake up dirt. She say Tiny been stepping out on me and she got doc-u-mentation, whatever that means. She make out like I be sitting at home waiting on him like some kind . . . some kinda . . . welfare mama. So I tell her again. We got a good relationship and that *is* all there is to it.'

'It sounds like she didn't exactly get what she was looking for then?'

'No way. Tiny and me got an understanding, man. He do his thing, I do mine. It's *our* bizniss. But she done the same thing to him, got herself all tied up in knots all over again and asked the same garbage questions. He didn't tell her different though.'

The lead Harmone looked like he had a sock in his crotch. But Richard didn't dare look long enough to tell. Just for the thought he bent his head over his lap.

With two long-nailed fingers Tareesa put out her cigarette. 'What she think I going to do? Go all sof and mushy for her and her cam-ra. No sir. *I* am a bizniss-woman.' Tareesa chuckled. 'But I sure did get a kick outta that lady. I sure did.'

The Harmones began to play a musical number and Tareesa stopped to listen. Richard was surprised to find that the group was quite good.

Hecklepeck was less sensitive to music. 'So it didn't bother you about being in Laurel's series?'

Eyes on the Harmones, Tareesa shook her head. 'My problem these days is dee-velopment. You newsbums oughtta be covering that garbage.' Still looking at the band Tareesa raised a hand in the air and waved.

'Yeah?' Hecklepeck quickly downed the last of his beer so when the waitress arrived with a new one he was ready.

Tareesa looked at Hecklepeck. 'You know how it goes, television man. The black folks have the land, the white folks want it. So the white folks get it. This block behind me? The way I hear it some company going to ee-rect some kind of urban shopping experience. Now you know most black folks don't get to *experience* shopping.'

Hecklepeck nodded and felt a little guilty just for being white.

'Most of my neighbours is gone and 'fore too long I'll be gone too 'cause I don't cater to the folks who's coming in.' Tareesa stood up. 'I feel like par-tic-i-pat-ing in some music. Go on and and enjoy the hospitality of my place.' She walked up on the stage where the three musicians were bringing the instrumental to a gut-wrenching close.

Tareesa consulted with them and the lead Harmone came to the microphone with a big grin. 'We're going to experience a treat tonight,' he crooned. 'Tess herself is going to sing for us. So sit back and en-joy. Here is the queen of St Louie soul.'

If not perfect, Tareesa's voice was full and round. She sang a blues song that she must have sung many times before. It fitted her as neatly as her blue sarong. All the nuances were in the right places. At the end of the song Tareesa disappeared into her office and the Harmones played on.

Richard was entirely caught up in the music. As a member of the headphone generation he had developed an educated ear for it.

Hecklepeck listened for only a few moments before he got up and went off. Richard hardly noticed. In the music he had finally lost his self-consciousness.

'Come on, young Richard, we have work to do,' Hecklepeck said when he returned. He put on his sheepskin jacket.

'What work? It's well after midnight.' Richard continued to watch the Harmones.

'We're going back to the station to look at those tapes.'

'Have you got a bug up your ass? Why don't you just mellow out and listen to the music?'

'Seeking truth and justice knows no hours.' Hecklepeck said piously. 'But you feel free to stay here. I'll just take the car and go back to the station.' He headed for the door.

'The hell you will!' Richard grabbed his jacket and hurried to catch up. Still officiating in the doorway, the bruiser glared at both of them as they left.

CHAPTER SEVEN

THE POLICE HAD LEFT. Station employees had gone home. Yet the big newsroom was as brightly lit as ever and almost as noisy. Nothing was ever turned off in the newsroom. The wire machines continued to clack out copy, the police radios screeched as loudly as ever and television sets made their fuzzy post-programming sounds all through the night. The news was there even if nobody else was.

The sound of a key turning in the outside door lock was barely perceptible in the newsroom din. The handle turned and the big metal door shuddered open. Photographer Art Macke shambled in, an empty laundry bag slung over his shoulder. With a boom the door slammed behind him.

Art was about to make a right turn towards the photographers' lounge. But something made him stop and listen. Had he just heard a sound coming from Laurel's office?

Art shook his head. Of course not, there was nobody there. Laurel was dead.

With his laundry bag he shuffled into the lounge.

Richard's Toyota bucked into the KYYY parking lot where it continued to protest with loud clangs after he turned it off. It was the only car on the public side of the lot. Behind the chain-link fence lurked the station vehicles, ridiculous in their question-mark paint.

Richard turned to Hecklepeck. 'Nighty, night,' he said unpleasantly.

Hecklepeck shook his head. 'You'd better come look at

those tapes,' he said. 'Even if I'm crazy and they have nothing to do with Laurel's murder, we can use them for the special show. This'll be our only chance to copy them. We do have to turn them over to the police.'

Richard knew it would be effective to include shots of Laurel working on her last project. He scraped the keys out of the ignition and slammed out of the car.

They found Art Macke sifting through a box of photographic equipment and placing certain bits in his laundry bag. 'Hey, Art.' Hecklepeck was not surprised to see him.

Art looked up. 'I'm trying to put together a new collection of equipment,' he said. 'The police will be keeping mine for a while.' Art's conscientious expression was somewhat undermined by his scruffy blond beard, ragged sweater and Army pants.

'That's a hell of a new equipment bag you've got. It's got a certain ... class,' said Richard disparagingly. 'What happened to the one the station gave you?' KYYY had provided all its photographers with leather-trimmed canvas bags, hoping they would keep better track of cables, light bulbs and other photographic minutiae.

'I dunno. Whoever killed Laurel must have made off with it. All my stuff was on the floor of the van. But the cops couldn't find the bag. They wouldn't have given it back to me even if they had.'

'That's interesting,' said Hecklepeck. 'I wonder if it doesn't have some bearing on Laurel's missing coat. I mean if you wanted to steal a fat, purple quilted coat without anybody seeing it, it makes sense to stuff it in a nice neutral canvas bag and take the bag.

'So what do we have? We still don't know if Laurel planned to meet her murderer in the parking lot or if they met by accident. But we *do know* Laurel was strangled with a mike cord and the cord was rolled up. We now think we know that the murderer stuffed Laurel's coat in Art's bag and made off with both of them. We think we know Laurel was killed because of her series. We. . .'

Richard yawned loudly and Art dropped the laundry bag on a chair with a dull thud. 'Let's get to work shall we? I'll scrounge around later.'

Richard looked questioningly at Hecklepeck.

'I phoned him from Tess's,' Hecklepeck said. 'We need him to help us identify what's on those tapes because he was Laurel's photographer for the *Mistresses* series.'

The three men sifted through the heap of tapes on Richard's desk, looking for the ones that belonged to Laurel. 'Ah,' commented Art, reading from a tape label. '*Cats in Crisis.*' That was truly one of your masterpieces, Richard.' Richard snatched the tape and put it on one of his piles. As Art was well aware it had not been his choice to produce the report on feline leukaemia. The story had not been a success either. The cats had not taken to the taping and appeared mostly as furry blurs.

'Go fuck yourself,' Richard muttered with unusual bitterness.

After a short silence Art began again. 'So. Heck. What exactly do you want to do here tonight?'

'You shot about fifteen tapes for Laurel,' said Hecklepeck. 'I want to cue each of them up to thirteen minutes forty-three seconds and see if I find anything that might be a clue to her murder.'

'Why?' asked Art.

'Because,' said Richard, 'he found some numbers taped to Laurel's typewriter that he thinks are time-code. Not me, however.' Richard stacked up some of the tapes identified as Laurel's. 'I'm not going to waste my time in the middle of the night on that shit. If I have to produce a special show I'm going to dub off shots of her ladyship at work. At least I know I'll be able to use those for something.' He gathered up half the tapes and marched off towards editing.

Art picked up the rest. He led the way into one of the editing rooms. Once the door to the soundproofed room was closed, Art asked, 'What's gotten into Markowitz?' He nodded towards next door where Richard had stalked with his share of the tapes.

'He's had a hard day,' replied Hecklepeck.

Art pulled himself up to the desk-high instrument panel in the centre of one wall and fiddled with some buttons. On either side of the panel were video-tape players and on a shelf above, a row of television monitors. Art leaned back and held out his palm to Hecklepeck, who slapped one of Laurel's tapes on it.

'I'm trying to think what was around thirteen minutes on those tapes,' said Art, as he put the tape in one of the players and pushed the 'rewind' button. 'I don't remember anything that you might call a motive for murder. Are you sure someone connected with the series did it? Someone at the station could have killed Laurel. She wasn't exactly popular.' Part of Art's talent as a photographer was his eagerness to enter emotionally into almost anything.

'Maybe,' Hecklepeck retorted. 'But we'd never have done it in the middle of ratings.'

Art grinned. 'Don't bet on it. A good murder is the best ratings-grabber I can think of.' He turned back to the machines. The first few tapes were disappointing. One of them was black at thirteen minutes forty-three seconds, indicating that Art had stopped shooting before he got that far on the tape. Another was a shot of Laurel walking in a park with a perfectly identifiable Tareesa. It was a shot that would probably have been used to set up an interview.

'I don't understand,' said Hecklepeck. 'In the first part of her series she protected the identities of all those women. What was Laurel going to do? Reveal them all one by one as the series went on?'

'Yep,' Art replied. 'There were four women. She was going to focus on one each day. She thought it would be more effective if she revealed their identities as she went along. It's never been done before,' Art wound up slightly on the defensive. He had thought it a wonderful idea at the time.

'Only on *The Dating Game*,' growled Hecklepeck.

They continued their search. 'Bingo!' said Art when he saw the next shot. It was the mayor and his press secretary leaving City Hall under cover of what they had expected to be darkness. 'I wondered if that shot would appear at thirteen minutes forty-three seconds. We staked out his office for hours and finally got them together at two in the morning.'

'Was Laurel planning to use that?' Hecklepeck asked

incredulously.

'Sure, everybody knows the mayor's having an affair with his press secretary.'

'Leaving City Hall together even in the middle of the night hardly constitutes proof. They could have been working late.'

Art's grey eyes looked puzzled. In his zeal he hadn't considered that. 'Well,' he said, 'even if it wasn't true it would still give Mayor Lucas a motive for killing Laurel. He wouldn't want her to put it on the air.'

'Are you suggesting that the mayor met with Laurel in our parking lot in broad daylight, crawled into the van, killed her and then left with or in her purple coat without anybody seeing him?'

'Maybe he hired someone.'

'Professional killers don't strangle people with mike cords. In this town they habitually use car bombs.' Nevertheless, Hecklepeck took a pen out of his shirt pocket and made a note in the reporter's notebook he had brought to the editing room.

Art cued up another tape. It was an interview with Rita Cullen. She was saying that her rôle as a mistress had hurt her career. 'Wow, Heck! I bet it was her,' Art declared.

'Okay, why?'

'Well, nobody would be suspicious if they saw her in the parking lot. She works here. She could have done it to keep Laurel from putting her on the air and ruining her career.'

'Ye-ess,' said Hecklepeck doubtfully. 'But she was the one who got involved in the series. So she was the one who was putting her career on the line. Why would she do that?'

'Maybe she and Wally had some kind of lovers' quarrel.'

'It still seems like a bizarre way to get his attention.'

'Wally always watches the news.' It was true. The station manager liked to check on the commercial spots.

Hecklepeck just motioned for Art to cue the next tape. It and the next several tapes revealed only general shots of people and locations. Hecklepeck routinely recorded them all in his notebook. With that they had finished reviewing their half of the tapes. Art took the stack next door to exchange for the tapes Richard had.

The next shot that seemed to interest Hecklepeck was that of a nice-looking but somewhat dowdy young woman. He recognised her shape. She was the woman he hadn't been able to identify in the first part of Laurel's series.

'Now she might have killed Laurel so as not to be on television.' Art was more tentative this time.

'Who is she?'

'She's some friend of Laurel's. She was really unsure about going on the air.'

'Friend? Laurel had a friend?' Hecklepeck didn't believe it.

'She lives in Laurel's building.'

'Why didn't she want to be identified?'

'Well, she did but then she didn't. Her name is Sonya something.' As Art recited the details, he admired the image on the screen. 'She was having an affair with some real estate/construction bigwig. He supports her. But she says he won't let her work or go back to school or do anything that might lead to her going out on her own. Sonya's really afraid of him. So Laurel thought if she went public she could make him loosen up. We shot the disguised interview and then covered the same ground in another interview where Sonya was recognisable. That way she could decide later whether she wanted to be identified.'

'But working on the principle that once an interview is shot it belongs to KYYY, Laurel was going to put Sonya's face on the air whether she approved or not,' said Hecklepeck distastefully.

'Oh, wow, I hadn't thought of that. Poor Sonya!' Art gazed at the screen with sympathy.

The next image, when they got to it, wasn't intentional. It was clearly something the camera had caught by mistake. Art had allowed it to run while he shifted positions from one shot to another. The camera had seen and recorded a slowly turning room as Art brought the equipment from his shoulder down to his thigh. There it had rested sideways while he'd looked for photographic possibilities. Art froze the image on the screen at exactly thirteen minutes forty-three seconds and the two men stared at it.

Had they been lying on their sides three feet up in the air they would have had the same view as the camera. They were looking at the top of an antique bureau or chest. On it were a pair of silver candlesticks, some china and a trail of white powder.

'What the hell is that?' asked Hecklepeck.

'I don't know. I don't recognise it.' Art backed the tape up until the camera came to rest on an elderly woman. 'That's Maggie Johnson. Her house. I was taking pictures of her and Laurel drinking tea.'

'Maggie Johnson. The mistress of one of St Louis' richest men, now dead. Still very prominent socially.' Hecklepeck waved his hand. 'Go back.'

Art rewound the tape back to the topsy-turvy shot.

'Do you suppose there's something significant about that shot? The chest maybe? Those candlesticks?'

'No way,' said Art. 'It was just a mistake.' He pulled his cigarettes out of the pocket on the right thigh of his Army pants and lit one. 'Unless Laurel was planning a new exposé: *Bad Housekeeping Among the Wealthy.*' He put on a mock announcer's voice. 'With newstape showing actual dirt. Or,' Art's voice got even deeper and more dramatic, 'maybe somebody used that bureau to cut some cocaine. Drug use among the wealthy!'

He looked over to see if Hecklepeck appreciated his act. But Hecklepeck was looking at the blue satin book of matches Art had laid down next to the tape machine with his cigarettes. 'Where did you get those matches?' he asked.

Art thought about it. 'I must have picked them up when we did the interview with Tareesa three weeks ago. But I don't usually keep matches that long.' He took the tape out of the machine and cued another one. A shot of an empty weed-covered lot filled the monitor screen.

'What's this?' asked Hecklepeck. There had obviously been a house on the lot. The front steps were still there: five concrete stairs, leading up to drop off into a foundation hole full of broken bricks and debris.

Art shrugged. 'Don't ask me. She just wanted it shot. I thought it was for some other story.'

'Where is it?'

'Over by the Central West End, on the corner of Evans and . . . what the hell's the cross street? It begins with "N". New. . .'

'Stead. Newstead?'

'Yeah. Newstead.'

'Near Tess's?'

'Well, yes, right behind there. In fact we went over there and shot it after we did the interview with Tareesa. But I don't think there was any connection.' Hecklepeck scribbled something in his notebook.

They reviewed the last few tapes quickly. There was nothing worth adding to the notebook. Art handed the last tape back to Hecklepeck and went to retrieve his laundry bag.

'How'd it go?' asked Hecklepeck, coming into Richard's editing room.

'I got some pretty good stuff,' said Richard, rewinding the last tape. 'I dubbed off about ten minutes worth of the Contemptible Consumer at work on her last project. There's one shot of her where her face is so bunched up her eyes bulge out. I'm going to work that one in somewhere if it kills me.' Richard's mood had improved.

He put the tapes on his desk and separated the copy he had made from the originals. The copy tape went into one of his drawers. Richard patted the pile of originals. 'You *are* going to put these back in Laurel's office so the police can find them in the morning, aren't you?'

'Absolutely,' replied Hecklepeck.

But Richard wasn't finished. He pointed in the direction of Laurel's office. 'And you're going to get my tapes, which you left in there as decoys, and put them back on my desk.' Richard spoke sternly. He wanted to be sure the switch was made. But he was too tired to do it himself.

Hecklepeck looked at him oddly for a second. Then he realised Richard didn't know that his decoy tapes had disappeared from Laurel's office. Better not to tell him. It was late. 'No problem,' said Hecklepeck. 'You go home and get some sleep. I think I'll just walk; I need to think.'

He watched Richard put on his jacket. Art, too, had filled his laundry bag and was leaving.

When they had gone, Hecklepeck debated with himself. Richard was right. The tapes belonged in the hands of the police but should they be left in Laurel's office? Somebody had already made off with the box of fake tapes. On the other hand it was after two o'clock in the morning. Surely no one would be coming to the newsroom to steal tapes at that time? The police, Hecklepeck reassured himself, would be on the job early.

He picked up some of the tapes and carried them to Laurel's office. At the sight of her desk he stopped. All her file folders had been neatly stacked on top of one another and – Hecklepeck's stomach gave a lurch – all her ink pens were lined up side by side in a neat row. Somebody had taken them out of the drawer where they had been tossed and arranged them on top of the desk. The police? Hecklepeck didn't think so. They generally left things as they found them. In fact the pens must have been lined up by someone after the police left. He shifted uneasily and stared at the pens for several moments. Was that person an employee at KYYY, after all? How, otherwise, had he or she got into the newsroom? Then he remembered the missing coat. Laurel had carried the things other women carry in their handbags in her coat pockets. Including her keys. Whoever murdered Laurel could have used her station key earlier that night. For what? To find what? Hecklepeck guessed it was the tapes.

He took his stack back out to the newsroom and set it down with the others. Casting around quickly for a container, he grabbed a cardboard box full of rolls of paper. These he dumped and filled the box with tapes. Putting on his jacket, he picked up the box and carried it to the door.

As he shifted the box to get at the door handle, Hecklepeck had the creepy feeling he wasn't alone. He turned and looked back at the newsroom, well-lit and reassuring, except for the row of dark cubbyhole offices on the far side.

Hecklepeck wondered if it wouldn't be better to look around a little before he left. No, he decided. It was best to safeguard the tapes. Surely, whoever had been in the newsroom had long since left, scared off by him and his companions.

CHAPTER EIGHT

'GOOD MORNING,' HECKLEPECK SANG INTO the telephone. Richard groaned. It dawned on him that he and sleep had parted ways, probably for the rest of the day. Something like despair washed over him.

'You're still asleep, aren't you little buddy?' Hecklepeck said sweetly. 'Well, just relax and listen to me. You can wake up while I tell you about our plans for the day.' Richard sank back on his pillows. He closed his eyes and gave himself up to misery.

'Art and I found some shots last night that puzzled us.' Hecklepeck looked over at the box of tapes sitting on his sofa. 'As I was running this morning, I thought it would be a really good idea to get another opinion about them and you're a smart guy.'

'Say it one more time like you mean it,' grumbled Richard.

'I *do* mean it. Anyway there isn't anybody else I can ask. I really think it's better if we keep this tapes business to ourselves.'

'So, okay. Whisper when you ask a *real* smart person to look at the shots for you.'

It did not deter Hecklepeck. 'Just come to the station and look at the tape with me.'

'All right,' sighed Richard, recognising the inevitable. 'What time?'

'Get there a little before nine and we may beat the cops.'

Hecklepeck hung up the telephone and rubbed the tummy of the shaggy black cat stretched across his lap. The cat extended himself further, presenting a greater expanse of stomach. Hecklepeck adjusted his stroke,

81

letting his hand travel up Colonel Chambers' middle and down again. He had named the breedless but handsome animal after a steamboat, one of those piloted up and down the Mississippi River by Samuel Clemens.

During his six years in St Louis the Mississippi had taken as firm a grip on Hecklepeck's soul as it had on young Clemens when he boarded the *Paul Jones* bound for the Amazon in April of 1857. The *Paul Jones* was headed for New Orleans out of Cincinnati. It was to return to St Louis with Samuel Clemens still aboard as apprentice riverboat pilot. His career on the river lasted four years and was, by his own declaration, the happiest time in his life.

Hecklepeck's affair with the Mississippi had been more academic. He had travelled down and up it once by barge and several times on the *Mississippi Queen*, one of the modern tourist steamers. But most of his river navigation had been by book. From the first steamboat to arrive in St Louis (the *Zebulon M. Pike* in 1817) to the famous New Orleans/St Louis race of the *Natchez* and the *Robert E. Lee* in 1870, Hecklepeck had read everything he could find about the heyday of the steamboat and its end in the greater efficiency of the railroads and barge lines.

Even barges were comparatively infrequent on the river now and the modern steamboat was usually a floating restaurant for the benefit of fun-seekers and tourists. Hecklepeck didn't begrudge it to them. If it seemed a sad fate for a noble craft, it yet dignified the waterfront with commerce. When he pictured romance, however, he saw working steamboats packed into the St Louis waterfront like books on a shelf, while crowds bustled in and around them.

Along with reading he had fed his passion with a large collection of steamboat fixtures, fittings and period furnishings. They filled his hotel suite and much of Mark Ginter's Cherokee Street antique warehouse, where he rented space. Most cherished was Hecklepeck's inlaid steamboat wheel. He took the big wheel whenever he faced a tough decision or needed to think, piloting himself and Colonel Chambers out over the tree tops among imaginary reefs and shoals. There with his hands firmly gripping the silky wooden handles, natural order prevailed. Thought was clear and dispassionate. He had vague ideas of setting the wheel in front of a river-view window someday in a house on a river bluff he would find and outfit.

Meanwhile he kicked off his running shoes, dumped the Colonel and bounced over to the kitchenette where he poured himself a cup of coffee. For now the big wheel overlooked Forest Park from the window of The Chase Park Plaza Hotel. There it was not entirely appropriate: the park was post-steamboat era and best known as the site of St Louis' famous World Fair. But Hecklepeck loved it nevertheless. In the winter-white rays of the morning sun, the park filled his window like a many-panelled nineteenth-century landscape.

He was happy living at The Chase. It was a comfortable existence. Breakfast was never more than a phone call away. Somebody dusted his table tops daily and turned down his sheets. His car was berthed in the hotel's parking garage while Central West End restaurants and shopping were just down the street. Most importantly, the Chase gave Hecklepeck a warming sense of impermanence. A media gypsy at heart, he did not want to think he had become stagnant.

He walked carefully back to his chair with the coffee and patted his lap in invitation to Colonel Chambers. The nomadic urge had brought him to St Louis. In two years he had tired of what passed as investigative reporting at TV stations in Washington, DC, just as he had tired after brief stays in five other cities.

The move to prime-time anchoring in St Louis had cost him Chris. She had refused to come with him. She wasn't interested, she'd said, in moving from place to place for the sake of his career. For the sake of hers she was going to stay in Washington, DC. At the time Chris was chief administrative assistant to one of the bureau directors at the Federal Trade Commission and looking upwards. She dreamed of power and the kind of influence that changed lives. And she'd got as far as the upper-middle bureaucracy before she'd stalled.

Six years later, still in St Louis, Hecklepeck occasionally wondered at the irony of it all.

Richard got to the station just before nine o'clock. He noted with irritation that Hecklepeck had not arrived and with relief that the police hadn't either. The chief assignment-editor was presiding over the newsroom in lonely splendour. Most reporters and photographers did not come in until nine-thirty.

There were only a few assignments on the storyboard, all follow-ups on Laurel's murder. Knowing it was the big lead of the day, the assignment-editor was punishing his rather limited imagination to come up with related story ideas. With his arms folded across his pudgy middle he stood on a chair and regarded the expanse of white plastic that hung from ceiling to floor.

So far, he had assigned research into other St Louis reporters who had died on the job. As far as he knew the list was limited to one, an elderly *Globe Democrat* writer who had suffered a heart attack during a mayoral news conference. But the assignment-editor was optimistic there were others.

He had also come up with an idea for a feature on the job-related dangers of consumer reporting in St Louis. What these were he hadn't a clue.

Richard tiptoed quietly behind the figure on the chair. He made his way among the news desks to Laurel's office. He assumed Hecklepeck had done what he had said he would and left the box of Laurel's tapes there. Richard planned to remove it before the police arrived. He would look at whatever Hecklepeck wanted to show him. Then they would promptly put the box back to be found by the authorities.

Richard stood in the office doorway, surveying the newsroom. He casually took off his padded jacket and smoothed his pastel-pink sweater. He intended to throw the jacket over the tapes and remove them to an editing room.

He leaned towards Laurel's cubbyhole, took a last look around the newsroom and slipped inside. Once there he wasted no time. Holding his jacket open with both hands,

Richard dived under Laurel's typing table to snatch up the tapes in one fell swoop. But what he swooped was air. Instead of embracing a box, Richard's arms travelled past each other. Hugging himself, he fell forward on his nose.

Hecklepeck drove slowly down Evans Street until he spotted what he was looking for: the house foundation he had seen on Laurel's tape the night before. He pulled into the kerb and put the car in park. On the back seat behind him was a square outline underneath a plaid blanket, the box of tapes in disguise.

Hecklepeck gazed at the three-dimensional reality of what he had seen the night before on tape and found it no more enlightening. The foundation was situated between two brick houses. At the turn of the century the houses had been substantial middle-class homes. Now, one was a shell and the other only half-standing.

Most of the block was in no better shape. There were a few houses that appeared to be inhabited, largely because they had newspaper stuffed into their broken window-panes. Life in those houses couldn't be better than miserable, Hecklepeck thought. It wouldn't take much to lure the inhabitants away.

What if Tareesa were right and the block were slated for some kind of development? From the looks of things it would only be an improvement. But Hecklepeck was well versed in the kinds of corruption that often came with development. He could well believe some of it was applicable here.

In any case the critical question was what, if anything, it all had to do with Laurel? He brought his attention back to the empty lot he had found on Laurel's tape. Except for the front steps, going nowhere, the lot was grass-covered, which appeared to be something of a blessing. The grass was winter-brown but somehow it had grown over the brick-and-broken-glass remains of a house. He was reassured to see that nature, even in an urban wasteland, could reclaim its own.

But it must have taken several years. Grass couldn't cover a debris-filled foundation hole overnight. Or even in the few weeks since Laurel had shot it. So why the hell was she interested?

Hecklepeck sighed and looked at his watch. He put the Jaguar into drive. But before he drove off he squinted at the number on the shell. It was '5302'. That would make the number of the empty lot next door either '5300' or '5304'. He drove slowly up the block until he was able to see the numbers were going up. That would make it '5304', he told himself. He made a mental note to follow up on it and drove around the block past Tess's on his way back to the station.

Fiddling angrily with his beard, Richard wandered out of Laurel's office. Hecklepeck, according to the newsroom clock, was now late. 'Rich, I wonder if you have a few minutes,' Wally Corette's hand landed like a breeze block on Richard's back.

Richard started. 'Uh . . . sure.'

'Then let's go to my office.' Wishing he weren't, Richard followed the station manager. The hall and reception area at KYYY were filling up with flowers. Some were from viewers offering seemingly sincere condolences to their favourite television station. But most had been sent by politicians and advertisers hoping to exchange floral tributes for advantageous press coverage and favourable ad rates.

Wally paused at his office door and waved at the flowers. 'You know, Rich. People really look up to us. Do you know what that means?' Richard shook his head. 'That means our responsibility to them is big. *Big*, Rich.' Wally opened the door and walked to the sofa formation at the far end of the office. With a gesture he invited Richard to sit beside him on the couch.

Richard sat in the furthest corner uncertain whether or not to cross his legs. Nor was he at all sure what to do with his hands. He knew absolutely, however, that his neck was twisting beyond its natural limits as he strained to look at Wally's chin.

'Part of our big responsibility, Rich, is not to let our viewers down in times of trouble.' Wally let this hang.

Richard attempted to clear his twisted throat and finally managed something like, 'uh-huh.'

'That's why it's up to you, Rich, to be certain that Bill Hecklepeck toes the line on this special. It's supposed to be a tribute, you know, a look back at all the good Laurel Michaels did for this community, not an investigative report.'

Richard gulped. Since the saliva couldn't help but take a wrong turn, he coughed.

'I just don't want Bill to go off pretending he's some kind of shit-hot detective. I want you, Rich, to keep him on the track. I'd really like to see the two of you put together something nice, something the station can be proud of.'

'Okay,' said Richard meekly. How, he wondered, did Wally expect *him* to control Hecklepeck? He unwound his neck and looked at his shoes.

'I bring this up, Rich, because of something that's happened,' Wally stretched out his legs casually but his voice deepened ominously. 'There seem to be some tapes missing. The police have informed me they can't find the tapes from that series Laurel was producing on mistresses.' Richard's stomach gave a warning lurch. 'It occurred to me, Rich, that you or Bill Hecklepeck might know something about those tapes.'

Richard's stomach threatened to erupt on to his shoes. Panic spread throughout his body, blurring his vision and drying his mouth. Wally knew about the tapes! Somehow he had seen the missing decoy tapes that had been left in Laurel's office. He had recognised them as Richard's work. And that was why he was coming after Richard for the real ones.

Trying to breathe calmly, Richard screwed his neck around to look at Wally. 'N . . . no,' he said with a little squeak. 'I don't know anything about Laurel's tapes.'

'No?' Wally stared at Richard coldly. But when he spoke again, his expression had turned to something resembling paternal. 'Well, I want you to understand, Rich, that if you do have those tapes or know who does, you can turn them over to me any time and the police won't have to know where I got them.' Slowly Richard's vision regained its clarity and he breathed a little easier.

'If that surprises you, Rich, I would do it because of our big responsibility to this community. We have to set an example and I don't think we want one of our team known as a person who steals police evidence.' Richard nodded solemnly.

Still on his chair, the assignment-editor contemplated the storyboard and turned four words over and over in his mind: *Can it happen here?* When hostages were taken in the Middle East or earthquakes racked South America, the KYYY newsteam regularly asked and answered that same question. It was the Channel Three response to any disaster that happened anywhere in the world. What the assignment-editor couldn't figure out was how to apply the question to Laurel's murder. After all it *had* happened here. He tried altering the question to: *Can it happen to you?* He didn't think that too many ordinary citizens were likely to be strangled with microphone cables. But anybody could be strangled. He wrote 'Stranglings' on the board and gazed at it fondly.

From the newsroom doorway Hecklepeck looked at the word with disgust. He snorted loudly but refrained from commenting since he had other business. He headed towards his office.

'Mr, uh, Mr . . . Bill?' One of the news writers, Joe Osifchin, was blocking his way.

Hecklepeck looked down at the little egg-shaped guy. 'Yes?'

'I have something . . . something I need to tell you.'

Hecklepeck sighed the long sigh of the long-suffering. He couldn't say no. His position required him to help out the little guys. 'Come into my office.'

Joe refused to sit down. Instead, he stood and wrung his hands. 'It's about Llll . . . rrrr . . . rrll.' He couldn't bring himself to say the name of a dead woman.

'Laurel? About Laurel?'

'Lllll . . . rrrr . . . Llll . . . rell, uh, she told me something I thought you ought to know.'

'Yes?' Hecklepeck took a deep breath and tried to be

patient. While this situation was probably hopeless, it was important to encourage the young and struggling.

Joe Osifchin recounted how Laurel, just before she left the station for the last time, had taunted him with her big story. 'She . . . she said she would give me a hint and then she whispered something. . .'

'Yes,' breathed Hecklepeck.

'Well, it was hard to hear. But it sounded like tootle . . . or maybe tootell.'

'Tootle? And she said this was the key to her story.'

'Yeah. She said if I were a good reporter I could figure out her story from that one word.'

'Well, it doesn't ring any bells with *me*.' *And I'm a good reporter.* Hecklepeck left the words unsaid but the implication was definitely there. 'Tootle? Tootell?' He shook his head.

There was an unmistakable thud in Laurel's office next door. Hecklepeck put his finger to his lips. He got up and crept around the corner to Laurel's cubicle. There was nobody there. But the box of decoy tapes was back! Richard's tapes were once again sitting on the floor under Laurel's typewriter.

Hecklepeck swung around and just caught a flash of baby-blue polyester leaving the newsroom.

Two fried eggs hung over the art department doorway. Side by side they looked like breasts. Hecklepeck had always thought the print lacked taste. But the former department head had been a little raw. He had covered the breeze-block walls of the square room with similar graphic guffaws, his idea of 'in' art jokes.

The oasis among the visual jokes was the corner around Rita Cullen's draftsman's table. She had surrounded herself with prettier pictures, selections from the kittens-with-big-eyes school.

Rita herself sat at her table with her dimpled hands folded on her blue lap and her head bowed. The platinum waves of her hair brushed the table top.

'Hey Rita,' Hecklepeck tried tentatively.

But Rita only bowed her head a little deeper and

mumbled something indistinguishable.

Hecklepeck came further into the room. 'I really need to talk to you.'

Rita said something that sounded like, 'Go away'.

'I can't. I have to talk to you. About the box of tapes you just returned to Laurel's office.'

At that Rita jerked up her head and Hecklepeck saw that she had a black eye. Encrusted as her right eye was with make-up and powder, it was unmistakably bruised and swollen.

'Jesus Christ, what happened to you?'

Rita merely shook her head.

'Wally did that, didn't he? Our esteemed station head, the man who leads us, beater of women.'

Rita burst into tears, snuffling into her dimply palms. Feeling inadequate, Hecklepeck spotted a box of Kleenex on another desk and held it out to her. She mopped up the tears, being careful around the black eye.

'What happened?' he demanded when she was calmer.

Rita shook her head.

'Let's see. Wally hit you. Could it be that he hit you because of the tapes? The tapes you took out of Laurel's office weren't exactly the ones you and he were expecting. Were they?'

Rita shook her head again but this time she raised her watery blue eyes and looked at Hecklepeck. 'They were all tapes of fat people.'

Hecklepeck nodded. The decoy tapes that had been taken off Richard's desk must have been his series on losing weight. 'You were expecting the raw tapes from Laurel's *Mistresses* series,' he prompted.

'Yep.'

'Why did you want them?'

'Not me. Wally. Wally was afraid I said something about him in that inverview I did. But I didn't. I swear I didn't. It was just going to be me in the series. Just me.'

Rita had suddenly turned into beaten egg-whites, folding easily into a soufflé of submission. It was a variation, Hecklepeck decided, of rolling over and playing dead: a survival trick, learned perhaps during an impoverished childhood in the Ozarks. But how much of what he was going to get would be air and how much substance?

'What I don't understand,' he said, 'is why anybody would want to go on television and talk about an affair she was having with her boss . . . particularly if that boss was head of the television station on which the interview was going to be aired. That seems plain crazy to me.'

'When Petie left I wanted Wally to promote me to head of the art department, but he wouldn't. I thought if I . . . ah . . . threatened to go public with our relationship, he would change his mind.'

In the grand old tradition of kiss-and-tell; but 'What do you mean "threatened"? Allowing yourself to be interviewed for television *is* going public.'

'Nooouh,' Rita breathed, lining up the magic markers on her desk like little soldiers. 'Laurel promised not to reveal Wally's name. It was just going to be me. I figured Wally would see it and know . . . hunh,' she issued a sigh, 'that I could have given out his name if I wanted to.'

Hecklepeck stared at a picture of a giant pickle lying in a water bed. Was Rita right in thinking she could manipulate Wally or did Wally control her? It was an interesting question. In either case there was something wrong with Rita's story. Hecklepeck silently reviewed it. Then he knew: Laurel would never have kept quiet about Wally. 'Laurel lied to you,' he said with certainty. 'Didn't she? She lied. You might as well tell me about it. The police are going to have to know eventually.'

'She called Wally on Monday and asked for an interview.' The words emerged on little puffs of air. 'She said she had to use him because otherwise the public could accuse her of covering up to protect her job.'

Interview. The word set off all sorts of bells in Hecklepeck's head. Just before she died Laurel had been waiting for a call from someone she was going to interview. Had it been Wally? Was the exposure of the station manager her big story?

It would have been a big story too, not by Hecklepeck's standards, but certainly by Laurel's. She would have gone after the boss, been the woman who stopped at nothing to get her story, even when it came to laying her very livelihood on the line. And what risk was there really? Not much. The strait-laced Babsons would have fired Wally immediately. Laurel's job would not have been threatened.

Hecklepeck realised that Rita was looking at him in a new, speculative way. 'So it all backfired. Wally must have been pretty angry with you.'

'Hunh. Not necessarily. Those tapes. You see if I could get those tapes and give them to Wally and he could see that his name's not on them anywhere, then he would forgive me and give me the promotion.' Rita clasped her hands and forearms, bringing her breasts into a crush. 'Help me. You're in the newsroom. If anybody could find those tapes you could. Look around for me. Ooooooh, please Heck.' Rita let her mouth drop open slightly and widened her eyes.

Hecklepeck looked away, only to find himself staring into the maw of a giant hooked fish, hanging on the opposite wall. He stared at it for several seconds before replying.

CHAPTER NINE

'*STRANGLINGS?* WHAT THE BLOODY HELL kind of news is that? How am I going to make a story out of that?' a KYYY general assignment-reporter muttered to himself. He gazed with envy at the *Dangers of Consumer Reporting* assignment on the storyboard. Now that would be a good story. He would start it with some music, something low and threatening. Then he would shoot a pair of feet, walking; the consumer reporter on the beat. Behind him one of his colleagues bit her lip. There weren't any dangers in consumer reporting. She would have to make them up, a fabricated news story. If she had been a male reporter, she would never have got stuck with a story like that. Her eyes filled with tears. It would really have been fun to do that piece on reporters who died on the job. Of course *it* had been assigned to a man.

Having descended from his chair the chief assignment-editor beamed at the reporters. He was too pleased with himself to notice the fallen looks. Nobody griped out loud. To be branded a complainer was never to get a good assignment and there were subtler ways of killing stories.

Richard's eyes passed over the group at the assignment desk, looking for Hecklepeck. He didn't see him. Nor was he with the group of policemen meeting in Ken's fishbowl office. He walked over to Hecklepeck's cubbyhole and peered in. Hecklepeck wasn't there. He moved on down the line to Laurel's office. It, too, was empty. But under Laurel's typing table sat the box of his tapes.

Richard stiffened. What the hell was going on? First the box was gone and now it was back. Who had taken it? Wally? Hecklepeck? How many people knew about it?

Jesus Christ, everybody! He peered out of Laurel's office. No. There was one group that didn't know. The police. They had just arrived and could not have had an opportunity to discover the box.

They weren't going to get the opportunity, if he could prevent it. The question was how to get the box out of Laurel's office. He couldn't wrap it in his coat and carry it out now. The police would certainly see him. The only part of him they wouldn't see as he stepped out of Laurel's office was his feet. From the knees down he was obscured by desks, chairs and piles of stuff. Richard carried the box to the edge of the cubbyhole. Steeling himself, he began whooshing it across the floor with his feet. It was a slow and unnatural gait. The box was heavy enough that giving it a good whoosh meant he had to bow to an angle of forty-five degrees. He crossed his hands behind him and pretended he was ice skating, hoping he appeared carefree, a fanciful guy indulging in a bit of whimsy. One reporter glanced up from her telephone, shot him a look of disgust and returned to her phoning. A photographer bumped into him but didn't stop even to apologise.

Richard let out his breath and eased the fluttering in his stomach. He was more than halfway; he was going to make it. This, he told himself, was why he had played all that ice hockey in college.

'Excuse me, Mr Markowitz?' Richard whirled around and planted himself, he hoped, squarely in front of the box. 'Er, uh, yes,' he managed.

Half the newsroom away Lieutenant Berger was standing in the doorway of Ken's office. 'I'd like to meet with you in here in a few minutes, if I may,' he said. Richard nodded, praying Berger wouldn't notice the box.

'Don't be nervous,' Berger reassured him. 'We're going to be chatting with everybody.'

Richard nodded again.

'Okay. As soon as we're wrapped up in here I'll come fahr you.'

Richard watched until Berger was once again involved with the group in Ken's office and then maniacally whooshed the last little distance to his desk.

94

He tore open the bottom drawer and hand over hand ripped out all his files. They fell randomly, spilling papers. Richard stuffed the box into the drawer and slammed it shut. Only then did he relax and only for a brief moment. His desk, he realised, was a foot deep in paper. Frantically he began to gather it up.

'I see yah're cleaning out yahr desk,' Berger was standing over Richard. Richard nodded. 'Sometimes when tragedy strikes it helps to wipe the slate clean and stahrt again,' Berger observed with a deep sigh. 'I know you want to get on with it but if you could spare a few moments. . .' He gestured towards Ken's office. Richard stumbled through the debris around his desk and followed him into the fishbowl.

Berger closed the door and went around to the desk chair. He patted his crew-cut and assumed an expression of deepest sympathy. 'I know this is a tough time fahr you,' he said. 'But you were close to Ms Michaels. We need all the help you can give us.'

Richard stared at Berger in horror. Berger had believed that business of Hecklepeck's about himself and Laurel? He was taking it seriously? Richard sat forward. 'Look, nobody was close to Laurel. She, uh. . .' He realised that he shouldn't actually say she was a raving bitch but he was at a loss for a milder expression.

'I know,' said Berger. 'Some women are like that. Hard to get to know. That's what makes them so, uh, captivating. Right, Markowitz?'

'No,' Richard yelped in utter outrage. 'I wasn't. . .' He was interrupted as the door behind him opened.

One of the other policemen stuck his head in the door. 'Excuse me, Lieutenant.'

'Give me a minute, Richard,' said Berger courteously. He gestured for the policeman to speak.

'That box of tapes that we found in the subject's office this morning. They're gone.'

'They're what?'

'They've disappeared, Mike.'

'That does it!' Berger sat forward in his chair. 'I want a twenty-fahr-hour patrol put on this place. As of now nothing goes in or out without our knowledge and approval. And let's get a search going. You go on down to headquahrters. Sign out a wahrrant. I've got a hunch,' Berger added slowly, 'that those tapes have considerable bearing on the death of Ms Michaels. I want to question whoever took them.'

The officer left and Berger turned back to Richard. 'Hey, buddy, I'm real sorry,' he said. Richard had turned paper-white.

Berger examined his stubby hands. First the back, then the front. The pathos was killing him. Here was a guy who had just lost the woman he loved. That Markowitz had loved Laurel, notwithstanding the fifteen-year-age difference, Berger was now certain. Richard's behaviour confirmed it. 'Richard, you want us to find Lahrel's murderer don't you?' Berger cajoled.

Richard nodded. He definitely wanted the police or someone to find Laurel's *real* murderer. They wouldn't though. They'd search the station, find the box with *Mistresses* written on it and believe that he, Richard, was the killer. 'I didn't do it,' he wanted to scream.

'Then you're going to have to help us. Tell us all you know about Lahrel's last movements.'

Richard nodded again. Inside he was screeching, 'I'm innocent, I'm innocent!' He saw them dragging him away anyway.

Berger sighed quietly. This wasn't going anywhere. Outside in the newsroom he caught sight of Hecklepeck. Maybe, he thought, it would be better to consult him about Markowitz. Berger knew that television people weren't like other people. What he needed, he decided, was an interpreter. He stood up and shook out his double-weave suit. 'Tell you what, Richard. You finish cleaning up yahr desk. We'll continue this talk later.'

Richard didn't hesitate. He bolted.

Hecklepeck watched as his colleague shot out of Ken's office. 'Found you at last,' he declared. 'Are you. . .' There was no point in finishing. Richard had passed right by, ignoring him completely. Hecklepeck continued watching as Richard hurried over to his desk, yanked open his file drawer, slammed it shut and fell into his chair in a slump.

'He's really taking it hard, isn't he?' Berger was at Hecklepeck's right elbow.

'He is?' Hecklepeck had forgotten his own fiction.

'Bill, I'd like to talk to you. Got a moment?' With a final, concerned glance at Richard, Hecklepeck acquiesced. The two men settled themselves in Ken's office.

Berger wanted to ruminate. 'This place has got me confuddled,' he began. 'If one of my men was killed, we'd be taking up a collection fahr his wife and family. That'd just be for starters. We'd get every copper from here to Hannibal to come to the funeral. Ahrganize a mile-long motorcade. The guy would be buried with full honours. Surrounded by his buddies.' Berger stopped, shaking his head. 'But here. I don't get it. It's business as usual.'

'Laurel wasn't much liked,' Hecklepeck offered.

It didn't satisfy Berger. 'Like's got nothing to do with it. It's about solidarity. Playing on the team and. . .' Berger wasn't sure how to express it.

But Hecklepeck understood. 'There isn't any solidarity in television, Mike. It's a solitary business. Almost everybody's in it for himself. The death of a colleague is an opportunity to cover a big story, the kind of story that could be seen by someone in New York or LA – a chance at the big time.'

'That's cold,' was Berger's comment.

'Maybe. Except you know the game when you come in. Laurel played it with distinction. If another of our reporters had been murdered, she would have been grasping for a piece of the action. She reached for whatever she thought would get her what she wanted and that was to be a network news star.'

'She was getting long in the tooth fahr that, wasn't she? Most of those women on the national news look like they haven't seen thirty.'

Hecklepeck nodded. 'I think that's why she was digging so ruthlessly for stories. She really wanted it and time was running out.'

'That poor kid,' Berger was looking now at Richard. 'How'd he get so involved with that woman anyway?'

This time Hecklepeck did remember and his conscience turned over. 'He's mostly, ah, star-struck, you know.'

'He seemed pretty cut-up to me. I tried to get some infahrmation out of him. The guy could hardly talk.'

'I'll talk to him.' Hecklepeck shifted in his chair. 'What's new? What do you know?'

'She was strangled with a microphone cable. But somebody kaboshed her first.'

'Yes, and?'

'We found a light-stand in that pile of equipment. There was some of her skin tissue on it. We think the murderer hit her with the stand. On the fahrhead. Knocked her cold. Strangled her.' Berger was unusually forthcoming.

'Could a woman have done it?'

'Sure. It wouldn't have taken any strength. She was out. Couldn't fight back. Why? You got one in mind?'

'No. Just asking. What about time of death?'

'Around one, one-thirty. She left the television station a little after noon and went across the street to eat some lunch. Around one she comes back and somehow manages to meet her assailant and get into that van without being seen. It's just a little hard to believe,' Berger sounded aggrieved, 'that all those newspeople going in and out across that parking lot didn't see anything. Aren't you guys supposed to be trained observers?'

Hecklepeck shrugged.

'Anyway, by two-thirty it's all over. I know this because that's when a busload of third-graders arrives fahr a station tour. Their bus driver parked in that area reserved for newscrews. Sat there the whole time they were touring. He used his eyes but he didn't see anything until those photo clowns arrived to drive the van away.'

Berger was now on a roll of grievances. 'What's got me flumboozled is that box of tapes from those repahrts she was working on. You know, the one I mentioned to you last night?' Hecklepeck nodded. 'They were put back this morning. While our Fahrensic Unit was getting ready to give them the treatment, they disappeared again. Whoever's playing cat and mouse with us is going to wish they'd never been bahrn.'

Berger was talking about the box of decoy tapes that Rita had returned to Laurel's office. Hecklepeck had to remind himself that the real ones were locked safely in his car. 'Any idea who took them?' he asked innocently.

'Nope. But we'll know better when we find them. We're going to search the station here shahrtly. We'll get that box. And the person who took it.'

Hecklepeck slipped a finger under his collar and tugged slightly. Why he didn't turn over the real tapes then and there was a question he could never quite answer. But Berger was obviously prepared to come down hard on whoever was withholding his evidence and, more than usual, Hecklepeck wanted to follow this story himself. 'You think it's someone who works here then?'

Berger rocked back in his chair. 'Yep, looks that way.'

'Well,' Hecklepeck stood up, 'I'll be waiting to hear the results.'

'By the way,' Berger added with just a hint of triumph. 'We found that coat, the pouffy, purple one. Hanging in the closet at Lahrel Michaels' apartment.' Hecklepeck digested that for a second before turning to leave.

Berger continued to rock, allowing himself to feel a certain mournful satisfaction. The case was off to a good start and he rated his chances of solving it as high. Berger failed to see that Hecklepeck didn't share his assessment. Hecklepeck should have been begging for the story. But he was out of his professional depth. He hadn't even asked.

'What the hell kind of trouble have you gotten yourself into?' When Hecklepeck reached him, Richard was still sitting dejectedly in his pile of papers.

At the sound of Hecklepeck's voice he leapt up and shoved the larger man halfway across the room into the wall. 'The box of tapes,' he whispered. 'It's in my desk. The police. Going to search.'

'All right. Calm down,' Hecklepeck grasped Richard firmly by the shoulders and removed him. 'I will take care of this.'

He went to the assignment desk and picked up a black

magic-marker. This, he took back to Richard's desk. Seating himself, he opened the file drawer. Checking to see that he was hidden from the police, Hecklepeck pulled the box of tapes out just far enough to reveal the word *Mistresses*. He scribbled over it with the magic-marker until it was no longer legible. Then he pulled the box all the way out.

While Richard hovered anxiously, Hecklepeck wrote the word 'Horses'. Then he scribbled over it. He next wrote, 'Organic Farming' and scratched it out. He continued this until the entire box was covered with marked-up labels. Finally he wrote, 'Art Show' and left it. The box looked as if it had been the repository of tapes from many series. 'You don't have the tapes any more,' said Hecklepeck, putting the box back in the drawer.

Richard was about to object wildly.

'Your box, your tapes,' enunciated Hecklepeck slowly and distinctly. 'They can't arrest you for this.' He stood up: 'Now let's go have brunch.'

CHAPTER TEN

'I DON'T KNOW WHAT YOU think this is going to accomplish.' Richard was luxuriating in the front passenger-seat of the Jaguar. Several bottles of beer and a stack of blueberry pancakes with whipped cream had restored his customary disagreeableness. He had even forgotten the blanket-covered box of tapes sitting amid all the other junk on Hecklepeck's back seat.

'Maybe nothing. But I think it's important for us to see all the women on that tape.'

'Yeah, but Maggie Johnson's not just a woman. She's rich and she's important in this town.'

'Look, Richard.' Hecklepeck was already parking the car in front of Maggie's pale-green stucco mansion. It was at the opposite end of Forest Park from his hotel, in the expensive suburb of Clayton. 'It may be difficult for you to believe but rich people sometimes commit murder too.'

'Maybe, but not ancient, old ladies. Anyway, I don't care,' Richard continued as he got out of the car. 'I would really like to do a nostalgia piece with her: *St Louis in the Forties*. This way I can meet her.'

Maggie had been at the forefront of St Louis society in the Forties and it was sheer pettiness that had put her there. In the beginning St Louis was shocked by her affair with the fertiliser king. At the time Warren Billings was emerging as one of St Louis' richest men. He had married Nonnie Sherman from New York City and used her money to turn Mississippi River fish into fertiliser. He had, however, little use for Nonnie herself. He preferred Maggie, a preference which had appalled St Louis at first.

It wasn't until it was discovered that Nonnie was living in

New York ten months out of twelve that public opinion began to shift and St Louis society had embraced Maggie. St Louisans take a disparaging view of their city but they have never allowed anybody else to do so.

'Shooooo-eeeee, whut we got he-yuh.' The big oak door had been opened by a tawny-skinned man of uncertain racial background. He had on an open shirt and black leather toreador pants. As he shook his head, his loopy gold earrings danced frantically.

'I'm sorry,' Hecklepeck said politely. 'We must have the wrong house. We're looking for Ms Maggie Johnson.'

The man laughed. As he did so he fluttered his hands around his face. He had a ring on every finger. 'This be the place,' he trilled. 'Y'all come on in. Miss Maggie'd luv to see yuh newspeople. She's dyin' to know about the muhder.'

Hecklepeck and Richard stepped into the lavish marbled hallway. 'Ah'll just tell huh y'all are he-yuh.' And the man in toreador pants slithered off into the back part of the house.

'What the hell is that,' whispered Richard, 'the butler?' Hecklepeck shrugged. 'Why does he talk like Scarlett O'Hara?' Hecklepeck shrugged again. 'And look like a matador? A matador in make-up.' Richard was silent for a moment. Then: 'It is really hot in here.' The hallway was so warm it was steamy, particularly after the cold out-doors.

'Elderly women almost always overheat their homes,' commented Hecklepeck as he removed his jacket.

'Miss Maggie'll see yuh in the back pah-luh,' the man had returned noiselessly. He was barefoot.

The back parlour was what most real-estate people would have referred to as a 'sunroom'. It was encased on three sides with French windows. They ushered in every available ray of early-afternoon sun. If the hall had been warm, the parlour was baking.

Maggie was seated on a massive Victorian loveseat with her back to the windows. A small woman, she was dressed conservatively in an expensive tweed suit. The brooch at her neck was worth a small fortune. She was clearly

102

vigorous for her age but rows of fine lines etched into sagging skin and a brown patchwork of age spots were telling no lies.

'Good afternoon. Won't you sit down?' Maggie dipped her elegantly permed head. She sounded like a less hearty version of Julia Childs. Hecklepeck seated himself next to Maggie on the sofa. Richard perched himself on an equally massive chair opposite.

'Birdie, would you get our guests some tea?' The coffee-and-cream-coloured man pranced out. Tea or any hot beverage was the last thing Richard wanted. He felt a prickling sensation in the neighbourhood of his left thigh. Glancing down, he saw a palm plant poking at him between the arm rest and the seat of his chair. He moved as far over to the right as he could and huddled there.

'Mr Hecklepeck, I would so easily recognise you anywhere.' Maggie looked at him with wavery dark eyes. 'But who is your little friend?'

Hecklepeck introduced Richard, who extended his hand but found he was looking straight into the sun. All he could see of Hecklepeck or Maggie were their outlines. Rather than risk putting his hand in Maggie's face, he dropped it and muttered something vaguely polite.

'How completely kind of you to come in person to tell me about Miss Michaels' death,' Maggie continued. 'I have been wildly anxious to know all the details.'

'Was she a friend of yours?' asked Hecklepeck.

'Why no. But I liked her immensely and she was going to feature me in one of her highly interesting reports.'

'Yes, I know,' said Hecklepeck.

'I thought you did. You are probably visiting all of us ladies who were spotlighted in the report.' Hecklepeck didn't bother to explain that it was not station policy to make courtesy calls on news subjects.

'Do you know when the presentation is going to take place now?' Maggie looked at the sizable diamond on her left ring-finger.

Presentation, thought Richard. Does she think she was starring in a Hollywood movie? He wondered if he had stepped into a horror film. He couldn't see anything but

103

endless suns even when he closed his eyes. Some plant was attacking him with intent to kill and the heat was stifling.

'Well,' Hecklepeck looked regretful. 'I'm not sure that Laurel's series will ever air now. I think it's been put on indefinite hold.'

'Oh, dear. How utterly sad.'

Birdie came in with an ornate silver tea-tray. He set it down on a side table. From there he poured and passed out delicate china cups of tea. It was a graceful performance if not strictly butleresque. When he'd finished, he left.

Richard noted with added sorrow that there was nowhere to put his cup. He was going to have to hold it.

'I would absolutely love to have a copy of those pictures Miss Michaels took here,' said Maggie.

'They seem to have disappeared,' Hecklepeck replied fallaciously. 'The police are currently searching the entire television station to find them.'

'My pictures? Are they so terribly interested in me?'

Hecklepeck said the police were looking for all the tapes. And Richard shifted his teacup to his left hand, wishing he could do the same with his body. His right hip had been taking almost all of his weight as he shrank away from the malicious palm.

'Hmmm. I would be willing to pay for a copy of those pictures. Do you think the station would sell them to me?' Maggie asked. Hecklepeck explained that it was against station policy to sell or give away its newstapes.

'How definitely too bad! Birdie and I have outfitted a media room. We love to watch movies now and again.' Richard tried to picture Birdie and Maggie watching movies together. He couldn't. Nor could he imagine on what sort of movie they would both agree.

Hecklepeck, in the meantime, had been taking what opportunities he could to look around the sunroom. He resisted the urge to get up and look more closely at certain pieces of antique furniture. Maggie had some beauties. Among them was the bureau that Art had inadvertently caught on tape. He had not had to look too far to find that it was right behind Richard, with the same silver candlesticks and pieces of china on top. The red-gold burl of the chest's finish was even more beautiful than it had appeared on tape and not for the first time Hecklepeck marvelled at how far short of reality newstape fell. He often worried that a news audience could look at one thing and see it as another because pictures just weren't the same as reality.

'That Laurel Michaels and I had such a really delightful tea together when she was here,' Maggie continued. 'We chatted for quite some time. I just found that I liked her immensely.'

'Yes,' said Hecklepeck trying to bring his mind back to the conversation. 'Yes.' Was that wealthy, cultured woman saying she found something to *like* about Laurel? 'She didn't say anything that might have indicated why she was killed?'

'Oh, too definitely not! We were having a holistic conversation and that, my dear Mr Hecklepeck, is the approach to health and a long life, not death in some sort of news vehicle.' Maggie wrinkled her nose, in contempt it seemed for the location rather than the murder.

'The word, uh, tootle or tootell doesn't mean anything to you does it?' asked Hecklepeck on a sudden whim. Richard gave the palm a vicious swipe and wondered what on earth his colleague was talking about.

But the word had an amazing effect on Maggie. Her eyes opened very wide and her mouth stretched into a huge garish smile. 'Tootle? Did you say tootle?'

Hecklepeck nodded. 'I guess it does ring a bell.'

'Oh, can you be trusted? I look deep into your eyes and I see that you can. You are an honourable man. Well, then you should know that tootle is the name that Birdie and I have for a little toot.' Maggie said it as if she were conferring a great and treasured secret on her two visitors.

'A little toot,' repeated Hecklepeck, entirely in the dark.

'Yes, yes, yes. Would you like to try one?'

'Sure,' he said in the interest of investigation.

The infernal itching of the palm and the ache in the teacup-bearing wrist suddenly seemed to be warning Richard about something. Toot did ring a tiny little bell with him. But no, he told himself. It just couldn't be. It wasn't possible.

'You and your little friend wait here. I'll be right back.' Maggie rose and walked towards the door of the room. As she went she was chuckling and muttering to herself. The words 'nose' and 'powder' filtered back to Richard and the ghost of a malicious, happy smile began to take shape underneath all his pain. He was going to enjoy this.

Maggie paused in the doorway and waved flirtatiously. 'Tootles,' she said. She burst into a new cackle of laughter.

Hecklepeck got up and stared after her, suspicious. 'What's got into the damn woman,' he asked.

Richard unfolded himself and stood up. He put his full teacup on the nearest available table. 'I can't believe it but she's going to get you a toot,' he said and began slowly to stretch his cramped limbs.

'What do you mean? That woman's out of her goddamn mind.'

Richard chuckled. 'That's one way to put it.'

Hecklepeck glared at him. He was prevented from saying anything by the entrance of Birdie, who skipped over to a converted, antique stereo cabinet at the far end of the room, selected a record and put it on to play.

'Ah'm so glad ya'll goin' to play with Miss Maggie and me. We luv company.' He danced out, waving his arms above his head and swinging his narrow hips.

'What's going on here?' Hecklepeck demanded.

'The music? Elvis,' smirked Richard. 'That's Elvis Costello.'

'Fuck Elvis. What are these crazy people doing?'

Richard deliberately seated himself in Hecklepeck's place on the loveseat. 'These people are about to offer us a toot,' he pronounced once again with enjoyment.

'*Toot . . . toot . . . toot.*' Maggie and Birdie had formed a train. They came loudly tooting back into the room.

Maggie had changed into something long and flowing. When she reached the loveseat, she sat in her old place next to Richard. Hecklepeck was left with Richard's palm-ridden chair. He took it.

Meanwhile Birdie had busied himself at the bureau. He

106

pulled out a silver tray and was conducting some delicate operation on it. Hecklepeck couldn't tell what but his darkest suspicions had taken shape and his irritation was growing. The music was so loud he couldn't hear it. The damn sun was blinding him and his left side was crawling with prickles. Nobody seemed to notice his distress, much less sympathise. In silhouette Maggie and Richard appeared to be conversing like old friends.

Birdie carried his tray over to Maggie. '*Toot est prêt*,' she shrieked. She picked up a tube of some sort and, bending over the tray, inhaled loudly through her right nostril. She then applied the tube to her left nostril and inhaled again. She made loud sniffing noises. '*Toot finis*,' she cackled and broke into wild laughter.

Hecklepeck now knew for certain. He had been inveigled into a cocaine party. The importance of that shot on Laurel's tape was not the antique bureau or the candlesticks, it was the line of white powder. And Richard, with his extensive education in recreational drugs, would have known. If only Hecklepeck had followed through on his early morning plan and shown the shots to his colleague, he wouldn't be in the situation he was now.

Richard was taking his turn at the silver tray with pleasure. He was thinking that he truly deserved it in compensation for a horrible morning and, as he sniffed, he wondered gleefully what Hecklepeck was going to do.

Hecklepeck, Richard knew, did not use drugs. Life seemed to offer him plenty of stimulation without them. It was true, he loved his beer, but as much for the taste of the brew as its soporific effect. Thus, it was doubly ironic to Richard that the drug community regarded Hecklepeck as a charter member. His reputation as the 'unanchored' anchorman had come about through a confusion of perception. Regarded through certain states of altered consciousness, the changes in Hecklepeck's mobile face were mind-blowing, particularly if the TV sound were turned down and the stereo up. The drug fraternity had discovered that to smoke a joint and watch Hecklepeck change expression in time to heavy metal was truly cosmic. It had made him something of a cult hero.

Richard watched Hecklepeck as he felt the cocaine taking effect and suppressed a giggle. What *was* he going to do now?

In fact Hecklepeck had developed a plan. He didn't want to refuse Maggie's cocaine and risk offence before he finished questioning her, nor did he want to participate. So instead of inhaling the drug, he was going to blow. He would scatter it to the four winds. If they offered more, he would be overcome with remorse: an expensive waste . . . his clumsiness . . . wouldn't dream of imposing further.

Birdie held the shiny tray in front of him. On it were four strings of powder. The tube, Hecklepeck saw, was a rolled-up one-thousand-dollar bill. He picked it up and looked over at Richard for support. He had forgotten about the blinding light. Not only was it impossible to distinguish Richard, but also, when he looked back at the tray, it was largely obscured by black sun-spots.

Hecklepeck placed one end of the tube where he could only guess it should go behind the lines of powder. He carefully applied his nose to the other end. So far so good. He began gently to breath in through his mouth, building up air for the big blow.

Birdie shifted slightly. The palm rustled. It stabbed Hecklepeck anew. He gasped involuntarily. Then with all his might he blew out through his nose.

The white powder had indeed disappeared from the tray. But it was not filtering through the baking sunlight. Instead the little granules were lining the inside of Hecklepeck's mouth. He had inadvertently sucked up all four rows of cocaine. Surprised and unthinking, he gulped.

'That sho' be one big toot,' chuckled Birdie. 'Not whut we call a tootle.' He carried the tray back to his bureau. Richard grinned.

Hecklepeck's lips, mouth and throat were Novocaine numb. He moved his mouth in an effort to say something and wasn't sure he could. The music was so loud he couldn't tell.

'He's long in the toot,' suggested Maggie. She and Richard laughed uproariously. Loud sniffing indicated Birdie was inhaling his share of the drug.

Suddenly Hecklepeck felt good. He was inside himself. That was a wonderful, more wonderful than usual, place to be. He wondered inanely if the outside looked good too. He got up and wandered over to a mirror. It did! He congratulated himself warmly.

Hecklepeck turned back to share his findings with Richard and Maggie. They were deep in some hilarious conversation. He returned to the mirror.

What an image, he thought. But not just an image. Behind that face was a brilliant man. He was capable of solving this Laurel thing blindfolded. He closed his eyes. He could feel his brain racing. It was flying along, solving puzzles he hadn't even presented to it yet. He wheeled around again.

Maggie, Richard and Birdie were dancing. Hecklepeck was surprised at how graceful they all were. He watched them fondly.

After a while Maggie sashayed over to him. She took his hand and guided him to the end of the room furthest from the stereo. It was almost quiet enough to talk.

Now Hecklepeck decided he had the chance to formulate the question that would reveal whether or not Maggie had killed Laurel. He had it right at the tip of his insentient tongue. It was brilliantly phrased.

'Did you kill Laurel Michaels?' Hecklepeck blurted through bubble-gum lips.

Maggie laughed. 'That's entirely too much,' she gasped finally. She laughed some more. 'I know,' she puffed. 'You want my alibi.' She giggled. 'When did it happen?'

'Yesterday.' Was it only yesterday? Hecklepeck took a moment to consider the mystery of time. It passes, he thought. He roused himself: 'Between twelve and one.'

Maggie began to laugh again. 'It couldn't have been Birdie or me. We were making chicken croquettes in the kitchen.' She howled with laughter at the idea of chicken croquettes. Hecklepeck found himself joining in. 'Between you and me,' Maggie chortled, 'we had powdered our noses first.'

She suddenly became serious. 'That Laurel Michaels was truly sweet. In fact I like all media people, William.' For a moment Hecklepeck wondered who William was. Then he remembered. What a paradox, he reflected. He was William. But William was outside him. He was inside. Fascinating.

From some stationary point in the back of Hecklepeck's racing brain came a rational thought: No matter what strange subjects Laurel had had in common with Maggie, cocaine wouldn't have been one of them.

'Of course we didn't do this when she was here. I just didn't think Miss Michaels was spiritually ready. Perhaps after a few more of our little chats. . .'

Even in his strange state Hecklepeck could imagine the tease line: 'Drug use among the very rich. Laurel Michaels has details at ten. . .'

Maggie looked shrewd. 'One has to be careful you know. Not everyone feels the way *we* do about our tootles. The way I see it, it's in nature and what is in nature is clean and good. Come here.' She led Hecklepeck over to the tape machine. Fumbling a little she removed the tape that was playing and inserted a new one.

The room filled with the sounds of the sea, the surf rolling out and rolling in. Maggie rolled her head back on her shoulders and took deep snuffly breaths.

'So soothing,' she crooned. 'So relaxing. Take a deep cleansing breath and, *shewwww*, let it all out.' Hecklepeck did. It felt wonderful and it didn't even occur to him that the last time he heard that tape it had been in Laurel's office.

CHAPTER ELEVEN

THE JAGUAR CAME TO A SILENT, if abrupt, halt at the corner of Skinker and Clayton Avenues. Other cars piled up, screeching, behind it. Richard hopped out, gave the newsboy fifteen cents, and grabbed a *Post Dispatch*. He climbed back into the Jaguar which sped off.

Inside he tore through the paper to the entertainment section. John Alden had written a piece about Laurel. 'He says St Louis has lost one of its greatest assets,' Richard reported. 'He ranks Laurel with the arch and the zoo as important St Louis institutions.' Richard considered. 'I don't know about the arch but the zoo seems appropriate.' Hecklepeck chuckled.

'Then he hits some of the highlights of her reporting. He remembers when she went after Mr Transmission – that guy who was doing phoney repair work. He mentions her nursing-home series and ... Oh, my God,' Richard shrieked. Still under the influence of the cocaine, he laughed wildly. Hecklepeck laughed too, even harder when he realised he didn't know why he was laughing.

'He thinks the city should put up a monument to Laurel,' Richard gasped. 'He wants KYYY to sponsor a telethon to raise money for it.' He began to laugh again.

So did Hecklepeck. He pictured a bronze replica of Laurel in one of her mechanic-suits; a caricature of some terrible saint, her pointed, prissy features screwed into a sanctimonious expression. Instead of a cross she fondled a pencil and her reporter's notebook. Sinners looked up at her in dread of something more awful than hell and damnation: public exposure.

Hecklepeck manoeuvred the car through the big

chain-link gates, around the back of the building, into a remote corner of the KYYY parking lot. It was a parking place designated for news vehicles but there weren't any general spaces left. The lot was fuller than usual because of all the police vehicles.

Richard began to laugh again as he got out of the Jaguar. 'They could put Laurel on the waterfront to bless the boats, maybe on top of the arch,' he howled.

'No!' Hecklepeck was full of mock outrage. 'She'd sink anything that floats.' He locked the car with the box of tapes still inside. 'She's more likely to be the patron saint of consumers. They could put her in one of the shopping malls. Rich old ladies looking for a bargain would genuflect and lay discount coupons at her feet. They'd hang price tags on her in gratitude for off-price TV sets and marked-down designer dresses.'

As they came around the side of the building Richard saw a blue Sedan parked in the restaurant parking lot across the street; one of a number of cars whose owners were having lunch at Holden's. Richard tried to remember why a blue sedan seemed important. But he couldn't get it together.

In front of him was the newsroom door. Just inside would be a policeman, checking everyone who went into or came out of the station, for the missing tapes. 'Are you ready to be frisked?' he asked Hecklepeck. Richard himself was ready. Over the years he had thumbed his nose at countless policemen who did not discern that he was under the influence of any of a number of illegal drugs. Squaring off against the pigs reminded him what it was like to be a child of the Sixties. With a swagger he threw open the door.

Inside a uniformed cop rose from his seat and held out his hands for their jackets. Hecklepeck and Richard handed them over. The policeman squeezed the jackets to see if there was anything in them. He went through the pockets. Then he picked up a metal detector and ran it up and down their legs and torsos.

'What the hell is he doing?' Richard asked Hecklepeck in loud undertones. 'Don't they know video tapes are made of plastic.' The policeman gritted his teeth.

'I bet if I did have a tape under my sweater that machine

112

would screw it up. The cops would never know what was on it,' Richard continued in even louder undertones. 'Anyway it's not like I could hide a video tape in my pocket. They're not exactly tiny.' The policeman ground his gritted teeth.

'Somebody ought to explain to these guys what the technical side of television is all ab. . .' Richard stopped suddenly and stared at the news-director's office. It was piled high with cardboard boxes. Berger and several of his colleagues were examining them. All of this Richard absorbed in passing, his eyes coming to rest on one box in particular. It was his box, the one with the substitute tapes and the myriad scratched-out labels. It was sitting in the middle of Ken's desk, right in front of Berger.

Several hours earlier the sight would have filled Richard with panic. Not now. Now he charged past Hecklepeck and burst into the office. 'I see you have my tapes,' he said. It sounded like a challenge.

Berger looked up at him in surprise. 'Yeah,' he said, 'We're about to look at them.'

'Okay by me,' Richard sank into the chair in front of the desk. He slid into a comfortable slouch.

Looking around, he decided that the police must have collected every cardboard box in the station. Not all of them contained tapes. Some were filled with papers, some with office supplies. One box even held the station toilet-paper.

Berger regarded Richard steadily. He was trying to assess the change in him. 'Feeling better are you, buddy?' he asked.

Richard nodded belligerently. 'Feeling no pain,' he said and began to giggle. He looked around to share the joke with Hecklepeck. But Hecklepeck had not followed him into Ken's office.

'You two've been having a few snahrts,' Berger guessed.

Richard hooted. 'Snorts! You might say that.'

'Sometimes a drink or two can work wahnders,' Berger commented. He ran his hand over his crew-cut and patted it gently. 'We picked up every cardbahrd box in the building,' he said.

113

'This, here,' he patted Richard's box, 'most closely resembles the one we saw in Lahrel Michaels' office.'

'Well, I wouldn't have thought it was that one,' Richard nodded at the box of toilet paper. He grinned widely.

'You don't seem to appreciate how serious yahr situation is,' Berger said sternly. 'It looks a whole lot like you've been playing us fahr suckers. This here box's been scribbled all over. Makes me wahnder why. Makes me think somebody wanted to hide something. Maybe some writing. Some writing that said "Lahrel Michaels".' Richard merely looked smug.

'That isn't all. We come across this box in yahr file drahwer. Yahr files're all over the flahr. Could be you took them out to hide something. The tapes, maybe.'

'I was redecorating,' said Richard impertinently.

Berger regarded Richard steadily. Without dropping his gaze, he took one of the tapes out of Richard's box and handed it to the policeman standing behind him.

The officer put the tape in Ken's play-back machine and pushed the button. He did it like an expert. He had become one over the course of the last few hours. The tape started.

Berger continued to watch Richard carefully. Behind him the monitor was suffused with a sickly yellow-green colour. Richard and the policeman watched with fascination as the camera pulled back and slowly gave shape to the putrid hue. The watchers became aware that it was somebody's rear end, a gigantic rump. Richard howled with laughter. The officer chortled.

Berger swung around to look at the monitor. The camera was pulling back even further. Some grossly fat woman in sickly green shorts was attempting to touch her toes.

To Richard it was hilarious and the policeman, too, appeared to be struggling for control. But Berger frowned.

'Okay, buddy,' he addressed Richard. 'I've been willing to go the distance with you. Now I'm going to get tough. Tell me about yahr relationship with Ms Michaels.'

Richard spluttered. 'I didn't have any relationship with that old bag.'

'If you can't come clean here we can talk at headquahrters.' Berger was finally running out of patience.

'But I didn't,' Richard protested.

'Fred,' Berger addressed the policeman over his shoulder. 'Take Mr Markowitz downtown. I'll be down shahrtly to question him.' Richard's mouth dropped open. He hadn't foreseen this.

The policeman stood, waiting for Richard to get out of his chair. When Richard did the officer placed his hand securely on his elbow and guided him towards the door.

'Next I suppose we could include that report on other reporters who died on the job.' Hecklepeck had spread the five o'clock producer's script across three desks. With cocaine-induced brilliance he was rearranging her entire show. 'No, I have a better idea. Let's bury the sucker after Sports along with that trash on the dangers of consumer reporting. Neither one of them passes the "Who gives a shit?" test.' As he talked, Hecklepeck moved script pages from one pile to another with abandon. He commandeered a fourth desk-top.

The producer shook her head. 'That story on reporters dying is a twenty-second reader. Leif Carlson is the only other St Louis journalist who died on the job and he had a heart attack.'

'Okay, but it'll still work with the consumer thing.'

The producer shook her head again. 'The camera went down. The dangers of consumer reporting story is out.' She sighed. 'And the stranglings story is pretty weak. Nobody strangles anybody anymore. They use handguns. . .'

Hecklepeck wasn't listening. He was watching a police officer conduct Richard out of Ken's office and across the newsroom. The policeman at the newsroom door also saw the pair. He opened the door and ushered them out with a little flourish.

Was Berger arresting Richard for Laurel's murder? Hecklepeck wondered. Why? What could he possibly have on Richard? He leaned back in his chair and closed his eyes to rein in his racing mind and think.

'So, in fact, more people die of jaywalking than strang. . .' The five o'clock producer saw Hecklepeck and

115

stopped. After taking apart her show and spreading it all over the newsroom, he was taking a nap! She looked at the clock. It was almost four-thirty.

Hecklepeck stood up. 'You finish up,' he said. The producer looked at the string of miscellaneous pages that had been her show. Out of the corner of her eye she saw the show director approaching to review his copy of a finished show script. She gulped back the rising panic.

Hecklepeck sauntered into the news-director's office. Berger was in the process of giving directions to one of his detectives. 'Get the news directahr to assign you a video-tape player. I want it going twenty-fahr hours a day. Until we find those tapes.'

Hecklepeck let out his breath slowly. If they were still looking for the tapes, why did they arrest Richard? he wondered fleetingly.

Berger continued: 'Divide up the building so you know which tapes you've looked at. Which you haven't. Work frahm the bottom up.' He nodded in dismissal.

They were going to look at every tape in the station, Hecklepeck realised. He pictured the stacks of old show-tapes stored in the basement; the shelves of file tapes in the editing-tape library and he looked at the piles in the newsroom. It was going to be a big job. Hecklepeck wished he could think of a way to hand the tapes over to the police without implicating himself. He made a mental note to give the matter some thought and, immediately, lost it.

Berger was looking at him curiously.

'What did you do with Richard?' Hecklepeck demanded.

'Don't worry. I just took yahr little buddy downtown to talk. I got to get some straight answers out of him. It might jolt him into saying something.'

Murmuring something in relief, Hecklepeck backed into the newsroom. He slipped into his office, sat down in front of the desk-top trash pile and unleashed his mind.

'Heck.' It was the night-time assignment-editor. 'They're calling for you out on the set. They want to line up their shots.'

Hecklepeck looked at his watch. It was three minutes to

show-time. He jumped up and headed for the studio, sprinting.

Over his shoulder, to the assignment-editor, he said, 'Get my make-up out of the men's dressing room.'

'I can't go in there,' she wailed. But Hecklepeck was out of hearing.

He slid into his seat on the set, reaching for his pink mirror. In its eye he straightened his tie, wet his lips and flattened a wave of hair. Lucky he was in such good face today! Hecklepeck dropped the mirror and faced the camera with drug-produced bravado.

The red light came on. The floor director cued him and Hecklepeck read off the teleprompter:

'TONIGHT WE REMEMBER LAUREL MICHAELS, OUR COLLEAGUE, YOUR FRIEND. ALSO, THE POLICE HAVE A NEW CLUE THAT THEY HOPE WILL LEAD TO HER MURDERER. THOSE STORIES AND MORE NEWS ON THE NEWS WITH ANSWERS . . . NEXT.'

As he read, Hecklepeck patted the desk around him in wide circles. When the camera went off he demanded: 'Where's my script?'

'You got it,' the floor director indicated three pages lying in front of Hecklepeck. A show script was usually closer to thirty sheets.

'Where the hell's the rest of it?' Hecklepeck was incredulous.

'Your alleged producer hasn't finished it yet. She's going to feed it to you piece by piece.'

' . . . why. Turn to KYYY, the news with the answers.' The show was beginning. Hecklepeck settled himself and took up his three pages. ' . . . Meteorologist Irwin Samuels, Sportscaster Bucky Ballwin and special consumer-reports with Channel Three's Cautious Consumer Laurr.rr-rr.ahhhhhhh . . . ' The show opening died a horrible, audible death.

In the control room, the show director swore loudly. 'Where the fuck is the new open?' he shouted. No one answered. 'Good evening,' said Hecklepeck graciously. His

117

regular viewers noted a slight stubble on his chin. He looked whiter and more tired than usual.

Pace it, Hecklepeck was thinking. Keep the show moving along. In his opinion the five o'clock show often dragged. 'As most of you know, Laurel Michaels died yesterday. She was consumer reporter here at KYYY for fifteen years. During that time she looked after your health and safety, she solved your complaints.' As he read, Hecklepeck listened to himself. He liked what he heard. The show seemed to be skimming along.

'What's he doing?' asked the show director. 'He's talking so fast I can't understand a word of what he's saying.'

'We have several reports on just how much Laurel Michaels meant to our community and, more personally, how much she meant to us here at KYYY. But first, we want to update you on the investigation into her murder. Joe Handy is at the scene where her body was so tragically discovered. Here he is with a live report.' Hecklepeck sprinted to the finish. 'Joe?' He swung around and looked expectantly at the monitor behind him. Nothing happened.

'Did you hear a cue?' asked one of the engineers.

'For God's sakes, just punch up Joe,' yelled the show director.

When Joe appeared he was standing in front of the now-familiar Maria Muldoni bungalow. Joe Handy was the reporter almost every local station has: white, male, with debatable good looks and skin-deep credibility. He wasn't talented enough to anchor but he also didn't threaten the men in management. He was assigned all the big stories at KYYY and he knew it.

In the background the bungalow door slammed. Out came the indefatigable Maria Muldoni with yet another plate of pasta. Maria had discovered the value of publicity.

Joe squared his shoulders. He held a black box in front of the camera lens. 'This is a video tape,' he pronounced.

In the background Maria Muldoni was giving a particularly scruffy-looking neighbour a helping of pasta.

'Laurel Michaels had a box full of these video tapes. She was using them to put together her story, '*Mistresses: Mystique or Misery*' Joe paused for effect.

118

The scruffy neighbour held a forkful of spaghetti high above his head. His mouth was wide open for the bite.

'The box is missing,' Joe declared in a low, thick voice.

The neighbour dropped the pasta into his mouth.

'Channel Three has learned that when the police find the box, they will find Laurel Michaels' murderer,' Joe pronounced intensely.

Behind him the scruffy neighbour demonstrated exaggerated delight. Or was the pasta choking him?

Mercifully at this point Joe's story continued on tape. It showed the police collecting boxes and looking at tapes. There was an interview with Berger in which he said, 'No comment.' Ken was also interviewed. He said he hoped the police found the murderer.

When the tape ended and Joe reappeared, the neighbour had vanished. Joe summed up: 'So, all efforts are being made to find those tapes. They are the key to the murder.'

He waved his box in front of the camera. 'It's hard to think a little box like this one could have so many big answers in it. Back to you, Bill.'

'It doesn't.' Hecklepeck appeared both disgusted and miraculously tanned. The night-time assignment-editor had arrived with make-up during Joe's story. Unfortunately it was Bucky Ballwin's and darker than Hecklepeck's.

'Finding that box of tapes in itself isn't going to solve this thing.' As soon as he said it, Hecklepeck realised that he couldn't explain about the tapes without incriminating himself. He turned abruptly to the third of his pages and raced through it. At the end he looked expectantly at the camera.

'If I didn't know better, I'd say he's been taking some kind of drug,' said the engineer in the booth.

'Just give me a two-shot with Sandler on Camera Three.' The show director bit off his words. 'My script says he's next.'

Ivan (he pronounced it 'Eeee-van') Sandler was the station commentator. He didn't expect to be on until later in the show. With his feet up on the anchor desk he was practising.

Hecklepeck wasn't expecting him either. His script called

for a taped report on Laurel's career. As soon as his camera light went off, he beckoned energetically to one of the floor crew. The crew member didn't come. The television audience watched as Hecklepeck beckoned again, angrily. Beside him Ivan mouthed his script and gesticulated.

Then almost simultaneously Hecklepeck and Ivan glanced at their monitors. In horror they swung into position and faced each other. 'We must have, uh, lost that report,' Hecklepeck improvised in his normal voice. 'Obviously commentator Ivan Sandler is here to fill in. Ivan?'

It was intelligible. The show director ordered a single shot of Ivan and Ivan began. Like most television commentators, he had an absolute horror of taking a position. Even on a subject as unequivocal as the murder of a colleague Ivan waffled. Laurel was sensitive but she was tough. Murder was bad but maybe some good would come of it. He was sad but he knew Laurel would have been happy to die in the line of duty. In his tight nasal voice Ivan wandered through a long list of dichotomies.

Hecklepeck, meanwhile, was in urgent, whispered conference with the floor crew. He had run out of script and his feelings of euphoria had suddenly gone away.

Ivan began to wrap up and still no script arrived. The floor crew lined up a camera for a two-shot. Hecklepeck prepared himself for a lengthy chitchat with Ivan. His head ached.

CHAPTER TWELVE

'WHO SAYS ONE PERSON DOESN'T make a difference?' Media critic John Alden silently offered the question to the row of television sets in front of him. Laurel Michaels had been murdered and the entire KYYY newscast fell apart. It was impossible to separate the two events. With thumb and forefinger Alden pulled at the hairs inside his right nostril and concluded that Laurel must have held the entire Channel Three newscast together. He gave the little hairs a final tug and brought his hand down to his typewriter. 'KYYY's lamentable performance Wednesday evening serves as yet another reminder that consumer reporter Laurel Michaels will be severely missed,' he wrote. 'The least this community can do is dignify her memory with a monument . . .'

In his office Hecklpeck tossed the show script onto the mound of trash on his desk. It slid to the floor. Hecklepeck sank into his chair. Tomorrow he would figure out a way to get into Laurel's apartment. He wasn't particularly hopeful about finding anything. The murderer, he was sure, had gotten there first with the key in Laurel's coat pocket. But Hecklepeck felt compelled to look and he would take the opportunity to visit the last of the women in Laurel's series: her neighbour, whom Art had dubbed, Sonya something.

So far, Hecklepeck brooded, his investigation was long on information and short on actual evidence. He knew a lot more than when he started but none of it seemed to add up to anything.

What seemed to be unassailable was that Laurel had

been on to some kind of big story. She had been planning an interview in connection with it, but before she could get the interview set up, she was killed.

Was the story, *Drug Use among the Rich?* Hecklepeck wrote the scenario in his mind: Laurel had somehow discovered that Maggie Johnson had a cocaine habit. Perhaps she figured it out from the tape of the white powder on the bureau. But Hecklepeck thought it more likely that the tape was confirmation, proof of something Laurel already knew. In any case she would have phoned, told Maggie she was going to tattle on her 'tootling' and asked for an interview. Maggie, or more likely, Maggie with her nasty friend Birdie would then have hung around the station until Laurel came out, inveigled her into the privacy of the van and strangled her.

But what if the story were *Sexual Exploitation in the Workplace?* Hecklepeck knew, because Rita told him that Laurel had phoned Wally the day before she died to ask him for an interview. She had planned to expose his relationship with Rita on the air which would have ruined his career. That was Wally's motive.

Rita's was equally strong. She had agreed to be interviewed by Laurel in the understanding that Wally's identity would not be released. When Laurel threatened to use Wally's name on the air, Rita stood to lose not only him but the job promotion she was trying to get from him.

What Hecklepeck liked about both Wally and Rita as suspects was that they worked at the station and could have been seen in the parking lot without arousing suspicion. It was hard to believe that Maggie and Birdie could have spent any time in the parking lot without calling attention to themselves. But maybe they had come around the back of the station through the little wooded area. Then they could have hidden in the shelter of the van until Laurel came out of the station, beckoned to her quickly and ducked back behind the van. Their exposure to the parking lot would have been extremely limited.

Hecklepeck mentally beat up on himself for not checking Maggie's and Birdie's cars. If they had come to KYYY to murder Laurel, they had probably driven and if so, they would have had to park somewhere in the neighbourhood. Maybe the car had been seen by somebody.

Or maybe it was Tareesa's car that somebody saw. Hecklepeck was a little fuzzy as to what big story Laurel might have had on Tareesa. It might have been *Sex and Politics* or *Small Businesswoman takes on Big Developer*.

The first story possibility revolved around Alderman 'Tiny' Payne and his infidelities. Tareesa had laughed about them and said she didn't mind. But maybe she did. Maybe she minded a lot and, as fierce as her pride was, maybe she didn't want the whole of St Louis to know.

The second story was hazier. The block behind Tareesa's nightclub was going to be developed, or at least that was the rumour. The development would force Tareesa out of business. Soooo . . . she'd commit murder to save Tess's. Possibly, but how would killing Laurel save her nightclub?

Hecklepeck did not see how. The only slim connection he had between the two was a taped shot of the grass-covered foundation that had been 5304 Evans Street. If Tareesa hadn't mentioned the possibility of development behind her club, the shot would not have linked up at all and Hecklepeck could have dismissed it. But there was that slim connection. He decided to go down to city hall and check the zoning records. The 5300 block of Evans had obviously been a residential block. If it were going to be developed, it would have to be rezoned.

'He . . . Heck, may I talk to you?' Ken stuck his head into Hecklepeck's cubbyhole.

Hecklepeck ushered Ken into the extra chair. They sat knee to knee.

'Wally and I have developed a plan of action,' the news director began. 'We want to coordinate with you.' It took some effort to get the words out. Ken was exhausted. His office given over to police work, he had spent a hard day in the newsroom, looking for something to do.

'Yes?' said Hecklepeck.

'Laurel's family lives in Darien, Connecticut,' Ken endowed the simple fact with significance.

Resisting the temptation to prod him, Hecklepeck merely said, 'Yes?'

123

'They want to hold the funeral there.'

'Yes? Yes?'

'Her body is to be shipped. They don't want to come here.'

Poor Laurel, thought Hecklepeck. Even her family didn't seem to care for her.

Ken let his last statement sink in. He let it sink in until, in Hecklepeck's view, it must have reached China and started back.

'Yes?' Hecklepeck finally prompted. At this point he didn't trust himself with the polite use of any other word.

'Wally feels the station should be represented at the funeral.' Aha, thought Hecklepeck, the heart of the matter.

'Who does Wally want to represent the station?' he asked innocently.

'Well,' Ken cleared his throat. 'Wally feels it should be someone who holds an important position here at KYYY, someone who really stands for what we do here, someone vital to our operation.' Someone Wally wants out of the way, added Hecklepeck to himself.

'Who?' he asked darkly.

Even Ken was capable of seeing it wasn't working. 'You,' he muttered. 'Wally wants you to go up to Connecticut Friday and stay for the funeral on Saturday. Tomorrow, after the police are through, he wants you to oversee the packing up of her apartment.' Ken dangled a key. He looked at the floor.

Hecklepeck snatched the key. 'I'd be very glad to pack up her apartment,' he said. Then with great regret: 'But I can't possibly go to Connecticut.' Ken looked up. 'It's ratings. My contract says I have to be on the air during rating periods. I can hardly do that from Connecticut.' It was true. Ken knew it. 'Why don't you go to Connecticut? It's really something the news director ought to do anyway. Nobody's more, uh, vital than you. You have KYYY written all over you.'

Ken nodded. He *was* the right person to represent the station. Wally should have thought of him in the first place.

'I know you have a lot to do,' Hecklepeck continued. 'So I'll just do the packing part for you. That way you can leave tomorrow if you want to.'

'You don't have to actually pack,' Ken said generously. 'A neighbour, Sonya . . . Sonya, uh, something, is doing that. She lives downstairs. You just have to check on it. Wally wants to be able to give his assurance that it was done right.' Hecklepeck regarded the key with great satisfaction before tucking it into his vest pocket. 'I'll take care of everything,' he said.

'Ken?' the evening assignment-editor stood in the doorway. 'There's somebody up front to see you: Alderman Payne.'

'I don't have time to see him now,' Ken snapped. 'I'm going out of town. Tell him I went home.'

Hecklepeck intervened. 'You should see him. It'll only take a few minutes. I'll go with you.'

'But my office . . .' Ken was doubtful.

'In the conference room. Come on.' Hecklepeck led his boss through the almost empty newsroom and down the hall to the reception desk.

'We've now looked at 294 tapes.' In Ken's office a very bored policeman pulled a tape out of the tape machine and stuck a numbered police seal on it. The cardboard boxes were gone and the office was filled with stacks of video tapes.

Beside him his partner lounged in one of Ken's chairs. 'Why is it called news when it's the same thing over and over again, day after day?' he mused. 'I mean, what's new about it?'

Alderman Walter Payne, known to everybody as 'Tiny', dominated the reception area. Tiny was almost as wide as he was tall and he wore his corpulence the way some women do a mink, stroking it, patting it. Tiny knew its worth. It had endowed him, a short man, with stature. Tiny had won four terms on the board of aldermen. He chaired the prestigious budget committee and led the powerful black caucus.

Tiny stood until Ken approached and offered a hand. They shook and Ken ushered Hecklepeck forward. The three men walked to the conference room; Ken apologizing all the way for not being able to use his office. 'We've just had a murder here,' he explained as if it were some event the station had hosted.

Tiny walked straight to the chair at the head of the oval conference table and, pushing gently on either side of his belly, settled in. His little black eyes darted around the room, picking up pieces of it for storage. Ken and Hecklepeck took seats on either side of him; Hecklepeck inquiring about work on the new budget.

Tiny slid around the budget on political platitudes: never enough money to go around. The poor have taken it on the chin long enough. Time for the mayor and his cronies to sacrifice a little. The rhetoric droned on like a distant chainsaw while Tiny's thin black moustache moved languidly up and down against the chocolate milk of his skin.

After a while he stopped and started again with no change of tone. 'I wish to extend my sincere condol-ensezz to you and the rest of the KYYY newsss team.' Tiny wanted the world to know a black man was capable of good grammar. He not only didn't drop his endings, he often stressed them.

'Yes,' said Ken. 'We are all very sorry about the death of Laurel Michaels.' His doughy face looked distressed but he brightened: 'I will be representing her KYYY family at her funeral in Connecticut Saturday.'

Tiny's eyes rested on Ken briefly, then darted off to the far regions of the room. 'I note-essed on the news tonight that the police are look-ingg for some tapes.'

'The tapes are the key to everything,' stated Ken. 'Whoever has those tapes could be the murderer. The police are reviewing every tape in the station right now. They don't think the tapes were taken out of the building.' For the first time Ken added it up. 'I guess that means someone at the station here is the, uh, killer.' He paused. 'I hope it wasn't somebody I hired.' There was another pause as Ken mentally reviewed all the people he had hired in his short tenure at KYYY.

Tiny massaged the loose flesh on his right hand and looked at Hecklepeck briefly. 'Laurel interviewed Tiny as part of her mistresses series, Ken,' Hecklepeck interceded.

126

'That interview is likely to be on those tapes.'

Ken looked distressed. 'Oh dear.'

'It would nottt be advantageous to my career to be part of a murder investiga-shun.'

'Oh dear.'

Hecklepeck sat forward. 'We obviously don't have that box of tapes,' he said, meeting Tiny's eyes for the briefest of seconds. 'But maybe you'd like to look at the second part of Laurel's series, the part that was to have aired the night she died. It's about Tareesa and . . . you.' Tiny pulled at the rolls of flesh under his chin and inclined his head slightly.

'Why don't you go get it?' Hecklepeck said to Ken. 'It's back on the show rack. The police have already seen it.' Ken went gladly.

Several minutes later the door opened and the evening assignment-editor came in. 'Ken wanted me to bring you this,' she said, holding out a tape. 'He says he's sorry but he has to make some travel arrangements.' Hecklepeck thanked her. He took the tape over to a tape player at the front of the room while Tiny moved himself around to watch.

Tiny showed little emotion as the piece played. Only when Laurel talked about his infidelities did he knead his upper arms back and forth, back and forth.

At the end Tiny leaned back in his chair. He looked at Hecklepeck and away. 'And will they air this?'

'Nope. Laurel's dead.'

Tiny rubbed his chest. 'It is the na-tchur of man to roam. You dig? I like to let my na-tchur run free. I don't think my constit-oo-ents would have any problem with that. But any connection at all with a murder is not desirable. Definitely not desirable.'

He rose, pulling up on his stomach with his hands.

'Before you go,' Hecklepeck stopped him, 'I'd like to ask you something.' Tiny sat back down.

'There's a block directly behind Tess's place, the 5300 hundred block of Evans Street?'

Tiny's eyelids seemed to drop a little, giving him a slightly hooded look. 'Yes, what do you want to know?' Was that wariness Hecklepeck heard in his voice?

'I understand the block is slated for development?' If anybody would know it would be Tiny. The block was in his aldermanic ward.

Tiny shrugged. 'There are rumours.' But this time his eyes did not meet Hecklepeck's even for the briefest of seconds.

Suspicious, Hecklepeck tried it from a different angle. 'There's the foundation of a house there, number 5304. Do you know anything about that?'

'There was a . . .' Tiny started out slowly, but he gathered speed as he went on, 'fire in one of those houses on that block. I don't remember which one. It was . . . four years ago. Four? Yes. The spring of '76. The house burned to the ground and an elderly woman did not get out in time. I was chairing the social services committee at the time. Naturally we held extensive hearings.'

In the newsroom the evening assignment-editor locked the city police-scanner in on the fire channel. They were calling for a hook and ladder to answer an alarm in a warehouse section near the river. The assignment-editor didn't hesitate. She picked up the two-way radio and said, 'This is KY333 to Barry Saire. Call me by landline please.'

Richard picked up another pile of papers from the floor around his desk. He was reconstructing his files. In Ken's office one of the policemen unenthusiastically plastered a sticker on a videotape. It bore the number 334.

The phone rang. The assignment editor grabbed it. 'Barry,' she said, 'there's a huge warehouse fire down on Laclede's Landing. I need you to get down there right away.' She adjusted the police radio while Barry talked, and then replied, 'Well, you're just going to have to take your dinner with you.' There was more protest from Barry. 'No, I don't know how you're going to carry mashed potatoes!'

'How's my furry little friend?' Hecklepeck loomed solicitously over Richard's right shoulder. An unsmiling Richard looked up at him. 'That bad, huh?'

Richard returned to his filing. 'Being questioned by the police wasn't one of the more pleasant experiences of my life. It was degrading.'

Hecklepeck leaned on Richard's desk where he could see his face. 'How come they let you go?'

'They had nothing to hold me on. When I told Berger that you made up that bit about me and Laurel, he seemed to lose interest in me.' Richard's tone changed from self-pity to deliberate malice. 'But I don't think he's very happy with you.'

Hecklepeck digested that. Then he pulled Laurel's apartment key out of his vest pocket. 'This will cheer you up,' he said. 'It's the, uh, key to all our problems.' Richard did not look impressed. 'It's the key to Laurel's apartment. We can go there tomorrow with a crew and shoot some tape for the special.'

Richard brightened a little. 'Not bad, Heck. I'll take all the visuals I can get for that thing. How did you get it?'

'I'll tell you over dinner. Come on.'

'It could be pretty effective. We'll be able to reveal the "real" Laurel by showing all the stuff in her apartment.' Richard spoke as he reached for his jacket. 'I wonder what the real Laurel was like,' he speculated as he followed Hecklepeck out the door. 'I'm assuming there was one. I mean there had to be one. Just because she acted like a fascist here doesn't mean she was one at home.' Richard paused before adding, 'You don't suppose she *was* a card carrying Neo-Nazi?'

It was dark out and the parking-lot lights were on. They walked around the TV station to the remote corner in the back where Hecklepeck had parked his car. 'Maybe she kept pet hamsters or something,' Richard raised the hope and then dashed it. 'If so she probably did consumer testing on them: have some more cyclamates, my little dears.'

He stopped at the passenger door to Hecklepeck's Jaguar. 'Oooo, Heck! How did you get all these dents on your car?' Hecklepeck hurried around to Richard's side of the car. 'It looks like somebody's been throwing rocks at it.'

'Not rocks,' said Hecklepeck. 'This brick.' He picked up a brick lying a few feet from the Jaguar. 'Somebody must have been trying to break the car window with it.'

'Yeah,' adjoined Richard. 'We probably scared them off.

Either that or they gave up. That's what happens when you work for an outfit like Babble Broadcasting. It's too cheap to buy a building in a decent neighbourhood.'

'Huh-huh,' murmured Hecklepeck. But he wasn't listening. Amidst the driving gloves, boots, books, snow-removal equipment and bag of kitty litter in the back seat, his eyes had distinguished a square shape draped with blanket. 'I think I better take the car back to the hotel parking garage. Whoever it was might come back.' He looked at Richard. 'If you follow me in your car and give me a ride back, I'll buy you dinner at Sebastion's.'

'Right O,' said Richard.

The assignment-editor flipped the switch that unlocked the police monitor and allowed it to scan all its channels. 'KY333 to Unit 5. Barry?' she said sweetly. 'Never mind. Go back and finish your dinner.' It had been a false alarm.

CHAPTER THIRTEEN

LAUREL HAD LIVED IN AN apartment complex not too far from Creve Coeur Lake. Driving there, Hecklepeck chuckled to himself. Broken-Heart Lake sounded so poignant, so redolent of romantic possibilities. It was actually a man-made pool in the heart of rapidly developing West St Louis County and St Louis had mongrelised the name into 'Creev Cur'.

West County buildings were decorated with construction signs rather than architectural detail. In his mind Hecklepeck indicted the area further. The first building he saw as he came off the Watterson Expressway exit ramp was hung with a banner. 'A Delano and Delano Construction Site' it read. In the last few years Delano and Delano seemed to have spread itself all over the metropolitan area, especially West County.

Of course, the entire development community was building in West County. Hecklepeck was always awed at the pace of construction there, possibly because his visits were so well-spaced. Each one revealed new office towers, hotels or apartment complexes. It was almost as though developers were vying among themselves to see who could bury the richest Missouri river bottom in concrete.

As he turned down the road to Laurel's apartment complex, Hecklepeck noticed that it also was a Delano and Delano project. He steered the Jaguar along a row of car shelters more predominant at The Pines than trees. He stopped halfway down the line.

Richard was leaning against a carport pole, his arms folded self-consciously across his middle. 'The body's already been taken away,' he announced catastrophically.

131

When murder calls came across the police radio, KYYY crews raced to the scene with one goal in mind: a shot of the sheet-covered victim being brought out and placed in an ambulance. Without it the story was likely to consist of an exterior shot and some police cars.

'Well then, we might as well go home,' rejoined Hecklepeck with a grin. 'The story's not worth airing.' Stories could be made or broken not on their merits but on the acquisition of a body shot.

'We will have to go home if I don't get a white balance.' In the shelter of a carport, Art Macke was pointing his camera at a patch of white on one of the KYYY vehicles. It was not so easy to find among the painted question marks, but every time the camera was used, its colour meter had to be readjusted against a white background.

Hecklepeck drove his car into the next carport and carefully checked all its locks. For lack of a better hiding-place the blanket-covered box of tapes was still sitting on the back seat.

'I got it,' said Art. He tipped the camera back to carrying position on his right shoulder and hoisted the recorder on to his left. Richard slung the tripod over his shoulder while Hecklepeck picked up the laundry bag filled with lighting equipment. The three of them went into the building.

Laurel's name was still inked to one of the metal mailboxes just inside the entrance. She had lived in Apartment 2A. Hecklepeck also noted that a Sonya Richardson lived in 1B; the Sonya 'Something', no doubt, from Laurel's report.

They climbed a short flight of concrete stairs to 2A. Hecklepeck unlocked the yellow door with his key. It swung open. For a few seconds the three of them stared into Laurel's living room in silence.

'She was a nympho,' breathed Richard. 'A news nympho.'

Laurel's living room looked like a souvenir shop. It was full of junk memorialising her twenty-five years in the television business. Pennants, tee shirts and preserved newspaper clippings traced the Laurel Michaels' story through television stations in New Haven, Dayton and

Tulsa. They covered the walls along with signed photographs of people she had interviewed: Ralph Nader; Robert Goulet. There were endless pictures of Laurel reporting and some framed pieces of fan-mail. Pillows embroidered with 'KYYY' and other station call-letters decorated the uninteresting modern sofa. Its end tables were covered with paperweights commemorating such occasions as the time Laurel addressed the St Louis Jaycees, and women's auxiliary trophies for her contributions to public service.

'Wow,' Richard continued. 'We'll have to handle this carefully. What about shooting it in the first person?' He turned to Art. 'You walk in with the camera rolling like you're Laurel coming home from work. The audience will see it as she would have seen it. It will speak for itself.'

'I like it,' said Art. 'I *reeeelly* like it. But we're going to have to find something to cover up those windows. I can't shoot into the glare.' There were no curtains.

'I'll do that. You set up the lights.' Richard was off in one direction; Art in another. Hecklepeck remained in the doorway. In spite of all the mementoes, he thought Laurel's apartment was a sadly impersonal place. There were no books, no magazines; nothing she had collected for its own sake simply because she liked it. Everything in the apartment was indentured to her career. Hecklepeck began a circular tour of the room, examining everything.

'I think this'll do it,' Richard returned from the back of the apartment dragging a bedspread.

Art was pulling pieces of lighting equipment out of his laundry bag. He stopped and stared. 'Did you take that off her bed?' he asked distastefully.

'She isn't going to need it,' said Richard. 'It's got to be packed up anyway.' He hauled the bedspread over to the picture window and held it up. 'I need something to keep it up.' He dropped the bedspread and surveyed the room. His eyes came to rest on one of the tables of paperweights and trophies.

Hecklepeck was learning more than he had ever wanted to know about Laurel's career in New Haven. He turned the corner to Dayton. Her memorabilia, he had observed, was carefully dated and hung in chronological order beginning with her college internships at the right of the front door and progressing right through her first real job in New Haven to her last in St Louis.

Richard picked up a table of paperweights and carried it over to the window opposite the Tulsa/Dayton wall. He took the heaviest trophy and placed it on the frame above the window, pinning the bedspread beneath it. Next he selected a paperweight.

Art positioned one of his lights next to the door. With a heavy-duty extension cord he plugged it into a wall socket on the other side of the room and flipped the switch.

Hecklepeck skimmed the Dayton and Tulsa wall. He slowed down, however, and observed more carefully when he reached St Louis. St Louis covered the rest of the room. Laurel had advanced fairly quickly through the smaller markets but she had never been able to get beyond St Louis. There were more than fifteen years of St Louis souvenirs on her walls.

Richard stepped back and rubbed his hands together. The bedspread was hung, affixed to the window frame with a row of paperweights and trophies.

Art adjusted his last light and turned it on. 'Let's try it,' he said. 'I'll come in and walk along here.' He gestured to the Dayton/Tulsa wall.

'I'll do the door,' volunteered Richard. 'It'll look really far-out if the door swings open to reveal all of this . . . this junk.' Art picked his gear and walked into the hall. 'Yell when you're ready,' said Richard. He slammed the door.

Hecklepeck walked around the window and resumed his observation. He had reached the 1970s and now recognised many of the events commemorated on Laurel's wall. There was a newspaper clipping announcing she had won a local Emmy. Hecklepeck remembered that year. He had finally been nominated for an anchoring Emmy. But he hadn't won. The news directors in other cities who judged the Emmy entries had never given the award to Hecklepeck. It always went to his less-successful competitors.

'Okay!' shouted Art. Slowly and dramatically Richard

134

opened the door. Art came in shooting. He walked his camera slowly down the Dayton/Tulsa wall. 'God, that's great,' he said at the end. 'It's really creepy, like some ghostly presence coming in and looking at old stuff. Let's get a couple more takes.'

When he had completed his tour of the living room, Hecklepeck went into Laurel's bedroom. He slid open the closet door, revealing an array of jump-suits. They looked like the wardrobe of a fashion-conscious paratrooper. Sandwiched between a lime-green jump-suit and a violet one was the purple coat. Hecklepeck stared at it for a moment with a sudden queasiness. He forced the sensation down and pulled out the coat.

In its pockets were several tubes of lipstick, a wallet and an assortment of junk. Laurel had lived in those coat pockets; there was more humanity there than anywhere else in her apartment. But pieces of her life were certainly missing. The coat had contained her keyring and her reporter notebooks. Somebody had taken the notebooks and probably destroyed them. The unknown person was also using the keys to eliminate other incriminating evidence. So far, Hecklepeck acknowledged to himself, that person was staying well ahead of the pack.

Hecklepeck pulled the coat off the hanger and examined it, squeezing its quilted patches with his fingers. The padding inside felt soft and slippery. He worked his way over the whole coat until finally along the back hem he felt something odd, a stiffness. His excitement rising, he took a pair of nail scissors from Laurel's bureau and cut the thread holding the lining to the coat fabric. The thread was a slightly different colour from the coat and had been hand-sewn rather than machine-stitched. He pulled back the lining. There in the coat hem were several sheets of paper.

It was a deep hem. Laurel had simply cut some of the stitching and inserted the papers in the pocket that was created. Then she had reattached the lining. In the pillow of quilting the crackle of paper must have gone unnoticed by both the police and the murderer.

'You've got to get this shot of Laurel all dressed up like a

135

mouse. She did some kind of children's programme in New Haven.' Richard was making his own set of notes documenting Laurel's career.

Art followed behind, shooting close-ups. He focused on the mouse picture. 'I'm going to pull back from her face so those ears are revealed little by little,' he said.

For a moment the gentle whir of the camera was the only sound in the apartment. It was broken by the turning of a key in the front-door lock. Richard whirled around to look. In spite of his cavalier treatment of the bedspread he was uncomfortable in the home of a dead person.

The door swung open to reveal a floor-to-ceiling pile of cardboard boxes. Richard grabbed for Art. 'Hey, you're fucking up my shot,' Art grumbled. He, nevertheless, turned to look.

From behind the pile peered a small elfin face. It registered alarm as round eyes took in the covered window, the tangle of electrical cords and, finally, the men themselves.

'We're from Channel Three,' said Richard quickly. 'Laurel's station.'

'We're just taking some pictures,' added Art, setting his camera down. 'Remember me? I met you before, with Laurel.'

The elf smiled slowly. Its little freckled face lit up. So did the whole cold apartment in Richard's opinion. He inadvertently took a step towards the door as the small child-woman emerged into the room. She looked for a few seconds at Richard and then at Art. 'You frightened me.'

'You must be Sonya Richardson.' Hecklepeck spoke from the back of the room.

'Yes.' Sonya shifted her gaze to Hecklepeck.

Her eyes were as beautiful as ever, Art noticed. He decided that the beauty lay in their rounded shape. The colour was what? He hadn't been able to decide last time he'd seen her either. Grey? Violet? In any case it was pale, a mere backdrop for her deep-brown lashes. Art, too, took an unmindful step in Sonya's direction.

'We're here to see if you need any help with the packing,' said Hecklepeck, coming into the centre of the room.

'As you can see,' she said with a little gesture, 'I haven't yet started. The police didn't give me a key until last night. In any case there's no real hurry. The shippers don't come until the end of next week.' She looked back at the door. 'I should get those boxes out of the hall.'

'I'll do it,' said Richard and Art simultaneously. They stumbled over each other getting to the door. Sonya smiled her slow, radiant smile in their wake. There was something odd about her, Hecklepeck decided. He wasn't sure what it was.

'How did you get landed with packing?' he asked.

Sonya tucked an invisible wisp of hair into the back of her shiny brown bun. 'Her parents called and asked me. It seemed like a nice thing to do.' Richard sighed slightly as he deposited some boxes on the carpet. He hurried out for more. Art was already collecting a second load.

'How long had you known Laurel?'

'About three and a half years. I moved here about three and a half years ago.' Sonya walked over to the sofa and sat down. As he watched her Hecklepeck realised what was odd about her. She couldn't have been more than twenty-two or twenty-three years old but she was dressed like a grandmother. Hecklepeck observed a skirt that reached mid-calf (an absurd length for such a small person) and a cardigan sweater. He noticed the clunky brown shoes and a brooch at her throat. Maybe more attractive clothing didn't come in her small size.

'That was you in Laurel's series, wasn't it?' he asked. Sonya turned hot pink. Art frowned meaningfully at Hecklepeck as he sat down the last of the boxes.

'Ye-es,' confessed Sonya. 'But I wish I hadn't.' She tapped the toes of her clunky shoes together before turning her enigmatic eyes on Hecklepeck. 'I have to ask you something.' Hecklepeck inclined his head and waited. 'Those tapes the police are looking for. They aren't going to be made public are they?'

He shook his head.

'If a certain person sees them, he will never forgive me.' Sonya frowned.

Hecklepeck felt for the sheets of paper folded up in the pocket of his sheepskin coat. 'Why?'

Sonya sighed. 'It's a long story.' She looked at him to see if he was interested in hearing it. 'When I graduated from St Mary's I went to work as a receptionist for a construction company. I didn't want to go to college. It seemed so frightening.' Sonya glanced at Richard and Art who were having a whispered conference by the front door. 'I fell in love with my boss. I couldn't help myself.' She stopped, bringing her gaze back to Hecklepeck. Behind the veil of her lashes her eyes were unreadable. 'It was very romantic,' she said quietly.

Hecklepeck was puzzled. It didn't seem possible that a girl as seemingly conservative as Sonya would get involved with her boss.

'I left my job and allowed him to set me up here in this apartment. For a while it was wonderful. . .'

Hecklepeck also couldn't imagine the man who would choose Sonya for a mistress. She was a Catholic schoolgirl; instant guilt.

Sonya continued. 'The thing is, he's married. He told me he was going to get a divorce, but he never did.'

And, here, Sonya was talking about her relationship with this married man to three strangers as if there were no moral considerations. It didn't sit right, not coming from her. But perhaps she really had been in love and her feelings had overcome her sense of propriety. Perhaps the man she was involved with enjoyed her innocence. Maybe that was what had attracted him in the first place.

'So it has to be secret,' Sonya wound up. 'Everything has to be secret.'

'We were wondering if you'd do an interview with us.' Richard interrupted.

'It won't be like the other one,' Art added quickly.

'Noo-ooo,' said Richard. 'We just want to ask you about Laurel and what it was like to be her neighbour.'

'This isn't for an investigative report or anything. It's for a feature piece. . .'

' . . . A special show on Laurel. Her life and times.' In their eagerness their sentences were blending into one long speech.

'We won't air it unless you approve.'

138

'Really,' Richard wound up. He could think of nothing more to say but he wanted the last word.

'Well,' pronounced Sonya, transferring her beautiful unreadable eyes from one to the other. 'As long as you don't ask me about anything connected with the interview I gave Laurel, I guess I can.'

'Great,' said Art. 'We'll do it against this wall, with the poster in the background. We can move that easy chair over.' Richard remained with his eyes fixed on Sonya for a second before going to help Art.

'But Laurel wouldn't keep the secret.'

Somehow Hecklepeck knew what was coming.

'She was my friend. I thought so anyway,' Sonya said. 'We did things together when she wasn't too busy. But when I agreed to be part of her story our relationship changed. I did it as a favour for her and she acted like I was some kind of criminal.'

In front of the Dayton wall, Art and Richard were arguing over the exact placement of the easy chair.

'We shot two interviews, one where I was disguised and one where I could be recognised. She said she only wanted the one where I was recognisable in case I changed my mind later. But she lied. She told me afterwards she was going to put it on the air anyway.' Was that anger in those eyes? Hecklepeck couldn't tell. Sonya rearranged some of the paperweights on the table at the end of the sofa and studied the effect.

'What about your, uh, former boss?' Hecklepeck asked. 'What did he think about this?'

'He doesn't know,' said Sonya pathetically. 'I never told him.' She adjusted one of the paperweights slightly.

'Laurel didn't try to interview him?' Hecklepeck couldn't believe she hadn't.

'She never knew who he was. I didn't give her his name.' Another of Sonya's deep-pink blushes suffused her face.

'Scrooch down in the chair,' ordered Art. 'You're much taller than she is.' Richard was playing the part of Sonya while he adjusted his lights.

'That's why those tapes are so important. If he found out, he would hate me. He'd probably stop supporting me and then what would I do?' There were tears in Sonya's eyes.

Get another job, Hecklepeck replied silently. 'You don't have to worry. They won't be aired now,' he said aloud. 'There's no chance that Laurel somehow discovered the identity of your, uh, friend is there?' He would have given a lot to know.

Sonya shook her head. 'I know Laurel didn't know because she kept trying to get me to tell her. If she knew she wouldn't have continued to pester me.'

Richard buttered in: 'We're ready now,' he said. Sonya cast a pleading glance at Hecklepeck as she let Richard lead her over to the easy chair. Richard sat in a straight chair directly in front of her and picked up a microphone. His knees were almost touching hers.

'Move back. You're in my shot,' growled Art, looking at them through the lens of his camera. Richard slid his chair back a scant inch. 'Here, let me do it.' Art came from behind his tripod. Almost before Richard could get out of it, his chair had been yanked back a foot by Art who returned to his camera. 'Nice framing,' he said with satisfaction.

Hecklepeck walked to the doorway. 'I'm leaving,' he announced. Art ignored him. Richard waved over his shoulder without turning. Only Sonya levelled her beautiful eyes in his direction. 'If you need help with the packing, let me know.' Sonya nodded. Her eyes stayed with him until he disappeared behind the door.

'Rolling,' said Art.

'You were Laurel's neighbour,' said Richard. 'What was she like?' He held the microphone up to Sonya's mouth. It was a long reach.

'Laurel was a genuinely nice person. I always thought of her as a good friend. . .'

As he walked down the row of carports Hecklepeck suddenly remembered he had once again forgotten to ask the make and model of a suspect's car. He'd have to call back and get the information.

He reached into his pocket for his keys and with them

pulled out the sheets of paper he had found in Laurel's coat. Then he got into the front seat of his car and studied them. They were Xeroxed copies of pages from a World War Two Army Manual; an explanation of how to rig a timer to an explosive device.

CHAPTER FOURTEEN

'HELEN, LOOK! IT'S *HIM*. OH, goody, goody, goody!'

In the KYYY parking lot a group of elderly people was gathering. They emerged in slow motion from Chevrolet Sedans and outmoded Cadillacs. One after the other they hurried eagerly over to the small crowd surrounding Helen Wheeler, President of the Webster Groves/Kirkwood Gardening and Seniors Club – known among its members as GAS.

Club Vice-President Peggy Hanford had spotted news commentator Ivan Sandler. But neither she nor Helen could put a name to the face.

'Yoo-hoo, Mr Um-hum. Could you come here a minute?'

For a second Ivan wondered from which part of the sky the attack was coming. Then he realised it wasn't an air-raid siren, just the stentorian tones of a human voice.

'We'd like to speak to you, Mr Um-hum, pull-eese.' Tall and gaunt to begin with, Helen had stuck her right arm straight up in the air and was waving a red bandanna. She was inescapable. Ivan changed course and walked towards the group.

Beside Helen little Peggy bounced. 'Oh, goody, goody, goody!' she chirped.

GAS members did not waste their time cultivating roses or coaxing clematis. They were aggressive vegetable gardeners. When the Collingwood Home for handicapped children had offered some of its land to the community for individual garden plots, GAS members had grabbed a substantial chunk. Over the years they had increased their holdings by taking over neglected and sometimes not-so-neglected plots. Gardeners too young to qualify for GAS membership had returned from vacations to find their tomato plants ploughed under and replaced. Other non-members had been driven out. They'd got tired of hearing the GAS method of staking tomatoes or the GAS approach to intensive gardening (more like insensitive gardening, according to some). But since GAS members spent the greater part of every day at the plots their advice was impossible to avoid.

February was a hard month for the club. It came at the end of a long winter, a winter with no gardening in it. February was the month when GAS members itched most to dip their knotty hands into damp spring soil. They had pored over the seed catalogues and established basement seed-farms large enough to plant entire acres. But it wasn't enough. GAS always tried to take on a community service project in February.

'We are here to demand an answer,' Helen Wheeler's tone was quieter but only slightly less shrill.

'Oh?' said Ivan assuming an expression of polite attention. He wondered if listening committed him to anything and decided it didn't.

Helen waved a copy of John Alden's latest article. 'We want to know what your station is going to do to remember Laurel Michaels. Is KYYY going to establish a memorial?'

At this the little group raised picket signs over their heads. Bouncing the signs up and down GAS chanted: 'We want a statue! Yes, we do.'

'Interesting,' said Ivan as the chanting continued. He looked around at the signs. They carried such slogans as, 'Laurel found the tumors for us consumers,' and 'Consumers all, loved Laurel'. Ivan moved a few steps away from the group in case anybody thought he was pro-Laurel. Then he took a step back towards the sign carriers so they wouldn't feel he was against them.

'Interesting,' said Ivan again, wondering what to do next. While he wondered, the chanting got louder and the pickets began to move. They formed a small oval in front of the station. Helen Wheeler stood in the middle.

The reason why was soon apparent. Television crews

from the competing two stations were coming around the side of the building. So were several newspaper and radio reporters.

Without hesitation Ivan ducked inside the front door. 'Get Wally out here,' he said to the receptionist. 'He's the one who should deal with these people.'

At the St Louis Public Library Hecklepeck headed for the microfilm room. One by one he looked through the books that listed the *Post Dispatch* reports for the spring months of 1976. He found what he was looking for in the March book: 'Fatal fire. 5304 Evans. 19 March, 1976.' Hecklepeck jotted it down and made notes of all the follow-up reports. He did the same with the *Globe Democrat* file. Then he handed the dates to the librarian and received several plastic cans of microfilm in return. He fed the first roll into a viewer.

It was a horrible story. As he pored over it, Hecklepeck remembered reading it on the news. The old woman who had lived in the house, Rose Dorfer, had been crippled. She'd lived on the second floor above a first that was vacant and boarded. When the fire had started with a small explosion just after midnight, she'd had no way to get out.

Mrs Dorfer, according to the newspaper, had been the subject of discussion for some time. She had been unable to care for herself. She wasn't eating properly and had no heat in her apartment except the oven in her kitchen. Day after day she sat in front of the open oven door in her wheelchair.

Neighbours, or at least one neighbour, an Earlene Gray, had been seeking help for Mrs Dorfer. Although she was black and Mrs Dorfer was white, Mrs Gray had taken it upon herself to give the old lady a daily meal. Her resources, however, were strained; she wanted the city to help out.

Who had Mrs Gray appealed to? None other than her alderman, Walter 'Tiny' Payne. Hecklepeck sat back in his chair. Rose Dorfer's death must have been something of a blot on Tiny's record, not that Tiny was noted for quick,

effective action, but he was adroit at avoiding the conse-
quences of inaction. This time he had been caught.

Hecklepeck checked the follow-up stories on the fire and
learned little new. There had been a lot of publicity
surrounding the case. Tiny had escaped lasting censure by
holding hearings on the plight of St Louis' elderly. After the
hearings it had all faded away.

The reporters had seen the pathos in the death of Rose
Dorfer and had pursued that part of the story energetically.
But to Hecklepeck they had missed a critical point: What
had caused the fire? Officially, the fire department said the
cause was undetermined. That had been reported. But
nobody had dug any further. It made Hecklepeck wonder.

At City Hall, three blocks away, he learned that the 5300
block of Evans had been zoned commercial in February of
1977.

'Wally won't come,' the receptionist hung up her phone.
'He says it would just incite those people even more.'

Ivan looked out of the thick glass door at the GAS
demonstration and reflected that Wally was right in his
'hands off' policy. It really wouldn't do to take a position on
something that was clearly going to be such a volatile issue
in the community.

Outside Peggy Hanford was handing out press releases
and Helen Wheeler was making a statement: 'The suggestion was made in the last two editions of the *Post Dispatch*
that KYYY should erect a memorial to the much-loved
Laurel Michaels. The articles said that if the station doesn't
have the funds it should sponsor a telethon to raise money
from the community.' She was reading her statement into
several microphones. 'We all know,' she continued, 'how
much money television stations make. We know KYYY can
afford a generous tribute to one of its best reporters.' A
pause for effect.

'But . . .' Helen's voice was once again approaching siren
pitch, ' . . . if KYYY is unwilling to pay for the statue by
itself, we are offering our services to organise a telethon.
The community will show Babson Broadcasting where its
priorities ought to be.'

146

Hecklepeck got out of the Jaguar and parked where he hoped it would be safe in the most crowded part of the KYYY lot. Before he did anything else, he swore to himself, he was going to find a safe place for the box of tapes in the back seat. There had already been one attempt to break into his car and get them. Who knew when there would be another? With the dark and dangerous turn his investigation had taken, Hecklepeck was more than a little apprehensive.

He headed for the newsroom door on the side of the building to avoid all the people at the front. But he didn't get there fast enough.

Looking around for fresh subject matter, one of the newspaper reporters spotted Hecklepeck. With the scent of an exclusive in his nose, he ducked behind a row of cars and, bent at the waist, scuttled over. The reporter might as well have advertised. The sight of him sneaking from one parked car to another brought the entire mob of newshounds down on his quarry.

Between the questions of the reporters and the chanted slogans of GAS, whose members had moved in behind them, it took a while for Hecklepeck to straighten it all out.

'We at KYYY want to honour the memory of Laurel Michaels too,' he said finally, for the benefit of the reporters. 'We could establish a memorial ourselves. KYYY has the money to do that. But we don't want to deprive the community of its chance to participate.'

One of the reporters, who knew Hecklepeck slightly, waved his hand in front of his own nose. 'That shit sure is starting to stink,' he whispered to his photographer.

'And we welcome the help of the Webster Groves/ Kirkwood Gardening Club.' Hecklepeck screwed his face around in an effort to look heartfelt. He had the awful feeling that blatant insincerity was showing.

'Just what is the station planning to do?' asked one of the reporters.

Hecklepeck shot a look of malevolence in her direction. 'Not decided,' he said. 'We're looking at the suggestion for a telethon. We're also considering other options.' Waving away new questions, he opened the newsroom door and ducked inside.

But he got no further than that. He was stopped by an open palm in his chest. 'I'm sorry. You media people had a chance to take pictures. Now we're trying to get on with police business.' The uniformed officer started to push Hecklepeck out of the door. He had had his fill of media people that morning. They had been coming at him from all directions.

'I work here!' said the aggrieved Hecklepeck.

'Come off it Mr Hacklespeck. Don't I see you on Channel Six every night? This ain't no media party. It's a po-leece investigation.'

Hecklepeck allowed himself to be edged back into chilly air. He knew from bitter experience that it was no use explaining to a viewer that he hadn't seen what he'd seen. He walked through the crowd of demonstrators to the front door of the station. There the police sentry, a more observant viewer, nodded him through with a mock salute and a smile.

In the newsroom the chief assignment-editor was once again poised on a chair in front of the big assignment board. He brandished his magic-marker in a circle over his head and drew a huge 'X' across the board. Behind him most of the news department uttered a ragged chorus of 'Right ons' and 'All rights'. The assignment-editor turned. Waving the magic-marker like a conductor's baton, he began to sing, 'We shall overco-uh-um.' Only one or two members of the chorus joined in. The others didn't seem to have the energy. They had draped themselves over and around the newsdesks in various poses expressing complete relaxation.

'I wish that guy would learn to sing,' muttered Berger at Ken's desk. Behind him the uniformed policeman silently agreed as he stuck the label '1,046' on a tape.

The police were the only ones doing anything, Hecklepeck observed as he came into the newsroom. They were stacking and collecting piles of newsroom tapes to be viewed and numbered. 'What's going on here?' he asked his lounging colleagues.

'We're staging a sit-down strike,' replied one staffer.

'Wally is trying to make us all take lie-detector tests,' said another.

'We refuse!' added a third. 'Ken left for Connecticut this morning so our boss is not here to defend us. We have no choice but organised protest.'

'We shall overco-um some da-a-a-ay.' The assignment-editor hugged himself and swayed. He was into it.

'Why?' asked Hecklepeck. The laid-back crew looked at him without understanding. 'Why does Wally want you to take lie-detector tests?'

'Us,' the assignment-editor stopped singing and looked down on Hecklepeck with fire in his eyes. 'Why does Wally want *us* to take lie-detector tests? You're not exempt, you know.'

'Okay. Why is Wally trying to make everybody take lie-detector tests?'

'To find the tapes. He wants to help the police so he's going to try to make one of us confess that we have them. It's a violation of our civil rights. What I want to know is,' the assignment-editor flung out his arms, 'are you with us?'

'Oh, uh, of course,' Hecklepeck had no intention of taking a lie-detector test.

The assignment-editor hugged himself again and began to rock anew. 'We shall overco-uh-um. . .'

One of the news writers pulled herself out of her chair and walked over to a monitor. She turned it to Channel Six. Her recumbant colleagues resettled themselves so they could see.

'We invited the media and gave a press conference,' one of the news writers told Hecklepeck. 'We want to see what they do with it on the noon news.'

'What about our noon?'

'It's been cancelled. They're putting on a game show.' The writer smiled serenely. 'The biggest story of the year is happening in our newsroom and we're airing a game show.'

Channel Six led with the pair of KYYY stories, the protest inside and the demonstration outside. Hecklepeck's statement was given considerable play.

From his chair the chief assignment-editor watched the televised Hecklepeck with suspicion. 'How come you're speaking for management?' he demanded.

'I'm not,' said Hecklepeck and explained how he'd come to give the impromptu press conference.

'I like it,' said the news writer. 'We're sitting in but you're taking over. That's really sending a message to management.'

'I wish I could sit in and eat at the same time,' grumbled a more pragmatic news staffer. 'I'm hungry.'

'Why don't I go get lunch for everybody?' Hecklepeck proposed with uncharacteristic thoughtfulness. 'I'm not supposed to be at work yet so there's no point in my sitting in and it would give you guys a chance to continue protesting without starving to death.' It would also be an opportunity to get the tapes out of the Jaguar, Hecklepeck added mentally. Tapes in disguise, under cover of burgers and fries.

Enthusiasm broke through the newsroom lethargy. Half an hour later Hecklepeck headed for the door with some cash and a list of fast-food orders.

'Hey, buddy, didn't I tell you to stay out of here.' The policeman at the door sounded mean.

'Ask anybody,' said Hecklepeck. 'I work here.'

'Yeah, and I'm the president. Didn't I just see you on Channel Six?'

'Yes, but. . .' Hecklepeck decided not to explain. He stepped outside.

'Don't try it again,' the policeman warned his back.

A Rolls Royce was parked by the kerb just outside the KYYY lot. As Hecklepeck walked toward his car, the tinted back window of the Rolls slid silently downward.

'Yoo-hoo, Will-yum.' Hecklepeck froze. Of all the voices he least wanted to hear, Maggie Johnson's was it. He nevertheless made himself walk over, thinking that if indeed Maggie and/or Birdie had killed Laurel, they certainly hadn't driven over in the Rolls. It would not have been missed in the Burger Chef parking lot.

In daylight and with the clarity of chemically unaltered vision, Hecklepeck saw Maggie differently. There was dissipation among the wrinkles at the outer edges of her eyes. Her painted mouth had a spoiled set to it. In spite of her perm and showy mink, she was a discernable fraud.

'Hullo,' said Hecklepeck unenthusiastically.

'Definitely come sit,' chirped Maggie. She slid over to the far side of the back seat and patted the place she had left for him.

He opened the door and reluctantly got in. In the front seat the terrible Birdie nodded and smirked. He was wearing a pouffy jacket patched together with many coloured rags. They were, Hecklepeck realised, expensive suede rags.

'I came right over, dear William, as soon as I heard you mention the need for money on the twelve o'clock news. We so want to contribute to a significant work of art commemorating Miss Michaels. It would do absolute wonders for the city as well as immortalise that sweet girl.' Maggie wriggled her black-kid fingers in Birdie's direction and received an alligator-encased chequebook. 'Let me make out a cheque to you personally. Will five thousand do?'

'No,' said Hecklepeck. 'I can't accept. . .'

Maggie pulled her gloves off one stubby finger at a time. 'Then let's make it ten. Birdie and I want you to have that statue, William. We know how much it means to you.' She wriggled her unsheathed fingers at Birdie and received a gold pen.

'No! If you want to contribute to a statue of Laurel, you should make out the cheque to KYYY or to our station manager, Wally Corette. It would be improper for me to accept it.'

Maggie stopped, eyes wide, lips drawn into an 'O' and gold pen poised. 'Oh. Well. If you want it that way, William.' She paused before bringing the pen down. 'I do see what you mean. We wouldn't want to get you in trouble.'

Maggie handed pen and chequebook back to Birdie. 'Well, I definitely will contribute to the KYYY statue fund

151

and when I do, William, I shall give the credit for my inspiration to you.'

'No,' Hecklepeck was irritated. 'Don't do. . .'

'It is as good as done. Let's definitely celebrate.' From the front seat a fawn-coloured hand presented a silver tray with a mound of white powder on it and a little silver spoon.

'Let's absolutely have a round together,' said Maggie with aggressive delight. 'To seal our collaboration, dear William.'

Hecklepeck shook his head. 'No, no thank you.'

But Maggie had broken into a grotesque grin. It lit her face up fiercely. She waved the tray in front of him. 'Tootle, toots?'

'No,' said Hecklepeck more firmly. 'I can't. I have work to do.' He moved as far away from her as he could. She came after him, waving the silver tray.

'You can't get a better toot than this. Birdie gets it from some of his little friends. They're musicians, don't you know. Musicians need their tootles to help their creativity.'

He didn't reply. His attention was riveted on the tray under his nose. He didn't dare breathe lest he again inhale the white dust by accident.

'You must come with us to hear them some time. What's the name of the group, Birdie?'

Hecklepeck turned his head so that he could pull in a little air through his mouth without taking in anything else.

'Thuh Hahrmoans,' Birdie said from the front seat.

'That's right, the Harmones. They really cook, as we used to say in my day.'

The Harmones had been playing at Tareesa's club. Hecklepeck pushed the silver tray away from his face in order to satisfy a sudden hunch. 'Did Warren Billings, your . . . your . . .' He realised he really didn't know how to describe Maggie's relationship with the man who kept her. 'Did Warren have any interests in city development?'

Still holding the tray, Maggie shrugged. 'Oh, my, yes! It was so, so important to Warren to make this city beautiful again. He wanted to have another World's Fair here. So he absolutely bought ugly old things to tear them down and replace them with beautiful new things.' She picked up the rolled-up bill and bent over the tray.

'Did he have a company he used?' Hecklepeck asked quickly before Maggie started sniffing.

She lifted her head and dropped the tube. 'He most surely did. It was called Billy-Do. It's a play on words. Warren always said it was just his little love letter to the city and, of course, to me. The company still exists but mostly on paper.' She was silent for a moment and then she said the name 'Billy-do' very softly.

'When did Warren die?'

The hand holding the tray was trembling. Maggie handed it over the front seat to Birdie and sank back into her corner. 'It definitely seems like such a long, long time ago. But it's really only been a few long years. Warren died in December of 1976.'

CHAPTER FIFTEEN

REPORTER JOE HANDY WAS TRAMPING around in the woods behind Burger Chef. 'This is going to be dynamite,' he raved. 'I've found just the place for the perfect stand-up. Come on, Phil.' Unaware that the rest of his colleagues were engaged in a sit-down strike, Joe was looking for a perfect background for his face. And he had noticed once on his way back from lunch that from the edge of the wooded area behind Burger Chef and KYYY there was a good view across the roadway to the city skyline.

While Joe surveyed the view from the woods, photographer Phil Cladstrip was napping on the hood of his car. He opened his eyes, moved his two hundred and seventy-six pounds and shuffled slowly around to the boot. In his view standing a reporter up against one background was as good as another. He felt no enthusiasm. He never did. He began sluggishly to unload equipment.

Joe watched from the spot he had chosen and demonstrated impatience. He jiggled the change in his pocket, shifted from foot to foot and sighed loudly. Union rules didn't prevent reporters from carrying photographic equipment but Joe did not.

Breathing heavily, Phil finally staggered over from the Burger Chef lot where the car was parked. He had the camera balanced on one shoulder and the thirty-pound tape recorder hanging from the other. A tripod was slung across his back. He carried a heavy bag of lighting equipment.

Joe bounded up a slight rise. 'If you set up here . . .' He

kicked a beer can out of the way. 'Then I'll be here . . .' He skipped over to a dead tree that was lying almost on the shoulder of the road. Sweeping away an old shoe and some newspaper, he propped his foot on the tree and leaned across his knee, a pose adopted at one time or another by almost all correspondents to connote intelligent analysis and complete candour.

Fat Phil was still struggling up the small rise. At the top he let the equipment fall into a heap, smiling between gasping breaths with born-again forbearance.

It took some time to set up the gear. All the while Joe exhibited impatience. Finally, Phil squinted into his camera viewer and announced, 'Rolling.'

With a sweep of his arm Joe indicated the St Louis skyline. 'Citywide . . . ' he said and stopped. After a few seconds he repositioned himself and repeated the sweep. 'Citywide . . . ' he proclaimed. 'The search is, uh, city-wide . . .' He stopped again and glared at Phil. 'You're just going to have to turn that thing off until I figure out what I'm going to say.'

Whistling 'Onward Christian Soldiers' under his breath, Phil turned off the camera and glanced around at his surroundings. There was lots of discarded junk in wooded areas. Phil remembered a recent newspaper article that identified such places as repositories for stolen purses. He wandered off to see if he could find any.

'Citywide . . . ' Joe muttered to himself. 'Citywide . . . citywide . . . citywide.' He scribbled something in his palm-sized notebook and began again, 'Citywide, the sear . . . '

'Look at this.' Phil was holding a canvas bag. Except for being empty it was identical to the one full of lighting equipment lying at the foot of his own tripod.

'Yeah? So what?' demanded Joe.

'It's Art's. It's the one that was stolen in the murder.'

'Yeah? How do you know?'

'It's got his initials here.' Phil turned the bag over and around until he found 'A.M.' written in magic marker.

Joe assimilated this for several seconds. 'Drop it,' he said. Phil didn't react. 'Drop it! It's evidence.' Phil finally let the bag slip to the ground. The two of them stared at it.

'This could be important,' surmised Joe with a flourish of his notebook. 'It could be the key to solving Laurel's murder. You should take a picture of it. Better yet. Let's put it back where you found it and take a picture of it.'

Phil obediently picked up the canvas bag. 'Even better,' said Joe, 'let's get some tape of me finding it.'

'Lunch for the troops,' Hecklepeck announced gaily to the policeman guarding the front door of the station. He was carrying two cartons full of greasy white bags and plastic-topped soft-drink cups. 'They've got me on KP today.'

The policeman grinned appreciatively. Hecklepeck set the boxes down on the floor with a clunk. 'Hey, I wonder if you could keep an eye on this stuff for a few minutes. I've got some more in the car.' The policeman dipped his head smartly.

'Help yourself to a coke and some fries,' Hecklepeck called as he went out. 'I bought extra.'

The policeman shifted the top box to get to the French fries underneath. It seemed heavy for a bag full of fast food. They must have put in extra grease, he chuckled to himself. He tasted a French fry gingerly. It was all right. It tasted good.

Hecklepeck returned with more boxes and went out again for more. All together it looked like he had purchased enough food for four newsrooms. 'Thanks, buddy,' he told the policeman. 'If you could just stand guard while I run these boxes down to the newsroom, I'd appreciate it. I'll be right back for the second load.'

'Sure,' said the policeman. 'I know you've got a job-action on against the management, but I'd hate to see a working man in any line of business go hungry.' He was an unusually enthusiastic member of the fraternal order of police.

'Yes,' replied Hecklepeck with a little smile. 'Our management would be interested in the contents of these boxes. That's why it's really important that they get to where they're going.' With that he set off down the hall. But instead of turning into the newsroom, he continued to the basement door at the end of the corridor.

*

'You're just going to have to take the test first,' Wally's words shot over the tips of his pointed Italian leather shoes, which were resting with his feet in them on top of his big desk. 'If you do it, other people will too. Those who still refuse will either know something about the tapes or be troublemakers.' He leaned back in his vinyl chair and half closed his eyes. 'I will deal with them.'

Rita's head hung over her chest. 'What if I fail?' The complaint was muffled in pink acrylic bosom.

'You don't know where the tapes are, do you?' Wally was impatient. 'You won't be lying.' Rita did not raise her head.

With a sharp sigh Wally got out of his chair, walked around his desk and pulled her up by her elbow. 'Look, you little bitch. You got me into this mess. Now it's up to you to get me out.' As he spoke, he drew her to the office door. 'If you help, I may still make you head of the art department.' Rita peered up at him. Wally shoved her out into the hall and towards the conference room where the lie-detector had been set up. She went reluctantly.

'I want to talk to you.' Wally accosted Hecklepeck, who was approaching with his last load of boxes. Hecklepeck glanced over his load and shrugged. He followed Wally into his office.

Wally strode to his desk and positioned himself behind it. 'Who the hell gave you permission to speak for this company? Do you know what you've gotten us into? You committed us publicly to a fund-raising campaign for a frigging statue of a consumer reporter. What the hell were you doing?'

'I did you a favour,' said Hecklepeck with infuriating conviction. 'It would have looked pretty shabby if this station hadn't agreed to do something.'

'It was way out of line. I am going to write a full report for your file. Come contract-negotiation time I'm going to see to it that Barry Babson gets a copy.'

'Okay,' said Hecklepeck affably. 'Is that all?'

'No. Stop by the conference room and take a lie-detector test. Do your part to help find those tapes.'

Hecklepeck looked down at one box of food and then over at the other. 'Help who?' he said with a sardonic little smile. 'The police or you?'

'We're all on the same side. You just take a test and be on that plane to Connecticut in the morning.'

'Actually,' Hecklepeck paused briefly before continuing in the blandest of tones. 'Ken's going to Connecticut. He's already left.' Wally's entire set of facial muscles went rigid. 'We discussed it. My contract says I have to be on the air during rating periods.'

Wally's lips barely moved but his words emerged with crystalline nastiness. 'You'd better start looking for work now because when I'm through nobody in this business will have you.'

Hecklepeck remained congenial. 'You have a nice day too.' He carried his precious cartons out to the hall.

'I knew it was important the minute I saw it.' Joe Handy was standing triumphantly in the middle of the newsroom waving Art's equipment bag. His idled colleagues were grouped admiringly around him. 'It was just lying there between an old purse and some newspaper.'

'Don't you think you should have left it there for the police?' asked one of the writers.

'Naw, I thought it would be better TV if we got some tape of me handing it over to the police.' Joe gestured at Phil who was once again in the sluggish process of setting up his equipment in front of Ken's office where Berger and his men were watching the tape monitor.

'Let me look at that.' Hecklepeck dumped the food boxes on a desk and reached for the bag. He examined it closely.

'Where was it?' he asked when he finally handed the bag back to Joe.

'It was towards the back of the little woods, away from Burger Death and the station – kind of under a big branch.' Joe turned his attention back to the larger audience. 'I can't wait to hand this over to the police . . .'

Hecklepeck tuned him out. The empty bag had been left in the woods for what purpose? He couldn't think of any unless the murderer just wanted to get rid of it. After using the bag to get Laurel's coat from the van to a waiting

159

car, maybe the murderer had simply dumped it. Behind the station like that, the bag was sure to be found but, abandoned there, it also said nothing about the identity of Laurel's killer.

'Phil, get ready!' said Joe sharply. After a huddled confab in front of the tape viewer, Lieutenant Berger and his men were coming out of Ken's office.

Joe positioned himself in front of the office door, holding Art's equipment bag conspicuously out in front. Phil was making a valiant, if not very intelligent, effort to be ready. Holding the unsecured tripod with his knees, he tried to balance his camera on it. With some difficulty he attached the camera to the top of the tripod. As he did the tripod's legs split open bringing the camera to knee level. Phil scooped it up just in time to shoot Berger coming through the door.

Joe smoothed his hair and adjusted his tie as Berger came into the newsroom. 'Lieutenant, I . . . ' he began. Berger looked at him. ' . . . wonder if you could . . . ' Berger looked away again. He walked right on by. It was clear Joe and the bag hadn't registered at all. Berger had something else on his mind. He strode on until he reached the centre of the newsroom.

'Have any of you seen Richard Markowitz?' Berger was grim. No one answered him. 'When is he due in fahr work?' Again, no one answered. Since Richard was on special assignment, no one knew when he was likely to show up.

'I saw him this morning,' Hecklepeck finally volunteered. Sitting at one of the desks, he was munching some French fries.

'In my office, Bill,' Berger marched back to Ken's office with Hecklepeck behind him.

'It looks bad, Bill,' said Berger sadly, in the privacy of Ken's office. 'Yahr friend Markowitz has the tapes.'

'What?' asked Hecklepeck.

'Well, he's got pieces of them, all strung together. Look.' Berger swung around and played the tape that had been loaded into Ken's machine.

The monitor showed Laurel talking to the camera,

followed by Laurel chatting with Maggie, followed by Laurel walking into Tess's place and so on. Berger shook his head dolorously. 'We found it on his desk. It goes on like that fahr about ten minutes. Nothing but shots of the victim.' He paused and added: 'He must have been really obsessed with her.'

'Richard? Obsessed?' Hecklepeck was outraged. He knew what the tape was. It was the dub Richard had made on Tuesday night while he, himself, was reviewing the time-code shots. These were the pictures Richard was saving to use in the special show.

Hecklepeck tried to explain. 'It's a show about Laurel so of course he dubbed shots of her at work.'

'Yeah? Where'd he get them then?'

'From . . .' Hecklepeck stopped short. He couldn't tell, he realised, without revealing the whereabouts of the tapes and he wasn't prepared to do that until he could assuage Berger's wrath with the name of Laurel's murderer. He had held on to the tapes too long to get away with anything less.

'You see,' said Berger. 'It doesn't look good. I'm going to have to hold him this time. Where is he?'

'I left him out at Laurel's apartment. He was doing an interview.' It was better for Richard to be arrested there, Hecklepeck decided, than in front of his colleagues and their cameras.

Berger beckoned to the officers waiting outside and began to bark out orders.

'We're just going to have to give Joe lots of extra time.' In the newsroom the producers were trying to decide how to fill their shows. Richard's impending arrest had obviated the need for lie-detector tests and the sit-down strike had ended.

'Okay, but after Joe, then what?' the five o'clock producer whined. She was answered with silence.

Joe Handy ceremoniously handed over the canvas bag to the uniformed officer on guard duty at the newsroom door. He was the only one of Berger's men who would hold still long enough to receive it. He had now received it five times. The perfect take was proving illusory.

CHAPTER SIXTEEN

'JUST TELL THEM YOU'RE PROTECTING a source,' said Hecklepeck persuasively. 'It's the time-honoured way out. That way no one will think you're a criminal.' Hecklepeck had arrived at police headquarters with an attorney friend before Richard had even been booked.

'It's not a bad idea,' conceded the attorney. 'I don't think they have enough to charge you with murder. But they're going to come up with something, probably concealing evidence. Protecting a source would at least be a defence.'

At the word 'murder' Richard had stiffened. He glanced wildly around the dingy room. 'I'm going to tell the truth,' he muttered.

'I'm asking you not to. I just need a little more time to complete my investigation.'

'Yeah? Do you have any definite leads?' Richard challenged.

'No,' admitted Hecklepeck. 'But I know I'm on the track of something. Somebody wants the tapes pretty badly.'

Richard looked at him with disgust. 'Everybody wants the frigging tapes. Including the police. I'm going to help them get them.'

'Come on, Richard. It will only be one night in jail,' Hecklepeck cajoled. We'll get a bond hearing tomorrow. If you tell them you're protecting a source they're bound to let you go. You'll be a hero, a journalist imprisoned in the fight to uphold truth and justice.'

Wally swung around and winked at himself in the mirror behind his desk. All they had to do was charge Richard Markowitz with murder and his part in the Laurel

Michaels affair might never have to come out. Ken had hired Richard. Wally would fire Ken and officially wash his hands of the whole messy affair. Wally's eye twitched and went into a series of spasms. If only he could be certain that those tapes would never be made public.

'Wally?' The speaker phone barked. It was Barry Babson in Tucson. Wally had been waiting for him to come on the line. 'What the dancing princesses is going on there?' Barry Babson was an avid practitioner of clean living. Wally could picture him tilting his cloud of white hair in a way that invited an unlikely comparison with Shirley Temple's curls. 'What's this about a work stoppage?'

'There's no work stoppage,' Wally assured Barry heartily. 'But the police have taken one of our news producers into custody. They haven't charged him with anything yet but they will. I always had doubts about that guy.' Wally reached into his top drawer for a cigar. 'He's very close to Bill Hecklepeck.'

'Hmmmm,' said Barry. 'We can't have Bill tied up in a murder investigation. You keep him out of it.'

'I tried. I wanted to send him to the funeral in Connecticut. But,' Wally issued a sigh, 'he refused to go.' Wally drew the cigar under his nose and inhaled.

'I'll just bet my Argyll socks and regulator clocks he had the ratings challenge in mind. He's a good man, Bill. Never deserts the sinking ship. You were right to try and protect him. You'll have to think of something else.'

Wally bared his teeth at the cigar. He pulled a clip out of his vest pocket. Snipping the end of the cigar, he said with a tight chuckle, 'We're being picketed.'

'Oh?'

'A bunch of old biddies wants to establish a memorial to Laurel Michaels.' Wally squeezed out another chortle.

'Isn't that cute? I hope you gave them your blessing.'

'They don't want my blessing. They want money.'

'Oh dear. See if they'll take your blessing instead.'

After some discussion of the budget, the conversation ended. Wally took a few little puffs on his cigar. Then he reached for his dictation machine and issued a memo. In it he did away with the position of art director. He moved the art department into promotion, making the artists answerable to the promotion director. It made him feel better to make somebody else unhappy.

Hecklepeck took a sip of coffee. 'I feel lucky to have found you at home,' he said to the woman on the other side of the linoleum table.

Earlene Gray smiled beatifically. She was a middle-aged black woman in a worn cardigan sweater who had a simple serenity about her. Hecklepeck had found her by the obvious expedient of looking in the phone book. 'I am not working this week because I am getting ready for my marriage,' she said. 'Therefore, you are indeed lucky. And so am I.'

Hecklepeck quickly congratulated her. Mrs Gray didn't live on Evans Street anymore; she had moved to a still poor but better neighbourhood on the north side of St Louis.

'Yes,' she said, cupping her hands around her thick porcelain coffee cup. 'I think my troubles are over. I'm going to have some support. Mr Baker's going to move in here with me and we will face the future together.'

Hecklepeck sighed. 'Sometimes I think that's the way it ought to be faced.'

'You're not married?' Earlene Gray clucked with her tongue. 'As fine-looking as you are and as successful? I should think there are lots of women who would be interested in you. All you've got to do is choose.' The appliances in the kitchen were old and there were great chips in the linoleum floor tiles, Hecklepeck noticed.

He took another sip of coffee and got down to business. 'I've come to ask you about Evans Street. About the fire next door to you that killed your neighbour, Rose Dorfer.'

'That was a terrible thing.'

'What happened?'

'I was asleep. All I know is something exploded and by the time I got some clothes on and got down to the street, the fire was going good. That poor old woman didn't have a chance. She didn't deserve to die like that.' Anger cut

165

across the pleasantness of Mrs Gray's face. 'She was crippled.'

Hecklepeck nodded. 'And you took care of her?'

'I took her food and cleaned her up sometimes. I wasn't the only one. One of the other neighbours shopped for her. We had to; she was helpless.' Mrs Gray swirled her spoon indignantly around the inside of her coffee cup. 'Now here's a question you can answer for me: why can't social services do something for a person like that?'

Hecklepeck shrugged as if he had no answer but he knew the reasons: lack of money; too many people in need; regulations that carefully restricted those who were eligible and for what. There were hundreds of Rose Dorfers in St Louis.

'We tried to get help for her. But nothing came through. We were all pretty close to going hungry ourselves at that time on that block.'

'Yeah, what happened there? You make it sound like there were lots of people living on Evans Street. It's practically uninhabited now.'

'You tell me. It was always a poor block but that spring there were several fires and after that it slid right downhill to the bottom. People started to move away.'

'Including yourself.'

Mrs Gray drank some coffee and used her paper napkin to wipe her lips. 'Including me. I was a widow with three young children. I could see what was happening on the block and when that company came and offered me money, not enough to buy another house but enough to rent one for a while, I took it. I knew it was all I was going to get.'

Hecklepeck crossed his fingers under the table. 'You don't happen to remember the name of that company do you?'

'Of course I do. It was Tudell.'

Hecklepeck sat forward eagerly. *Too-tell.* Had she just said . . . 'Too-tell?'

'No,' Mrs Gray chuckled. 'Too-dell. Here, I'll write it down for you.'

In the aldermanic press room at City Hall, crews from all

the major stations were waiting for a press conference to begin. They had been waiting for more than twenty minutes. 'What's he got to say this time?' one of the photographers grumbled to another.

'Don't know,' was the reply. 'He's got some announcement to make.'

Alderman Walter Payne finally appeared. Gazing at some spot above and beyond the group of press people, Tiny waited until the rustling and the whispering had stopped. 'I am con-cerned about the pace of develop-ment in this city. It is true that we need develop-ment. It provides jobs for our workers, pulls in needed tourist dollars and in most cases it makes our city better to look at.

'But too much develop-ment, uncontrolled develop-ment, over-develop-ment will only result in crowding, traffic and pollution. The St Louis of the future may well be a city that is not pleasant to live in unless we do some care-ful planning now.

'Therefore I am going to propose the appoint-ment of a commission to take a close look at develop-ment in St Louis. Such a commission would . . .'

'Dipped in honey and sugar-coated,' a photographer muttered.

'Yeah,' another replied. 'He must be covering up something pretty awful. I wonder what it is.'

Tiny came to the end of his remarks about develop-ment. 'Before I throw it open to questions, I would like to add a little personal announce-ment. I am going to be getting married soon. Miss Tareesa Wells, pro-priatress of the distinguished Tess's nightclub, and I will be tying the knot.' The reporters and photographers clapped politely.

Richard sat in the city hold-over cell and tugged pathetically at his beard. The cell was a dirty rectangular box permeated with the smells of previous sojourners. In an effort to cheer the unhappy prisoner, someone had had the place painted bright yellow. But all that effulgence in such tiny quarters only made Richard feel distinctly queasy. He swallowed hard and reminded himself it was only for one night.

He tried to blot out his surroundings with pleasant thoughts. Sonya. Richard didn't think he'd ever forget Sonya's look when the police arrived. She was obviously a deeply emotional girl. He had seen shock and what he hoped was concern on her face as he was marched out between the two officers.

Of course Art had stepped right up to console her. Richard gave his beard a savage twist. Art was no doubt taking unfair advantage of the situation. He was probably even now planning to take Sonya out to dinner and who-knows-what afterwards. Richard put his head in his hands and moaned in jealous agony. He had completely forgotten the other man in Sonya's life, the one who paid all her bills.

On the screen the beautiful blonde betrayed her husband with his best friend. 'My my my my my my my.' Tareesa Wells shook her head and took another drag of her Kool. In her shaggy pink coat she was watching KYYY's four o'clock soap opera in the TV station's reception area where everything aired by KYYY was shown on a big colour monitor.

'I knew that was coming,' commented the station receptionist from behind her desk. 'She's already been to bed with everybody else on the show.'

Tareesa shook her head. 'This ain't one of my stories.'

Hecklepeck came down the hall and into the reception area. 'Hello,' he said to Tareesa.

Tareesa ignored him while she put out her cigarette, holding it carefully between her powdery-blue nails. Then she patted the vinyl sofa beside her.

Hecklepeck sat down. 'Don't you want to go to my office? It's more private there.'

'This fine. Who that?' Tareesa asked over her shoulder to the receptionist. Her eyes were still on the television screen.

'Oh, that's Marcia Wellborn. She's married to Bill Wellborn but the marriage is on the rocks. She owns an incredibly successful boutique and he's unemployed. Marcia's also the grandmother of little Cecilia who is the

168

daughter of Jackie but nobody knows exactly who her father is . . .' The receptionist stopped for air.

'You wanted to see me?' Hecklepeck interjected quickly.

The station conveniently went to commercial and Tareesa lowered her eyes from the monitor to Hecklepeck. 'Yeah, television man. I got to consult you. About a matter of zoning. Cain't nobody develop nuthing without zoning, right?'

'Um-hum.'

'Suppose some part of the city is zoned one way and you got an interest in getting it zoned some other way. How you go about it?'

'You're not talking about that block behind your nightclub are you?'

Tareesa looked at Hecklepeck keenly. 'How you do it?' was all she said.

'Well, you make a filing. You get signatures from people who live in the area and then you post your intentions for a certain period of time so that anybody who wants to object can object.' Tareesa's eyes went to the deodorant commercial that was showing on the monitor. 'Then there's a hearing in front of the zoning board and eventually the board issues a ruling.'

'Ain't nobody asked me.'

'Yes?'

'Ain't nobody asked me my objections 'bout that block behind me.' Tareesa did not take her eyes off the TV monitor but something in the set of her face showed how serious she was.

'I see.'

'Whut I want to know: could some guy in government, some Mr Almighty Im-portant, get the zoning changed without all that, that procedure?'

'It's been known to happen.'

Tareesa muttered something under her breath that sounded like, 'Go fo yo mo, mo fo.'

'What?'

She stood up, her eyes flashing, and stuffed her cigarettes in her purse. 'Take care yourself, television man.' Muttering furiously to herself she made for the door.

'Wait,' Hecklepeck stood up. 'I hear you're getting married. Congratulations are in order.'

Tareesa turned, a furry pink beast with smouldering eyes, and said something vicious with a lot of 'mos' and 'fos' in it. Then she shouldered her way outside.

Sonya Richardson put another pile of Laurel's correspondence on the fire in her grate. 'There,' she said gaily, 'that's one less thing we'll have to pack.'

'I'll drink to that,' Art Macke raised his second glass of wine. After work he had joined Sonya for a picnic supper on the packing boxes in Laurel's apartment.

Thoughtfully, Sonya watched the papers burn. Then she went over to a wall of pictures and took some down. With a crash of broken glass they went into one of the crates. 'Oh dear,' said Sonya, peering inside. 'I think I broke one.'

Art reached for the bottle of white wine and looked for Sonya's glass. It was still full so instead he refilled his own. Sonya was working out her anger at Laurel. Art understood that and in his view it was righteous anger. Laurel had really treated Sonya shabbily. How much healthier, he reflected, to work out feelings by breaking a few pictures than by committing murder.

She picked up a staple gun that was almost as big as herself and applied it to the box she had just packed. It was an industrial staple gun, Art noticed, and had the logo 'Delano & Delano' on one side.

'Where did you get that?' he asked.

'This?' Sonya brandished the staple gun with both hands. 'I got it from a company I used to work for.' She dropped it and came over to where Art was sitting on one side of a tablecloth-covered packing box. Sonya had arranged their dinner on top of it. To Art it looked like a lot of little bits of things, rather than a real meal, but if he kept on drinking wine the way he was, he wouldn't miss eating.

'Let's watch the news,' he suggested. Sonya nodded. He turned on Laurel's television set and sat back. There were new developments surrounding the murder of Laurel Michaels, Hecklepeck was saying. Reporter Joe Handy had the story.

170

Sonya knelt down and nibbled delicately on a chicken wing.

'Police Lieutenant Michael Berger,' announced Joe Handy, 'has uncovered one of the missing tapes. It was in the possession of KYYY producer Richard Markowitz.' Here, the screen showed a photograph of Richard at the station Christmas party. It was the only picture of him anybody could find. In the middle of a drunken imitation of Barry Babson, Richard looked capable of murder and worse. 'Markowitz has been charged with withholding evidence. A bond hearing has been set for ten-thirty a.m. tomorrow.'

Art looked meaningfully at Sonya to see if she understood that his rival was a prime murder suspect. He noted that her expression was devoid of pity and he silently drank to that.

Joe then launched into a subject dearer to his heart: the discovery of the equipment bag.

'That's my bag,' said Art and he explained the bag's disappearance at length.

On the TV screen Joe saw the bag, registered discovery, walked over to it, walked around it, poked it, lifted it with a stick, transported it to the car and so on. The report ended as he handed the bag over to the authorities, a climax somewhat undermined by the expression of boredom on the policeman's face.

An outraged Hecklepeck reappeared on the screen. 'Producer Richard Markowitz has told the police he is protecting a news source,' he ad-libbed. 'We at KYYY can only applaud his journalistic integrity and stand behind him in his hour of need.'

Sonya wiped her lips on one of the tiny linen napkins she had provided. She got up and picked up another pile of papers. One by one they were fed carefully into the fire. Sonya watched them burn.

The KYYY station receptionist walked across the lighted parking lot, her unfastened rabbit-fur coat flapping on either side of her. She approached a group of journalists who were staking out the big story of the day. They were

171

also roasting marshmallows over a kerosene fire burning in a barrel.

'Here,' the receptionist said, shoving a stack of papers into the hands of a reporter who had just devoured his share of the feast.

'Wha's zis?' he demanded. But the receptionist was heading towards her car. It was past quitting time.

The other journalists crowded around and grabbed at the papers. The reporter with the mouthful of marshmallow would have lost them all had not one of them stuck to his fingers. He examined it in the light of the fire. It was a short press release from KYYY station manager Wally Corette.

Wally wanted the press to know that he and he alone officially spoke for KYYY TV. 'Any other self-styled spokesman,' he wrote in the release, 'is unofficial and should not be relied upon to deliver accurate information.'

'It is, therefore, necessary to set the record straight,' Wally continued. 'KYYY is a news organisation. As such we cannot take an advocacy role, even for a dead employee. While KYYY applauds the efforts of GAS members, the station cannot actively support them in any way, financial or otherwise.'

The release went on to say: 'Regarding another matter, KYYY cannot and must not tolerate wrongdoing on the part of an employee. Producer Richard Markowitz, who was arrested this afternoon for obstructing justice, will be placed on leave without pay until such time as the charges are dropped or he is proven innocent in a court of law.'

The reporter tried to whistle under his breath. But his lips stuck together, preventing any sound from getting out. 'It's lucky those GAS people have gone home,' he said to one of his colleagues.

'Yeah, but this'll bring them back tomorrow,' she replied. 'All hell's going to break loose.'

CHAPTER SEVENTEEN

THE NEXT MORNING HECKLEPECK SWUNG the big steamboat wheel to the right and brought it back just to the left of centre. He was steering a dangerous course. On the one side was the six-headed monster, Scylla: Berger and his men waiting to snatch him as soon as Richard spoke up about the tapes. That Richard would have to talk, Hecklepeck had little doubt. It was a question of sooner or (he hoped) later. On the other side of the channel was Charybdis, the frightening whirlpool of death; the whirlpool that had sucked up Laurel and was waiting, waiting oh so patiently, for a chance to suck up the last, outstanding bit of incriminating evidence: the tapes.

As if the silent, watching presence of Laurel's murderer were standing behind him, Hecklepeck gave the wheel an involuntary little jerk. That was the creepy part. Unseen to everybody, the murderer had been on stage since the beginning of the drama: standing in the shadows until the victim appeared, lining up ink pens in Laurel's office, going through her coat pockets, creeping around her apartment and daring to spy on Hecklepeck.

The murderer knew that Hecklepeck had had the tapes. He or she had tried to break into the Jaguar for them and the attempt was his or her only failure – because it alerted that man of action, Hecklepeck.

Hecklepeck smiled as he remembered marching past the police guard with the boxes of fast-food-disguised tapes. At least he could rest easy about their safety. All that was left in the back of the Jaguar now was an empty cardboard box covered with a blanket.

Colonel Chambers had taken Hecklepeck's smile as an

173

invitation. With a throaty growl he launched himself on to the top of the wheel and stood poised between two spokes. Breaking into a loud, somewhat specious purr he butted his head into Hecklepeck's chest, overcome with affection. Hecklepeck gave him one long stroke beginning at his ears and ending at the tip of his shaggy tail. The Colonel's already excessive rumble intensified and he stretched blissfully. It threw him off balance.

'Okay, Chambers,' said Hecklepeck, scooping him up. 'I see you're in desperate need of attention.' He carried the cat over to an armchair, lit with the morning sun.

Colonel Chambers collapsed into Hecklepeck's lap and then, as though unable to help himself, rolled over and presented his belly. Hecklepeck petted him fondly. 'Development of the 5300 block of Evans is the key to this thing, Colonel. I'm convinced of it.' He looked at the ecstatic animal. 'Why? Because Laurel as much as said so. She said that Tudell was the key to her big story. Of course, the idiot she said it to didn't quite hear it right, but nevertheless, that's what she said.' Hecklepeck curled the fur on Colonel Chambers' tummy around one of his fingers.

'And *we* know that the Tudell Company was buying up property on the 5300 block of Evans. We also know that Laurel was very interested in a house that burned down on that block. Mysterious explosions. World War Two Army ordinance manuals that explain how to attach bombs to timers. It sounds suspiciously like the burn-'em-out-and-build school of urban development. Doesn't it, old boy?'

The Colonel lifted his head and fixed Hecklepeck with a yellow-eyed stare. 'Sorry.' Hecklepeck resumed the tummy rub. 'Yep. The big developer wants to build a shopping centre on that block. But, woe is him, *people* live there. So he sees to it that there are a few fires on the block. Suspicious, yes? But who can say? Those houses are firetraps with tricky old wiring, accumulations of combustible junk and dry, seasoned wood. Hard to say if fire is the work of an arsonist or the smouldering of oily rags in the basement.

'A few such fires and the residents who are left are

willing to take fire-sale prices for their property. Then all our friendly developer has to do is apply for a zoning change. It's time-consuming. But it's time well spent. The profit potential is huge. And when everything is finally in place, Mr Developer comes in like a hero, builds a beautiful new building and reclaims a dying neighbourhood.'

Colonel Chambers lifted a tufted black paw and batted at Hecklepeck's hand. Hecklepeck rubbed him behind the ears. 'Nasty, huh? Laurel really did have a big story and so do we, if we can figure out the missing pieces.'

With one hand on the cat, he reached towards a phone book with the other. He just managed to grab it without dumping the animal on the floor.

The Colonel was miffed but not enough to give up his seat. Flipping his tail on Hecklepeck's knee, he watched him turn to the 'T' section. 'The first thing to do,' Hecklepeck announced, scanning the list of businesses, 'is to go talk to the owners of the property, that Tudell Company.'

But Tudell was not listed. For several seconds Hecklepeck stared at the place where it should have been between Tucson Trucking and a Dr Tudor. Then he sighed. 'I was afraid of that,' he said, mollifying the cat with a scratch. 'Tudell was probably only a dummy corporation in the first place. It was a way for Mr X Developer to do business without anybody knowing it was him doing business. Of course, if he's smart he has incorporated the company in his mother-in-law's name or his nephew's or his maid's and it won't be traceable. But I need to find out by checking to see if Tudell's incorporated and to whom. For that I'll have to go to Jefferson City.' The Missouri state capital was two hours away by car.

Hecklepeck rubbed the Colonel's again-exposed tummy and reviewed the situation. The only new idea he had was that the answer might well be on tape, *not* the tapes the killer was trying so hard to get but one he or she might not have known about: a possible loose end that could still be caught. Hecklepeck started up. He wouldn't lose much, particularly not much time, by checking.

Colonel Chambers landed on his feet and stared at the carpet in disgust.

'Bail denied,' Judge Herschel Black swung back and forth in his big leather chair. 'Mr Markowitz, I'm going to leave you in jail until you remember the name of this mysterious source of yours. I appreciate your journalistic scruples but *this* is a murder investigation.'

Richard stared at the judge in shocked silence. On either side a bailiff appeared to lead him away.

Wally came down from behind his desk with his hand extended and his mouth drawn out to 'smile' position. He ushered his visitor over to the sofa and waited while she settled herself and delved into an expensive leather pocketbook.

Maggie's hands emerged from her purse clutching a cheque. 'Mr Corette, I definitely wish to make a contribution to the Laurel Michaels statue fund. A ten-thousand-dollar contribution.'

The corners of Wally's mouth stretched a little further as he reached for the cheque. It alone would pay for a cheap statue. He wouldn't have to use station funds and could get those GAS crazies off his back.

Maggie pulled it out of his grasp. 'Just a minute, Mr Corette. I want the cheque to be listed as a contribution of the Billy-do Company.'

'Billy-do? Sure. Whatever you wish.'

'I thought we might just have a little bronze plaque at the bottom that says "Courtesy of Billy-do".'

'Yes, uh, that is possible. Of course, we would have to look at our budget and consider quite carefully.' Wally went for the cheque again but Maggie still held it back.

'I also feel so very certain that you will want to know just the exact person, who, I guess we can say – ' Maggie looked over her shoulder to Birdie who was wearing fake fur and sweat pants, '– inspired me.'

'Oh, yes I do,' said Wally, irritably polite.

'He is absolutely one of the pillars of this community. I just feel that it is so important for you to know what a truly rare treasure you have in him.' Wally's smile stiffened.

'The person who motivated me to make this teeny, tiny gift was Mr William Hecklepeck.'

Wally sucked in his smile. In the sudden vacuum his mouth trembled.

'We shall . . . we shall NOT be moved . . .' Arms linked, several hundred protestors swayed in time to the music. They formed a human chain that entirely encircled KYYY. The protest had been gathering momentum since daybreak. It had grown beyond GAS to include every would-be elderly militant with any kind of cross in St Louis. In death Laurel had done what most politicians would like to do: she had united Left and Right and all the degrees in between in a single cause.

Forming a wider circle around the station were the police. They sipped coffee and chatted in the warmth of their cars, riot gear on the seats beside them. Although complaints from area businesses had been vociferous, they had orders from City Hall not to interfere. The mayor was waiting to see how the balance of St Louis voters felt about the statue issue before he took a stand.

'The mood out here is tense.' In front of the human chain Joe Handy delivered a live report. KYYY and other local TV stations were interrupting the morning game-shows with enthusiastic updates. 'There is some talk of storming the building. It's just a rumour but in the present atmosphere anything is possible.' Joe saw himself reporting it all while the mob took over his own television station. As long as he had a microphone in his hand he would never give up.

Richard sat dejectedly in the yellow hold-over cell and smelled himself. All prisoners must share that one curdled scent, he thought. Did their personalities merge too? Would he leave jail a rapist or murderer? No. He would probably never leave jail. The other prisoners would kill him before he had a chance to become one of them.

He had yet to meet any. But he was sure the marshal would soon take him over to the City Jail where he would be thrown in with hordes of them. Richard could easily imagine the terrible things they would do to him.

177

He began to bang on the yellow door.

Hecklepeck passed KYYY for the second time in his navy-blue Jaguar. Even if he could get into the parking lot there was nowhere to put the car. Instead he turned into the abandoned gas station next door and parked the car in the shadow of a rusting gas-pump island.

As he approached the human chain in front of the newsroom door, he held two fingers in a 'Peace' sign. The woman with the headband forming the left half of the link smiled and raised her arm to let him through. However, the tattooed man on the right frowned. Hecklepeck took a chance. 'Stop flag-burning,' he whispered in the man's ear. The man immediately moved so Hecklepeck could pass.

'Mr Hacklespeck, come on in. Sorry about yesterday.' The policeman at the door had finally figured out that Hecklepeck did work at KYYY. 'It's just that all you anchormen look alike to me.' The policeman chuckled at his own egregious joke. Hecklepeck shot him a look that would have withered a cornfield and hastened across the newsroom, down the main hall to the basement door at the end.

Old show-tapes rested on several rows of shelving that stretched floor to ceiling. Hecklepeck walked down one row, checking dates. They were in amazingly good order. It was because the police had looked at them and refiled them, he decided. The newsroom secretary was never very careful about where she put the show reels.

Hecklepeck stopped when he got to March, 1976. There it was: 19 March. He breathed a sigh of relief. Often, old show-tapes were removed and never returned. Hecklepeck grabbed the tape, sprinted back up the stairs and into the editing rooms.

He shoved his find into the arms of the editor on the morning shift. 'I need you to cue this up,' he said.

The door of the hold-over swung open and Lieutenant Berger walked in. 'You wanna talk?' he asked Richard. Richard nodded glumly. From journalistic hero to abject traitor, he thought. But what did Hecklepeck expect? It wasn't fair to expect him to rot in jail forever without even being paid. Other journalists who went to jail rather than reveal their sources were not suspended without pay. They could afford to have principles.

Richard looked up at Berger. 'I can tell you where the tapes are,' he muttered.

Laurel had covered the fire that killed Rose Dorfer. Hecklepeck wondered why he hadn't remembered that. She had been hanging around the station as usual reviewing tapes or editing, or something. When the fire began in the early hours of the morning, she had called a photographer and gone to report on it.

It was a connection. Hecklepeck felt the pounding of his pulse as he watched her story. One minute and forty-seven seconds. Laurel had written a straightforward, if somewhat lifeless, account. There was nothing in it about developers, nothing that differentiated that fire from any other fatal blaze and nothing that linked the blaze with Laurel's own murder.

Hecklepeck asked the editor to re-cue the tape. He watched the story again and then again. It wasn't until the fourth playing that something caught his eye.

'Freeze it,' he said to the editor. 'Now back the tape up. A frame at a time. Stop there.' Hecklepeck stared at the screen. What he saw, or thought he saw, was the face of someone he recognised. Yes, it was a familiar face. It had to be.

Joe Handy threw down his microphone in disgust. 'We might as well relax for half an hour, until the noon news,' he said to his crew. Joe was disappointed. The mob had opted not to storm the Bastille. Its chanting was becoming sporadic and individual protesters spoke of breaking the chain for lunch. The story was fizzling short of historical significance. Joe consoled himself with the thought of warming his hands and joined fellow journalists already gathered around the kerosene fire.

On the outskirts of the KYYY parking lot, Berger consulted with the lieutenant in charge of crowd control. 'I want to get him and fahr or five of my men inside.' Berger nodded towards Richard who slumped in the back of an unmarked car. 'In an ahrderly fashion, no trouble.' The lieutenant was only too glad to have something to do.

'Give them their mem-or-i-al . . . to remember their Lau-au-au-ral.' The St Louis press corps bored easily. The group around the burning barrel had developed a new version of 'The Stars and Stripes Forever'. 'It's not for her glory . . . We're just sick of this story . . . So give them their mem-or-i-al . . . Hey! . . . Give them their . . .' Taken with its own cleverness the press corps began to march triumphantly around the barrel.

None of the journalists noticed the phalanx of riot-geared policemen making its way across the parking lot. In the centre were the homicide officers and Richard. The group moved swiftly until it reached the chain of protesters in front of the station door. There the lieutenant in charge of crowd control explained to Helen Wheeler that the homicide detectives needed to cross the line to continue their investigation. 'So if you could just break it,' he finished, his voice muffled by his riot helmet.

Next to Helen, GAS Vice-President Peggy Hanford misheard him. 'They want us to break it up. Oh, the pigs, the pigs, the pigs!' she shrieked. She threw herself at the nearest policeman and began to pummel him with her fists.

Peggy's shriek drew protesters from the other sides of the building. At the sight of Peggy seemingly under attack they rushed to her aid. Surrounded, the lieutenant in charge of crowd control unhooked the two-way radio from his belt and called for reinforcements.

The press corps also heard the shriek. Reporters and photographers fell over each other to get at their cameras and notebooks. By the time most of them were in position they had no way of knowing what had happened. The parking lot was full of screaming protesters and ducking policemen.

Berger had not waited to see the mêlée develop. At the first sign of trouble, he grabbed Richard and shoved him into the station. His men followed. 'Now let's find yahr buddy,' Berger growled, prodding the unwilling Richard towards the hall.

Hecklepeck replaced the tape on the basement shelf. It was the safest place for it. The police had reviewed the tapes in the basement archives and were unlikely to do so again. Since they had searched and found nothing, nobody else was apt to bother. Hecklepeck had already explored that line of reasoning when he was looking for a place to hide Laurel's tapes.

He walked around the corner to the shelves of tapes from 1977. There, filed just after the 7 January newstape, was *Mistresses No 1*; after 7 February, *Mistresses No 2*; and after 6 March (the 7 March, 1977 tape was missing), Hecklepeck had placed *Mistresses No 3*. He checked each of the months until he reached May, 1978 and *Mistresses No 17*. They were all there. Giving himself a mental pat on the back, Hecklepeck went back up the basement steps and into the hall.

'*No* tear gas. The chief just got off the phone with the mayor and he wants you to keep hands off.' Lights flashing and siren screaming, a police car carrying a couple of captains sped towards KYYY. One of the captains was talking to the lieutenant in charge of crowd control by two-way radio.

'But we've got to do *something*!' The lieutenant looked over the battlefield. Some of his men had been backed up against the station wall. Others were fending off protesters by swinging their night-sticks. However, they no sooner drove off one group when they were threatened by another. The lieutenant wasn't sure how much longer they could keep it up without someone getting hurt. 'We're really taking a beating,' he told his superiors.

'Come on. Things can't be that bad. It's just a harmless group of old people.'

From opposite ends of the hallway Berger and Hecklepeck approached each other, gunfighters poised to draw. Still thrust forward by Berger, Richard found himself in the crossfire. With his eyes he pleaded for Hecklepeck's forgiveness.

181

But Hecklepeck was looking at Berger. Never had he seen the police lieutenant appear so angry.

'The book,' said Berger when he was within spitting range of Hecklepeck. 'I am going to throw the goddamn book at you and I am going to throw it so hard that you will never get up!'

'I think I know who did the murder,' said Hecklepeck. 'If we work together we can collect enough evidence to make an arrest tonight.'

Berger wasn't going to be deterred. 'Fahr stahrters I am going to charge you with withholding evidence. Just as soon as we go out to yahr car and pick up the tapes.'

'The tapes . . . ' Hecklepeck began. He never finished; his words were stopped by the sound of an explosion. Although it came from outside, the blast was strong enough to send a shudder through the entire building.

Richard sank into a crouch at the base of one wall and covered his head with his hands, a response learned in elementary school tornado drills. Berger hesitated for only a second before sprinting towards the outside door. Hecklepeck was right behind him.

In the parking lot the fighting had stopped. The protesters had drawn into groups and, hugging each other, were gazing in the direction of the explosion.

Hecklepeck followed their eyes to the gas station next door. 'It's my car,' he said in disbelief. Where he had parked the sleek blue Jaguar sat a smouldering shell. Doors and windows had completely blown out and the car's body slumped on bent tyre rims. Pieces of the Jaguar lay in a wide circle around it as did bits of all the junk Hecklepeck had kept in his back seat. Book pages were interspersed with scraps of cloth and cardboard, as well as other items.

Much of the mess was indistinguishable, but here and there something stood out with chilling clarity. The lens from a pair of sunglasses was discernable, as were parts of a ballpoint pen and a discoloured glove. On one side of the car lay the handle of a snow shovel, its twisted blade on the other. Everything was covered with a fine khaki dust.

It looked to Hecklepeck as though somebody had placed

an explosive *under* the car, in fact, directly under the place on the back seat where the box of tapes had sat. The thrust of the blast had been straight up. That was obvious. The hole in the Jaguar's roof was two feet in diameter.

'The tapes!' The words tore out of Berger's gut. He wheeled around and addressed the lieutenant in charge of crowd control. 'Round up those demonstrators and take them downtown. I want to question every single one of them.'

'But the mayor . . .'

'To hell with the mayor! Round the biddies up.'

Given something to do, the police acted with speed and efficiency. Within minutes the KYYY parking lot and the gas station were cordoned off. Fire trucks arrived. They were followed quickly by forensic units and paddy wagons.

All of this the protesters watched from their huddles in relative silence. They allowed themselves to be ushered into the police vans without protest. The press, too, was subdued. As they went about their work, reporters and photographers communicated in hushed tones.

Lieutenant Berger was everywhere. He oversaw the collection of evidence and supervised the rounding up of witnesses. The lieutenant did not need to be told that the bomber and Laurel Michaels' murderer were likely to be one person and he was determined to miss nothing that might lead to that person's identification. It wasn't until some time later that he remembered to look around for Hecklepeck. When he did, Hecklepeck had disappeared.

CHAPTER EIGHTEEN

EARLY ON MONDAY MORNING BERGER sat at his desk and sighed. He sighed again, a long heartfelt expiration. Without realising it, he was singing an entire chorus of sighs. Berger's normally maudlin personality had sunk to despairing over the weekend. Half of St Louis, much of the police force and the entire press corps had been in that parking-lot on Friday but nobody had noticed anything unusual in the gas station across the street. Somebody had marched up to Hecklepeck's car, stuck a bomb to its underside and walked off in perfect anonymity.

To make matters worse Hecklepeck himself was still missing. Berger had been able to ascertain that he had walked from the TV station to his hotel on Friday afternoon. There he had rented a car at one of the rental desks. But where he and the baby-blue Buick LeSabre had gone from there was a mystery. It was hard to believe that someone as well-known as Hecklepeck could drive anywhere in St Louis County without being recognised. Yet nobody had reported seeing him. On Saturday and Sunday the police had watched all roads leading out of the area in vain.

Monday morning provided Berger with new impetus to find the anchorman: a forensic report. In the wreckage of Hecklepeck's car, it said, there were pieces of cardboard and leather, fragments of plastic and glass, bits of plaid blanket and cotton cloth. The powder had been identified as kitty-litter, for crying out loud. But there was no trace of video tape.

Berger read the words again and ground his teeth, before sinking into the next sigh. Where, then, were

185

Laurel Michaels' tapes? Had Hecklepeck hidden them or had someone else got hold of them? Either way only Hecklepeck had the answer and Berger longed to get hold of him. To make matters worse, something was niggling at the back of his mind. From there Berger heard the echo of Hecklepeck's words, 'I think I know who did the murder.'

Johnny Burnham swung his helicopter down over Highway Forty for a look at Monday's rush-hour traffic. It was an unusually warm morning for February. The mercury was already above the freezing mark and was expected to climb as far as fifty before the day was out. With a silk scarf tucked into his leather flight-jacket, Johnny was feeling sexy. It was a relatively new feeling for him. He had never felt that way before retiring from the helicopter charter-service and taking up part-time traffic monitoring for K000 Radio. The move had made him a minor celebrity, particularly among a certain group of women.

'This is Fabulous Phil Barnes, a little honey . . .' – here the voice coming across Johnny's radio became guttural – ' . . . to go with your morning toast. Does that move all you ladies out there? No? Well, let's see what is moving as we check in with our AM 1350 Sky Supervisor. What's the traffic doing on this beautiful day, Johnny?'

'It's behaving itself,' Johnny spoke into the mike attached to his sizable earphones. 'Moving briskly for this time of the morning. Some minor delays on Highway Forty where there's a bit of a slowdown approaching the downtown area but no major tie-ups. And if you're in a big hurry you could avoid Forty altogether. Forty-four will get you downtown in no time. Only other trouble spot: construction on the Watterson Expressway just south of Seventy.'

'Sounds like it's hardly enough to keep you awake.'

Johnny chuckled. 'That's okay. I got my share of excitement at the pad this morning.'

'*Wellll*, let us in on it.'

'I saw the man everybody in St Louis seems to be talking about.'

'Darn! I guess that leaves me out. I don't hang out at hangers. Helicopter hangers, get it?'

'Yeah,' said Johnny. 'William Hecklepeck.' It didn't occur to him that this information would be better shared privately with the police than broadcast over K000 Radio. He was too taken with the effect he knew it would have on Cathy. Cathy was a waitress at the North County Steak and Shake. She had promised to tune in and listen as she served the breakfast crowd from behind the counter.

'The disappearing anchorman. Well, I bet that made your day.' It didn't do much for Phil who saw other television and radio personalities as so much competition.

That helicopter pilot had recognised him. Hecklepeck felt sure of that as he walked along the highway away from the heliport. In any case he didn't dare use his rental car; he was going to have to find a phone and get some help.

He wondered who to call. There was always Richard. After blabbing about the tapes, Richard would be feeling guilty and eager to help. But he was too obvious a choice.

Anyway, what Hecklepeck needed was organised help, efficient help. He still had an errand to run.

He walked into the parking lot of the North County Steak and Shake in the direction of the outdoor phone-booth and made up his mind to take a chance. He put some change into the coin slots and punched 411. When information gave him the number he wanted, he hung up, re-fed the coin slots and pushed the correct buttons. The phone was answered almost immediately.

'Hello,' said Hecklepeck. 'You'll never guess who this is. William Hecklepeck. Yes, that's right.' He explained that he needed to be picked up and described his whereabouts. The person on the other end wrote it all down and rang off.

Using the phone booth to shelter himself from the people eating breakfast in the Steak and Shake, Hecklepeck waited. He had spent a long, quiet weekend in Jefferson City at the home of a friend of his. He hadn't dared come back to St Louis for fear of being caught. But he hadn't wanted to risk wandering around Jefferson City either. So he'd stayed indoors playing gin rummy with the pilot he had hired to fly him down.

Yet the trip had been successful. On Friday afternoon in the office of the Secretary of State, Hecklepeck had learned what he'd needed to know about the incorporation of the Tudell company. He only needed one more piece to complete the puzzle.

After twenty minutes of waiting, Hecklepeck heard a siren in the distance. He pulled up the collar of his sheepskin jacket and wished he had on less identifiable clothes.

The siren was getting nearer. A maroon Pontiac pulled into the Steak and Shake lot and rolled towards the phone booth. Hecklepeck peered at it from behind the cubicle. Recognising the driver, he went round and got in.

The Pontiac pulled out on to the highway just as a police car turned into the heliport next door, its siren screaming.

'How was your trip to Connecticut?' Wally asked News Director Ken Marshal, who was seated on one of the uncomfortable chairs in front of Wally's desk.

'Well . . . ' Ken shook his head. The whole experience had bewildered him. 'It was held at the Darien Polo Club.'

Wally grunted. 'We need a policy on Hecklepeck,' he said. 'It is imperative that we disassociate ourselves from him as much as possible.'

'We don't know he's guilty.'

'Certainly he's guilty. He had the tapes didn't he?'

Ken was silent. He couldn't argue with that.

'Ivan Sandler will anchor and while we have to make some show of covering the news, I don't want Hecklepeck mentioned on our air more than is necessary.'

Wally waved Ken away and dialled Tucson.

After a short wait Barry Babson came on the speaker phone and pronounced, 'You are what you eat.' Wally identified himself. 'Oh, it's you,' Barry sounded as if his wisdom had been wasted.

'Yes, I have some highly disturbing news for you. . .'

'Mr Hecklepeck has been the biggest supporter of our

statue drive. . .' GAS President Helen Wheeler was addressing an emergency meeting of the group. Members had come into her garage with the fresh scent of defrosting soil in their nostrils. The unseasonable warm weather made them long to sink their itchy fingers into the soothing ground and garden until they knew peace. Failing that, they were looking for something to take their minds off their misery.

'He spoke out on our behalf on television. He risked his job for us. And now,' Helen's voice rose to a peak somewhere above the heads of her listeners. She dropped it way down, 'is his hour of darkest need.'

'Oh, dear, dear, dear me,' Peggy Hanford hugged herself.

'Our mission is clear. We must help Mr Hecklepeck.' This brought on a chorus of cheers. 'And we alone can do it.'

Helen surveyed the room, searching each face for less than enthusiastic signs. Satisfied, she went to the door leading to her kitchen and ushered out William Hecklepeck. 'Mr Hecklepeck needs to get into a certain office building without being recognised. He needs our help.'

In the KYYY newsroom the chief assignment-editor twisted a magic-marker-stained rag. He and Ken surveyed the big assignment board. The assignment-editor was proud of it. It was almost three-quarters filled with magic-markered assignments.

'Take Saire and Partridge off the Hecklepeck story,' Ken said. 'Handy can handle it alone.'

'*Alone?*' the assignment-editor shrieked. 'But the other stations have a bunch of crews covering it. They've got one staking out that radio station. Four or five others are cruising the area of the latest sighting to be ready if there's a bust. The newspapers have even more people out on the street. Nobody wants to take any chances after everybody missed the beginning of that riot yesterday.' The chief assignment-editor did everything but set his clock by the competition.

'Our policy is that that's playing into his hands,' said Ken. 'Wally believes it's just what Hecklepeck wants: public attention. Nobody knows better than Hecklepeck how to manipulate the media.'

In the news-director's office Richard Markowitz waited for Ken. He was preoccupied with guilt. Because of him Hecklepeck was doomed to a life on the run. *He* had caved in, blabbed under pressure, betrayed the man he admired most. He wasn't fit to crawl, not even worthy of sliding on his belly. Richard was grovelling internally and enjoying it greatly.

'I've just had a little confab with Wally,' Ken said when he finally came into the office. 'We think Joe Handy should host the Laurel special since he's been covering the story.'

'The special? We're still airing that special?'

'Of course. Tyre Country is sponsoring it. We can't let one rotten apple spoil the whole, uh, pile. We have to forge ahead. Why should this Hecklepeck thing ruin all the good work you've done producing the show?'

'All the work?' Richard emerged from his inner snivelling in consternation. 'I haven't done any work.'

'What have you been doing for the last six days?' Ken slid his chair back from his desk and further away from Richard.

'I . . . uh. . .' How could he explain the last six days to Ken? He had spent two of them in jail, for Pete's sake!

Ken was moving his chair back some more. 'I've been out of town,' he said, 'on official station business. I could hardly be responsible for your failure to produce in Connecticut.' Ken's chair thumped into the objects behind it and he started. 'Hrrrmph.' He settled himself. 'If there is, ah, no special, it seems to me that is has to be your fault. Of course, you could still do it. There's a day and a half left.'

Richard sighed deeply. Yes, if he hustled, he could do it. He'd have to string a lot of Laurel's old stories together to fill time. It would be shitty but he could do it. He directed a malevolent look at Ken and went out into the newsroom.

'Ree-shard, there's a call holding for you on line two.'

The chief assignment-editor made a curlycue in the air with his magic-marker. 'It sounds like some weirdo talking through his socks. He won't hang up; he's been holding for five minutes.'

Richard grimaced and picked up the phone. 'Richard Markowitz,' he said.

'Sebastion's. Back room. Seven-thirty.' But the voice wasn't filtering through socks. Rather, it rang with the unmistakable mellifluousness of William Hecklepeck.

CHAPTER NINETEEN

IN THE KYYY PARKING LOT the burnt-out barrel of kerosene was the only remnant of Friday's demonstration. The lot was filled with the usual number of week-day cars, some of them draped with their owners soaking up the noontime sun.

On the hood of a beige Honda, one reporter took a blissful drag on his after-lunch cigarette. 'We could stage another sit-down,' he said propping his head up on the windshield.

Leaning against a nearby Datsun, the five o'clock producer shook her head. 'It would never work twice in a row and we'd just get fired.' She turned her face to the sun so that it would tan.

'What the hay?' asked one of the writers rhetorically. He was sitting cross-legged on the Datsun's hood. 'We could take a stand but we'd just end up in the unemployment line. Anyway, who's to say Wally the walleye isn't right? Heck could be a murderer you know.'

'He probably is,' the five o'clock producer sounded vindictive. Her face, however, remained impassively presented to the sun. 'Whether he is or he isn't, we ought to be covering the story.'

Nobody replied. For several minutes each was alone with his or her thoughts and the seductive warmth. Then: 'We have to *do* something.'

'Yeah.' But reportorial principles were not as compelling as the sun's rays.

In the centre of downtown Clayton, a small group of people was gathering with picket signs.

'What's going on?' one St Louis' County policeman

asked another as they drove by in their cruiser.

'I don't know,' replied the policeman behind the wheel. He pulled the car over to the kerb to watch. 'Do those people have a parade permit?'

One of the group in the park raised his sign so that the policemen could read it. The policeman in the passenger seat groaned. 'That's the group that made all the trouble in the city on Friday. The Last Gasps or something like that.'

The other policeman picked up the two-way handle to call headquarters.

GAS was bringing its Laurel Michaels statue-drive to the heart of St Louis County – 'Where the money is,' as Helen Wheeler had put it. When everybody was there and the pickets distributed, the group started to march and chant with an enthusiasm that was unusual even for them.

'We want a statue! Yes we do!' The cry rose up among the glass-fronted high-rises and echoed back. It wasn't long before a crowd of office workers had gathered to watch.

Reluctantly the two policemen got out of their car and walked over to the old gentleman in overalls who seemed to be leading the march. 'We would like to see your parade permit,' one of them said.

'If you please,' added the other, trying to be polite.

The elderly gentleman stopped dead in his tracks, put his hands on his hips and shouted loudly, 'We don't have one.'

'Shhh,' said one of the policemen. He didn't want to attract any more people than had already gathered.

'Freedom of speech!' yelled the elderly gentleman. He hoisted his picket sign high into the air. 'Freeeeedom of Speeeech!'

'We can't let you demonstrate here without a permit.'

'Well, what are you going to do? Arrest me?' the old man bellowed. At the word 'arrest' all the demonstrators converged on the policemen and the ring of spectators moved closer to hear what was happening.

While almost everybody in downtown Clayton was focused on the ruckus in the park, two elderly women in gardening clothes hurried along the sidewalk with a man in overalls between them. The man had a tweed hat pulled way down over his face and he walked with a stoop.

The trio ducked into one of the high-rise buildings across from the park.

In the KYYY newsroom Richard was feverishly organising the special show. Around his desk were piles of tapes with old Laurel Michaels' stories on them. The trick was to get them in some kind of order. Chronological? By subject? Then he had to put together some kind of biographical piece for Joe to voice. He could use the tape they had shot at Laurel's apartment for that. But filling an hour-show was going to be difficult. It would probably take him most of the night.

Richard's task was harder because he couldn't keep his mind on it. He tried desperately to remember when Laurel had done *Dead Meat*, her series on St Louis butchers, and to decide if it would be tacky to air it in conjunction with her comparison of local undertakers. He couldn't make any headway. Between the problems and any decisions intruded the question: What is Hecklepeck up to now?

The policemen had been arguing with the old gentleman and his friends for over an hour. They didn't want to arrest him; they really didn't. It didn't look good to drag respectable senior citizens away in handcuffs.

But the old man and his companions didn't seem to be getting the message either. They had been shouting and screaming about their civil rights in tones that reached to the outskirts of the crowd and into the microphones of the news media: tones that made the policemen cringe.

Just as the police were about to give up and call for reinforcements to arrest the demonstrators, a piercing whistle came from somewhere outside the crowd.

The old man suddenly dropped the sign he had been waving. 'I beg your pardon, Officers. We didn't know we needed a parade permit. Next time we will certainly obtain one.'

Within ten minutes the park had emptied completely except for some television newscrews who were still putting away their equipment and the two somewhat-stunned policemen.

'Our commentator is taking his place and I think you'll see I've arranged to keep any mention of *him* to a minimum.' Wally wanted a drink and a cigar badly but he knew Barry Babson would not have approved. The head of Babson Broadcasting had arrived from Tucson late that afternoon via corporate jet and limo.

Barry nodded, not a hair in his white mane moved from its place. They were seated at the sofa-end of Wally's office, waiting for the news to begin.

'When you want to know why, turn to KYYY, the news with answers. With our Channel Three news family, Anchorman Ivan Sandler, Sportscaster Bucky Ballwin and Weatherman Irwin Samuels.'

'Good evening,' Ivan looked puzzled. He wasn't sure if it really was a good evening or if he had inadvertently expressed an opinion.

'A group of demonstrators was forced to leave a Clayton park this afternoon after trying to demonstrate without a permit. We'll have that story and an update on the search for a man suspected of murder.' Ivan was sitting in that man's chair but he couldn't say his name.

'But first we're going to go over to Weather Central to get the details about this beautiful weather . . . at least those of you who aren't polar bears have to agree it's pretty nice.' Flat-out calling the weather beautiful was far out on a limb for Ivan. While Wally was working to undermine the news, to Ivan it came naturally.

'KYYY Meteorologist Irwin Samuels says it will go down in the record books as one of the great thaws. Can we really go as far as that, Irwin?'

Just before seven-thirty that evening Richard walked into Sebastion's. Sebastion's was one of the most fashionable bars and restaurants in the Central West End. It was also Hecklepeck's hang-out. Guy (pronounced Gee with a hard

'G') Sebastion was something of a friend and Hecklepeck usually patronised his restaurant several nights a week.

Not knowing where to find the back room, Richard stood uncertainly inside the doorway of the bar section and wondered what to do next. In earthy reds, hunter-greens and golds the decorating theme was *Twelfth Night*; a play that seemed to possess Guy Sebastion, possibly because he shared his name with one of the principle characters, but more likely because it expressed the basic dilemma in Guy's life, his bisexuality. Guy seriously couldn't decide if he was meant to be a man or a woman. He dabbled in both, sometimes appearing as Sebastion but also dressing as Sebastion's twin sister, Viola.

Richard stared at a tapestry until he saw that it depicted a woman with a man's body fondled by a man on one side and a woman on the other. He blushed and dropped his eyes. It was then he realised that almost everybody in the place was looking at him.

Richard made himself walk across the bar to the restaurant section. As he did, it occurred to him that this was a strange crowd for Sebastion's. It seemed older and not very chic. A number of patrons looked as if they had come straight out of their gardens.

'May I help you?' The head waiter was at his podium in the restaurant doorway. Richard cleared his throat and tried to explain discreetly what he wanted. He had the feeling everyone in the restaurant was listening.

The head waiter looked Richard over carefully and then motioned for him to follow. They went through the restaurant to a hallway at the back. The head waiter gestured at a door and left. Richard opened the door.

Underneath a ceiling mural of copulating hermaphrodites, Hecklepeck sat at a table elegantly set for four and covered with dishes. Two elderly women in overalls sat on either side of him. All three were tasting something in a sauce that looked delicious.

'What the hell is going on?' demanded Richard.

'We're fortifying ourselves to catch a murderer,' replied Hecklepeck with a smile. But his eyes were very, very serious.

CHAPTER TWENTY

'HE ASKED ME TO TELL you that he still has the tapes,'
Richard said into his telephone receiver. He was sitting at
his desk in the newsroom with his feet propped up on a
pile of video tapes.

'I know, but they weren't really in his car,' Richard went
on after a short pause. 'So they weren't destroyed.' He
listened some more before saying, 'No, I can't tell you
where he is. I don't know. Just come to the TV station at
seven-thirty this evening.'

Richard marked a name off a list on his desk. Then,
consulting it, he dialled another number. 'Hello. I'm sorry
to disturb you so early in the morning. My name is Richard
Markowitz. I have a message for you from William
Hecklepeck . . .'

Berger poured himself another cup of coffee. He didn't
want it, he just had nothing else to do. He had been
officially relieved of his duties. But the orders that would
take him to the Traffic Division had not yet come
through. He was in limbo.

He sipped his coffee. It took a tremendous effort to lift
the cup to his lips. He wouldn't have bothered at all if
coffee weren't so bad for him. Berger wasn't considering
suicide. *That* was against the law. But he saw little point in
taking care of himself. What future did he have in Traffic?

He imagined himself arriving at the scene of a fatal
traffic accident the way he had done at so many homicides.
What if it were nobody's fault, a driver losing control of his
car and crashing? There would be no investigation, no
arrest, nobody to hold responsible for the poor guy whose

blood was all over the front seat. A fresh wave of sadness swept over Berger as he pictured the imaginary victim. Pointless. Traffic was a pointless way to die. Better to be murdered and at least help put a murderer behind bars.

'Mike, there's a phone call for you on line three.' The detective avoided eye contact. Like the rest of Berger's colleagues he didn't know what to do or say.

Berger had spent the morning in an aura of silence. Now he lifted up the phone. It wasn't easy. 'Lieutenant Berger,' he said.

'Mike, this is Heck. I want to make a deal.'

'It's too late. I'm off the case.'

'Well, they'll have to put you back on. I'm not dealing with anyone else.'

'I was wondering if you were going to show me the script for the Laurel special sometime this afternoon.' Ken's face appeared above a pile of tapes. Richard brought his feet to the floor with a crash.

'Uh, it's not, uh, finished,' he said.

'But you *will* have it done by eight o'clock tonight?'

'Oh, absolutely. Everything's under control.' Richard meant it. Hadn't he joined forces with Justice and with Hecklepeck? It was an unbeatable combination and that was fortunate because his entire career was at stake. Beneath his assurance the pit of Richard's stomach throbbed.

'Maybe you could tell me a little about it.' Having ascertained that there would be a special, Ken wasn't particularly interested in content. He needed the information, however. 'We want to promo it during the newscasts.'

'Well, uh, we're going to be showing a whole new side of Laurel.'

By evening the cold weather had returned with a vengeance. It arrived in conjunction with some snow showers. Initially the snow had melted on contact with the warm ground but it was now rallying to form little icicles on the KYYY parking-lot fence.

Behind the fence a plain white van nestled among the garishly decorated KYYY vehicles. Under the anti-crime lights it shone, luminescent except for the black expanse of its windows. The windows were tinted to hide the van's interior and two chilly detectives, sitting in the front seat, were invisible.

So was the rest of the law-enforcement chain that surrounded the television station. Every once in a while a shadow took on a policeman shape. Otherwise the lot was still.

At seven-thirty a Rolls Royce pulled up to the front door of KYYY with a gentle hum. Without cutting the engine, Birdie disembarked and went around to hand Maggie out. They were both wrapped in fur.

Birdie saw Maggie in through the front door and went to park the car. Then he followed her into the station.

Several minutes later a KYYY newscar drove into a parking slot near the police van. Photographer Art Macke turned off the engine and got out. He leaned against the hood waiting for his companion to work her own way out of the vehicle.

Sonya Richardson was wearing a cloth coat that was too long for her little frame. Fluffy earmuffs sandwiched her tiny face. At Art's request she carefully locked her door and the two of them went in through the newsroom door.

While Art was waiting for Sonya, another car had pulled into the KYYY lot. Rita Cullen rose out of her yellow mustang in a pink parka. She looked over at Wally Corette's car parked in the spot designated for the general manager before drifting in through the front of the station.

Almost twenty minutes went by before the next arrival. A wine-red Lincoln Continental approached the front door of the station. The Continental's purring ceased, indicating the driver meant to park it right there in the fire-lane.

'Shee . . . ' one of the invisible policemen in the van let out a disgusted snort.

Alderman 'Tiny' Payne dismounted carefully. He settled his bulk for comfortable walking and went around to the front passenger door. With a flourish he opened it. A spiked heel shot out, catching Tiny in the groin. He held himself and groaned. The policemen snickered.

Tareesa stepped out of the Continental and flounced towards the entrance of the station, leaving Tiny to close the car door and catch up. 'Forgive and forget' did not seem to be one of her mottoes.

One of the policemen picked up the two-way radio. 'They're all in,' he said, 'including the suspect.'

So Art *was* going out with her, Richard thought after he directed the photographer and Sonya to Studio B. There was a time, four days ago, when he would have been jealous. Now he had more important matters on his mind. Richard actually felt a contemptuous sort of pity for his colleague. It was the pity that someone about to witness an historical event feels for the short-sighted slob who can't see the larger picture for his own petty concerns.

'Where's my script?' Joe Handy demanded. He had approached behind Richard.

'Your script?' asked Richard, his mind still on Art and Sonya.

'My script. The one I'm supposed to use to anchor the Laurel Michaels special. The special that begins in about ten minutes.'

'Oh,' said Richard. 'Oh. You're, uh, not going to be anchoring after all. They've found somebody else.'

'Somebody else. Who? Not Mr Ivan I-can't-take-a-stand Sandler?'

'No. It's not like that,' Richard struggled for a way to put it. 'It's just that they've changed the entire concept of the show.'

'Who is *they?* Ken?'

'Well, not Ken exactly.'

'Not Ken?' It must have come from higher up, Joe decided. 'Wally!' he declared. Richard shook his head. He wasn't about to explain that he and he alone had taken it on himself to dump Handy. If he did, Joe would tell Ken; the special would be cancelled and he, Richard, would be fired. The two steel bands that had been constricting his stomach all evening tightened some more. Richard burped to relieve the pressure. He would be glad when it was all over.

'Oh my God. It must have been Babson himself.' In Joe's mind it couldn't have been worse. 'Oh God, Rich, tell me. I need to know if I should put together a new audition tape.'

'It will be anchored by one of our top reporters, Joe Handy.' Wally and Barry were back in Wally's office after an expensive, tasteless meal served at Barry's hotel. It was food Barry had had to go out of his way to find. It was not easy to spend a lot of money and get bad restaurant fare in St Louis.

There wasn't so much as a crack on his exterior but inside Wally was crumbling. An evening without alcohol, without any cigars, without even red meat had shaken him up badly.

'I think you'll see that this special is a heartfelt, er, tribute to Laurel Michaels.' Wally tensed in an effort to put the words together properly. 'It should put to rest all this ridiculous talk about KYYY management not, er, caring about its employees.'

'And we do,' Barry smiled piously. 'We care about each and every member of our Babson Broadcasting family. But we simply can't afford to erect statues of them. This show is costing us enough.' Barry said it as though he believed it.

Wally wasn't sure whether to let him go on believing or to tell him the truth. He decided on the truth: 'We, er, sold almost all the advertising time. We're making money on this special.' He had made the right choice. Barry's righteous smirk widened.

Richard walked into master control with a small stack of tapes in his arms. On one of the many monitors in front of him the show director was studying a shot of a speaker stand. Behind it stood a particularly hairy member of the floor crew.

'Okay, Melvin, you can relax. It looks okay,' the director said via loudspeaker. He turned to Richard. 'Are those your tapes? Where are the rest of them?'

'This is all there are.'

'All? You told me yesterday that you were going to have about twenty tapes.'

'I reworked the show and decided we didn't need them.'

'Well, I just hope you have something to fill this show with. It's going to be pretty boring without any visuals.'

Richard smiled a secretive smile. 'Heh . . . eh . . . Handy has a lot to say,' he said lamely.

The director looked at Richard as though he'd lost his mind. 'Hearing Handy talk is like listening to grass grow,' he commented. 'Let's see what he's gonna say. Where's your script?'

'I, uh, don't have a script. We're just going to wing it.'

In Studio B, Sonya Richardson looked at the hairy member of the floor crew with a little moue of distaste. She and the other subjects of Laurel's *Mistresses* series were sitting on metal chairs set up for the studio audience. Studio B was so called to distinguish it from the news studio, Studio A. 'A' did not, as its name implied, begin a string of studios leading through to 'Z'. 'A' and 'B' were all there were.

'B' was most noted for the Sunday Mass which was taped there every Saturday evening. The Mass was KYYY's answer to public-service programming. It cost next to nothing to produce and the archdiocese did all the work, scheduling priests and inviting worshippers.

Tonight the altar and other Mass accoutrements had been piled up in one corner of the studio. KYYY's all-purpose special set had been erected in their place. It consisted of a carpeted platform backed by sky-blue canvas flats. The flats allowed the show director to change the on-air backdrop at will by electronically projecting slides behind the image of the anchorperson, a technique known as 'chromakey'. In front of the flats was a speaker stand and several potted plants.

'I didn't come here to be on television,' Sonya whispered to Art. They were sitting at the back of the audience section, as far away from the set as possible.

'Don't sweat it. They can't do that without your permission. Not if they don't want serious trouble.'

Sonya was silent for several seconds, then: 'Who are all these people? Why are they here?' Art explained, realising that she would have no way of knowing who else had been interviewed for Laurel's *Mistresses* series.

Sonya frowned. 'Why are we all here?'

'I don't know,' said Art. 'But I bet this is Markowitz's idea of a joke, his idea of an audience for his special.'

A few rows in front of them on the far right sat Tareesa and Tiny. Tareesa had moved as far away from Tiny as her folding chair allowed. She was immobile, her face stony, but static electricity seemed to flow from the strands of her straightened hair and the pink fur of her coat. Tareesa was clearly charged with emotion.

Tiny, too, was still; his bulk carefully draped over his chair. Only his eyes moved. They travelled ceaselessly around the room, resting now on a member of the floor crew, now on the ceiling, now on the speakerless podium.

In the chairs on the far left, Birdie whispered something to Maggie and she fiddled with her sapphire bracelet.

In the far, back corner of the studio Rita sat on the Mass altar. 'Hey, Rita,' a member of the floor crew boomed. She started and smoothed her hair.

'Stay tuned for a special remembrance of KYYY consumer reporter Laurel Michaels who was brutally murdered one week ago tonight.' The situation comedy that aired on KYYY between seven-thirty and eight had ended. In master control the show director turned to Richard. 'Where the hell is Handy? I've only got a two-minute break before this show starts. I need to set up an opening shot now.'

'He'll be here,' said Richard nervously. 'Just set up on that speaker stand. There'll be somebody behind it when the show begins.'

In studio B, a camera operator futilely aimed his camera at the speakerless speaker stand. The floor director pulled his vial of valium out of his back pocket and stared at it thoughtfully. He reserved his valium for the hectic uncertainty of newscasts. During long, drawn-out specials, like the one about to begin, he drank coffee. Now he wasn't so sure.

There was a squawk in his headset. 'Thirty seconds,' he announced to the crew behind him.

'Thirty seconds?' shrieked the camera operator. 'There's no Anchor.' The floor director shrugged and weighed the valium in his left hand against the styrofoam coffee cup in his right.

The door at the back of the studio opened. Lieutenant Michael Berger and another man entered. The lieutenant leaned against the back wall of the studio just inside the door while the other man came towards the set. When the floor director saw him, he tossed his coffee cup in a nearby trash-can and hastily swallowed the valium.

Behind the speaker stand the new arrival clipped the waiting microphone to his vest and plugged in his earpiece just as the red camera light came on. The floor director delivered a cue. Too late. William Hecklepeck was already saying, 'Good evening, St Louis.'

CHAPTER TWENTY-ONE

'ONE WEEK AGO TONIGHT,' HECKLEPECK began purposefully. His borrowed suit was not up to his usual standards, either of fit or quality. 'My colleague, this station's consumer reporter, Laurel Michaels, was murdered. She was strangled in the back of one of our television news vans. In the week that followed there have been false accusations, public demonstrations and talk of missing evidence. It has been a week few of us will ever forget.

'But if we are to get on with our lives, we must put this past week and Laurel Michaels' death behind us. I know of only one way to do that. It is to discover the truth, to answer the questions why was Michaels killed and who killed her? Tonight, I am prepared to shed some light on those questions.

'I will be working from my notes without a script so I ask your forbearance in the face of technical difficulties. What you will see is live television in its purest form. I would like now to get one of our breaks out of the way. When the commercial is over we will begin on the night before Michaels died.'

In the studio there was the sound of audience members shifting uneasily on their metal chairs. Some of them looked around at the door. The group of plain-clothes men standing there made it obvious that escape was impossible.

'Holy Shit! Punch up the first commercial. This is going to be some show,' the show director was rising to the challenge. 'Richard, why didn't you tell me?'

Richard looked smug. 'You'd better get that first tape

ready,' he said. 'Heck'll need it after the break.'

The director continued to look at Richard. Something had just occurred to him. 'You know who did it, don't you?' he asked. The look of smugness on Richard's face settled into truly sickening complacency. 'For goodness sake, *who?*' the director begged.

'I can't tell you,' simpered Richard. 'But I'll give you a hint. The person is here at the station. There could be an arrest during the show.'

'Here? Holee Shi . . . in the studio audience, it's gotta be all those people in the audience. We'd better get a camera on them. Even if Heck doesn't want the shot, we can put it up on a monitor in here and watch.' The show director began to issue orders to the floor crew.

Wally had been on his feet from the time Hecklepeck first appeared on the air. They took him directly over to the bar where he automatically poured and gulped a shot of Jack Daniels. As Wally listened to Hecklepeck's opening speech, he poured and drank two more.

Barry watched Hecklepeck impassively, leaning slightly towards the television set. Although he could hardly miss Wally's behaviour, he gave no sign, merely pursing his lips as the general manager barrelled out of the office.

Wally had no thought but to stop Hecklepeck. He flung open the door to Studio B, throwing it against the concrete wall with a thud. Inside were two uniformed policemen flanked by Lieutenant Michael Berger and the group of plain-clothes men. It was an impressive and unexpected showing.

Wally took a step backwards. 'I, uh, just checking to see if everything's okay.'

'That's fine, Mr Cahrette. Now that you're here though, we'd like you to stay.' Berger gestured at the rows of folding chairs. 'You may be able to help shed some light on all this.'

Over Berger's shoulder Wally saw Rita and snarled. He chose a chair well removed from her and yanked a cigar from his inside jacket pocket.

'If Heck really is going to announce Laurel's murderer, I'd

better save some time for it at the top of the show.' In the newsroom the five o'clock producer was speaking to the evening assignment-editor. She was producing the ten o'clock newscast in Richard's absence.

The evening assignment-editor nodded. 'Yeah,' she said watching Ken Marshal come out of his office and walk across the newsroom, 'unless Heck's gone stark raving mad and is having delusions.'

The producer considered this briefly. 'Either way it's a lead story. I wonder if a minute forty-five is enough time for it?'

Ken slipped through the newsroom door into the frigid air. If he was at home rather than in his office, nobody could blame him for whatever Hecklepeck was about to do. He got into his car.

'Laurel Michaels was devoted to her job.' The commercials had ended and Hecklepeck was back on the air. 'So much so that she had no private life to speak of. It was therefore a safe guess that her murder was connected with her work.

'Eight days ago, one day before she died, Laurel Michaels aired the first segment of a five-part series on the rôle of mistresses in St Louis society. There is evidence that Michaels was killed because of work she did in connection with that series.

'To refresh your memories I am going to replay that segment just as it was presented one week ago on Monday. I would urge as you watch that you pay special attention to what Michaels says at the very end. There, you will find, she provides the first clue to her own murder.

'Do we have the tape?' Hecklepeck asked the floor director. 'Okay, let it roll.'

There on the screen was the living Laurel of eight days ago in her hot-pink jump-suit and olive-green suit jacket, her face hard with anger. In master control Richard grinned. Laurel had been angry with Hecklepeck and, in a way, she had won that argument. Hadn't Hecklepeck just introduced the same story he had refused to be connected with eight days ago? Wherever she was, Richard imagined,

Laurel was wearing her awful little smile of vindictive triumph.

'Hey, that woman's in the studio!' The show director was comparing Laurel's piece on one monitor with the Studio B audience on another. He had connected a disguised, shadowy figure with the real Tareesa, sitting in the audience. 'She looks like she could spit nails.' The show director inhaled sharply, 'Holy Moly, roll me over with tongs, there's lovely Rita. Laurel interviewed *her*?'

'During the rest of the week you will learn the identities of these women and hear their stories. Their situations, you will find, are not enviable.' The taped Laurel wrapped up the second airing of her series just as she had the first. In retrospect her words took on a new importance. 'They are characterised by neglect, abuse and, even . . . crime. Join us tomorrow for part two of *Mistresses: Mystique or Misery?*'

Hecklepeck looked sternly into the camera for a beat or two before he began. 'Laurel Michaels meant what she said. She was going to reveal those women one by one in the four parts of her series that were to follow. She also planned to expose the men with whom they were involved.

'I am not going to share their identities with you. Not all of them really consented to appear and some did not know what they were consenting to. But every single one of them, the women and their men, would have been hurt by Michaels' series. In her search for a story Laurel Michaels threatened the very foundations of their lives: their careers, social standing and human relationships. It could be argued that all of these people had ample motive to kill Michaels. But she was also working on a bigger story, a story that involved the perpetrator of a serious *crime*.' Hecklepeck paused. Well aware of the libel laws he wanted to choose his words carefully. 'This reporter has learned,' he said slowly, 'that that person will be charged with the murder of Laurel Michaels.' Hecklepeck referred to his notes.

'Now, you've been hearing a lot about tapes in the past week. The tapes referred to are the ones that were shot for Michaels' series. You may have heard that they were destroyed when my car was blown up on Friday. But the tapes were not in my car. I had previously placed them under police protection.' The studio audience tensed. Maggie slid her index finger under her sapphire bracelet and twisted. Rita slumped further down on the altar while Wally puffed aggressively on his cigar. In the back of the studio Berger grinned and shook his head. Sneaking tapes past police guards in boxes of fast food in order to hide them in the basement was not his idea of police protection.

'There are about five hours of tapes. It was hard to say what, if anything, on them was significant. But here once again Michaels herself came to our aid. She left a notation in her office.' To simplify matters Hecklepeck did not explain about the time-code reference.

'The notation narrowed down the search to a certain number of shots. Of these, only one stood out. I would like to show it to you now.' Hecklepeck waited while the engineers punched up the shot of the house on Evans Street. '5304 Evans Street,' he continued, 'burned down in March of 1976. It is located several blocks north of the Central West End, where millions of dollars in development money have created one of the wealthiest neighbourhoods in the city.

'At the time of the fire this house was the home of an elderly, handicapped woman. Rose Dorfer died in the blaze. Now, you may well wonder what this picture of a house had to do with a series of stories about mistresses. I found the answer in the KYYY television coverage of that fire. There I recognised a face in the crowd, somebody who didn't belong there. Michaels was the reporter on that fire story. She must have made the connection too.'

Rita slid off the altar and walked to the studio door. 'I want to use the ladies' room,' she announced.

Berger shook his head. 'You'll have to wait until this is over. Nobody is allowed to leave.' A pained look passed over Rita's face. She returned to her seat.

'I decided the fire merited a closer look,' Hecklepeck was continuing, 'after I discovered that less than a year later the entire 5300 block of Evans was rezoned from residential to commercial.'

Tiny searched the chair seat with his rear for a tolerable place to sit. Beside him Tareesa snorted uneasily.

'This is a sad and all too common story in our cities: A series of mysterious fires tears into an already-poor neighbourhood. People start to move out and soon it's not hard to persuade those who are left to sell their homes dirt cheap. After the block is cleared the developers move in. That's exactly what happened on Evans Street.'

'Wow! I shot that house for Laurel. I didn't realise how incredibly significant it was,' Art whispered in Sonya's ear. She didn't alter the set of her face but Art was in no need of encouragement. He went a step further: 'My God, I could have been killed too.'

'Last week, I visited a former resident of Evans Street, a Mrs Earlene Gray. Mrs Gray remembers the spring of 1976 very well. Shortly after the fire that killed her neighbour and several other fires, Mrs Gray received an offer to buy her house from the Tudell Company.'

In the newsroom Joe Osifchin bounced up and down. 'That's it!' the egg-shaped writer said excitedly to the five o'clock producer. 'Laurel told me that.'

'She told you the name of that company?'

'Yesss.' Joe hugged himself excitedly. 'Only I thought she said 'tootle'. But she didn't; she said *too-dell*.'

'Well, why didn't you tell anybody?'

'I did,' he said proudly. 'I told Hecklepeck. I gave him the key to the whole story.'

'You've probably never heard of Tudell. It doesn't advertise. It's not listed in the phone book. In fact Tudell is a dummy corporation, set up to do business quietly for a better-known St Louis Company.

'On Friday,' Hecklepeck went on, 'I flew down to Jefferson City to the Secretary of State's office. There I checked Tudell's incorporation records. According to the records, Tudell is owned by relatives of Raphael and Peter Delano. You will almost certainly recognise the name Delano. Delano and Delano is one of the biggest development companies in St Louis.

'Once that connection is made it's easy to see where the

Tudell Company got its name: two Del-anos.

'This morning the police picked up Peter Delano at his office in St Louis County. Rather than face court charges, Delano has agreed to testify against a company employee, Sonya Richardson.'

Richard was watching when Hecklepeck made the announcement. He almost laughed as he saw Art spring away from Sonya's side with a howl of fear. But the laugh caught in Richard's throat at the sight of Sonya. All her sweetness had vanished and her freckled face had paled, giving her a spotty, unhealthy look. Still it was her eyes that held Richard. For once their message was clear. It sent a sickening shock into the pit of his stomach. Sonya was full of self-righteous pride. She stared at Hecklepeck as though he had just acknowledged her contribution to the good of mankind.

'Is that her?' asked the show director. Richard didn't answer but the approach of Berger and his men told the show director it was. 'Okay, we're going to take that shot. We're coming to you, Camera Three.'

'*No,*' screamed Richard, 'Heck didn't want that. Go to break. Go to break.' He was too late. All of St Louis watched as Sonya was handcuffed and led out.

CHAPTER TWENTY-TWO

'YESTERDAY I WENT TO THE Delano building in Clayton and talked to Peter Delano,' said Hecklepeck after a lengthy commercial break. 'In a way he was expecting me. Monday, eight days ago, the day before Laurel Michaels was killed, he had a similar conversation with her. At that time Delano told Michaels that he had made some disturbing discoveries about the way his father, Raphael Delano, ran the company. Delano Senior had a stroke last year and is now living in a nursing home. Without warning Peter Delano was forced to step up from his position as manager of construction to head of the entire company.'

Hecklepeck cleared his throat. 'Shortly after he assumed his new title a young woman named Sonya Richardson came to see him. He says that she told him she worked for the company in a very special capacity. In exchange for this specialised work she did, she had received an envelope of cash from Raphael Delano every month and she was allowed to live in an apartment complex built and owned by the Delano and Delano Company.

'Peter Delano says he was slow to catch on. He told her he had no intention of giving her a lot of cash without knowing what for. That's when Richardson explained that she was the company arsonist; that it had been her job to set fires in houses that stood in the way of Raphael Delano's development plans. Further, she said that unless Peter Delano continued the arrangement, she would go to the police with it.

'So Peter says he did. He wasn't at all comfortable with it, but he didn't think he had a choice. Until Michaels came along with what she knew . . .

215

'Now, how did she know?' Hecklepeck shifted, presenting his right shoulder to the camera. 'Michaels originally set out to do a simple exposé of people's sex lives. She discovered that finding people to interview was not all that easy because they didn't wear their sex lives on their sleeves. So she ended up working with the famous and with people she knew. One of those people was a woman who lived in her building, Sonya Richardson.

'Richardson had given out that she was supported by a mysterious lover because she had to find some way to explain the fact that she didn't work but had an income. When Michaels came and asked her to be in the series, she agreed, possibly to put pressure on Peter Delano, possibly because she enjoyed living the lie. Only Sonya Richardson really knows.

'It is impossible to say what first made Michaels suspicious. She had some Xeroxed pages of a World War Two Army ordinance manual sewn in the hem of her coat. The pages explained how to rig a timer to an explosive device. Maybe Michaels found them in Richardson's apartment.

'Maybe she remembered seeing Sonya Richardson at the scene of the Evans Street fire. Maybe she went back to check the tape and recognised Richardson in the crowd of people watching the firemen in the early morning dark. I'd like to show that tape now. Richard, if you don't mind.' On the screen appeared a freeze-frame of a crowd of people herded behind a piece of yellow police tape. Many of the group were black. Richard had highlighted one of the white faces and it bore an undeniable resemblance to Sonya.

'This tape is likely to be crucial evidence in the case against Sonya Richardson,' came Hecklepeck's voice. 'It will place her at the scene of the fire just as it did for Laurel Michaels. After that Michaels worked back, the way I did, through Tudell to Delano & Delano – to the office of Peter Delano.' Hecklepeck reappeared on the television screen and addressed the camera.

'Then she made her big mistake. She telephoned Richardson and asked her for an interview. But

Richardson put her off. Instead she staked out the station, waiting for Laurel Michaels to appear. We know that Michaels met her murderer in the KYYY station parking lot and they moved into one of our news vans either for privacy or to get out of the cold. There was some discussion; they sat on the van floor, Michaels in a cross-legged position. At some point her assailant picked up a light stand and hit her with it, head on. Michaels was bigger than Richardson. She would have warded off the blow had she seen it coming but she was taken by surprise. Once Michaels was unconscious Richardson allegedly strangled her.

'Before we close I would like to say a word or two about my colleague . . .'

'Close? There's still fifteen minutes left in this show,' the show director was ready to think the worst.

'It's all right,' said Richard. 'The last tape I gave you is a bunch of Laurel's stories edited together. All we have to do is put it up. It'll more than fill the time.'

'Oh, good. Cue it up, Mark. Let's punch up that chromakey shot too. If we don't use it now, we won't get a chance. Behind Hecklepeck on the television screen appeared a gigantic head. Truly bigger than life, Laurel was making one last appearance.

In his green-and-gold living room, reviewer John Alden looked at his pocket watch and retched. Hecklepeck had been on camera forty-six minutes minus five minutes of commercial, minus roughly four minutes of tape. Thirty-seven minutes! Not even the president would dare to stand in front of a television camera for that long without some kind of visual relief. It violated all the rules of good television. Alden retched again. But how could he pan a newsman who had just solved a major murder case after doing some superb investigative work? Alden retched for a third time and made for the bathroom.

' . . . journalism in St Louis can never be said to be the same without her,' Hecklepeck wrapped up his little eulogy and waited until the floor director signalled that he was off the air. He had tried to keep his remarks as short and ambiguous as possible. Laurel, he felt, would have forgiven him that much. He had, after all, avenged her death in the only way she would have appreciated: on camera. He walked out of the studio, into the hall.

'Well, we pulled it off,' Richard emerged from master control.

'You had doubts?'

'Of course not,' but Richard didn't seem very pleased with himself.

Hecklepeck regarded him sympathetically. 'You know, Richard, she was a nasty piece of work. She wasn't sweet the way she appeared. She burned poor, defenceless people out of their homes. She killed people.' Hecklepeck continued more thoughtfully. 'She was probably into fires although it's unusual for women to be firebugs. That's probably why Delano kept her on retainer as it were. She was a highly unlikely arsonist, didn't fit the police profile.

'I also think she liked designing and rigging explosives and then seeing the way they performed. She could have set that fire on Evans Street with some gasoline-soaked rags but she did it with an explosive device. Mrs Gray heard an explosion.'

Richard gulped, his expression queasy. 'Where'd she learn how to do that?'

'That's a good question. Making bombs is not all that easy. The old Army ordinance manuals would have been one source. They show up all the time at flea markets. Libraries have them. They were meant to be taken into the field by Army troops so they had all kinds of weird instructions in them, like bomb-making. And Sonya wouldn't have had any trouble getting dynamite or fuses or even detonating devices from Raphael Delano. Those things are used all the time in the construction business for demolition.' Hecklepeck looked glum. 'I just wish I'd known she was going to use her expertise on my car.'

But Richard was not going to be distracted. 'She's such a little person, so petite . . .'

'She didn't need to be strong. Laurel had already been knocked out so the strangling itself would have been easy.

Sonya may have used a piece of Art's equipment to tighten the mike cable, the way you use a stick to secure a tourniquet. We'll never know because she coiled up the microphone cable afterwards.' Hecklepeck hit his palm with his fist.

'She is a neat little person. She likes playing around with wires and cords. Anybody else would have dumped the thing and gotten the hell out. Not Miss Sonya. Although she could have been discovered at any moment, she sat and, incredibly, coiled the cord. It was the act of someone who was incalculably cool under pressure. Then,' Hecklepeck was swept away by his story, 'she bundled Laurel's coat into Art's equipment bag and took it to her car, which was parked in the Burger Chef parking lot. This is a woman with nerves of steel. Next she realised she didn't want to be caught with the bag; she had plans for the coat but the bag was a problem. So she dumped the coat inside the car and took the bag back into the woods where Joe Handy found it.

'The rest is history. Sonya went through the pockets of the coat. She found Laurel's notebooks and some documents, which she destroyed. She then used Laurel's keys to get into her apartment. There she hung the coat up in the closet and went through the apartment to see if there was anything that would implicate her.' Hecklepeck paused to reorder his thoughts.

'At some point Sonya must have reviewed the situation in her mind. She knew Laurel had been shooting tapes for her story. Sonya wouldn't have known exactly what was on those tapes but it must have worried her to have them knocking around. That's where we came into it.'

'We?'

'We had the tapes, remember? We looked at them after we got back from Tess's the night of the murder.'

Richard nodded. 'How could I forget? You were supposed to leave them in Laurel's office and get my tapes back. You never did,' he said bitterly.

'With good reason,' replied Hecklepeck. 'When I went into Laurel's office to make the switch, there was evidence that the murderer had been there. Someone had cleaned everything up and lined up all Laurel's pens in a creepy way. I couldn't take the risk that they would come back before the police discovered the tapes.'

'Why didn't you tell me?' demanded Richard.

'I didn't really have a chance, and how was I to know things would get so far out of hand?'

'Hmpf.'

'What I didn't realise then was that the murderer knew I had the tapes. Either Sonya was still in the newsroom when I walked out with them or she was lurking around outside. If I'd checked around, it might have been all over then.' Hecklepeck sighed. After a few moments he began again. 'I didn't and Sonya was hotter than ever to get her hands on the evidence.'

'So she hung around here,' Richard looked around the hall as though Sonya might be lurking there. 'She must have been watching us all the time.'

'Yeah, if I'd just had the sense to check the make and model of her car, I think there's a good chance that somebody around here may have seen it because she must have been hanging around in the vicinity of the station for days.'

'Yeah,' said Richard conversationally. 'Like that weird guy in the blue car that we kept seeing around here.'

'What blue car?' Hecklepeck's tone had a dangerous edge.

Richard told him about the blue car the five o'clock producer had seen on the day of the murder. Then he described how he himself had seen it the day after the murder.

'I bet that was it,' said Hecklepeck in an aggrieved tone. 'Why the hell doesn't anybody ever tell me anything around here?'

'You mean? That car? That blue car was Sonya's? And she was using it . . . to spy on us? I thought it was just some guy who worked around here. Or at the most maybe a sexual pervert.' Richard shook his head. 'But not Laurel's murderer. That never occurred to me.'

'Next time come tell me and don't try to think.'

*

It was a St Louis spring afternoon that felt much more like summer. Warm, humid air hung over the KYYY parking lot where a small crowd had gathered around a modest platform next to the station's front door. Between the platform and the door stood a life-sized figure draped in white sheeting.

One of the big studio cameras had been brought outside and was trained on a speaker stand at the front of the platform. 'Ten,' mouthed the floor director. He was holding out ten fingers and more carefully than usual counted down to 'Zero' when he pointed to the speaker stand. He pointed vigorously several times before the woman behind the lectern spoke. 'Good evening,' said GAS President Helen Wheeler, reading from an index card. 'KYYY, Channel Three, has kindly given up some of its newstime so that we could bring you this special dedication ceremony . . . live.'

The group looking up at Helen was mostly GAS members but even that venerable organisation had made a poor showing. GASers didn't leave their gardens in May, not for any business that wasn't horticultural.

'She sounds like shit. You should be up there doing that.' Side by side Richard and Hecklepeck were leaning up against a car at the back of the lot.

'No way,' said Hecklepeck. 'As I told Ken, it was important for his image that he should be the only one to appear during the ceremonies.'

'Bullshit, you just didn't want to be connected with it.'

Hecklepeck grinned. 'Well, I didn't like or approve of Laurel Michaels. I don't see why everybody thinks I'm her biggest champion.'

Richard chuckled. 'They just want you to repeat your success in the ratings,' he said with sarcasm. KYYY news had risen to new heights in the February ratings book. The special show on Laurel had captured an an unbelievable fifty per cent share of the audience. 'So, here we are kicking off the May book by bringing back our very own martyred reporter in the five o'clock newscast.'

'It's going to take more than that. That's old news.'

'Yeah, we're going to have to arrange to kill somebody in

front of a live camera if we want to top Laurel's murder.'

'. . . would like to introduce KYYY's new general manager, Ken Marshal.' Helen continued from the podium. 'Mr Marshal was recently promoted from his post as news director. Since his promotion he has wholeheartedly endorsed our statue campaign. Mr Marshal?'

Ken walked to the lectern and looked over the crowd. Then he looked beyond the crowd, giving the impression to viewers at home that thousands had come to see the unveiling of Laurel's statue. 'What can I say,' he said. 'On an occasion like this, what is there to say?'

'Crap,' said Richard. 'Crap is the word I'd use.'

'Have you heard that lovely Rita is joining our former leader, the love of her life, in Detroit?' Hecklepeck asked.

'You're kidding. Wally hired her again? I thought they hated each other.'

'Maybe that was the attraction.' Hecklepeck shrugged. 'It makes about as much sense as Wally being fired from here and getting a job in a bigger market for more money.'

'Yeah,' rejoined Richard, 'and Ken, who is truly feeble, being promoted to take his place. It is, as I said, crap.'

'. . . so hard to find words to express my feelings at this moment,' Ken had kept his remarks short. 'I would now like to introduce the woman who made it all possible, Maggie Johnson.'

Maggie swished to the microphone in green silk. 'Such a truly great reporter,' she gushed. 'I felt it was a project definitely worth doing and that's why I willingly put up the money through my corporation for the beautification of St Louis, Billy-Do. From the beginning I was totally . . .' Here Maggie giggled a little, '. . . totally committed to the idea.'

Richard looked at Hecklepeck and they both laughed.

'Did you read the cover article in this month's *St Louis Magazine*?' Hecklepeck asked. Richard shook his head. 'It's an interview with Alderman 'Tiny' Payne. In it he explains why he decided not to marry Tareesa Wells. He said marriage would interfere with his ability to serve his constituents.'

'I suppose he didn't mention that she wouldn't have him?'

222

'You guessed it. She's never going to forgive him for easing the way for Delano and Delano to get the zoning changed on that Evans Street block. His aiding their development plans was forcing her out of business.'

'And the special commission Alderman Tiny established, allegedly to put the brakes on development, didn't appease the Lady Tareesa one little bit.'

'Nope,' said Hecklepeck. 'But I'm sure she's pleased to be working with Billy-do on that multi-cultural development for Evans Street. The new Tess's will be in the centre.'

'Billy-do.' Richard shook his head.

'Before we unveil the statue I want to tell you a little about the so-talented artist, Bob Keshia,' Maggie continued from the podium. 'He's only twenty-eight years old but Mr Keshia's work has earned him a national reputation.'

'He comes from Milwaukee and did a sculpture for some obscure park in New York. You might call that "national",' commented Richard. 'I call it unheard-of and cheap.'

'Have you seen any of his stuff?' asked Hecklepeck. Richard shook his head. 'He does those sculptures you see in parks that make you look twice to be sure they're not real people. You know, statues sitting on park benches, eating brown-bag lunches.'

Richard nodded. 'Who belongs in front of a TV station?' he asked. They stared at the sheet-covered statue for a few seconds, speculating.

'I've got to go in. They're going to tack some news on the end of this and I have to be there to anchor it.' Hecklepeck started to walk off but paused. 'Hey, I told Helen and Peggy Hanford I'd take them for a celebration dinner at Sebastion's between shows. Want to come?' Richard nodded but his attention was focused on the front of the station.

Helen, Maggie and Ken had descended from the podium and were grouping themselves in a semicircle behind the draped figure. They each picked up an edge of the covering and prepared to pull. In front, a breeze lapped at the sheet revealing bronze underneath.

'One, two, three,' counted Ken. The sheet slipped off and there she was, hurrying to catch an interview with some-

223

body. The forward motion pinned back the skirt of her suit to reveal a perfect pair of legs in mid-stride. In her right hand was a microphone, held like a torch over and before her. Beneath it her face was charmingly determined.

She was nothing at all like Laurel. The artist had had plenty of video tapes from which to work. Maybe the thought of reproducing them in bronze depressed him; maybe he didn't have the capacity. In any case Bob Keshia's statue bore no relation to any journalistic reality. His was the vision of the television reporter as created by television.

In the newsroom she came to be known as 'Barbie'.